# THE SALT GARDEN

TYNDALE HOUSE PUBLISHERS, INC.
WHEATON, ILLINOIS

## Cindy McCormick Martinusen

Visit Tyndale's exciting Web site at www.tyndale.com

*The Salt Garden*

Edited by Lorie Popp and Ramona Cramer Tucker

Designed by Zandrah Maguigad and Alyssa Force

Published in association with the literary agency of Janet Kobobel Grant, Books & Such, 4788 Carissa Ave., Santa Rosa, CA 95405.

Scripture quotations are taken from the *Holy Bible*, New Living Translation, copyright © 1996. Used by permission of Tyndale House Publishers, Inc., Wheaton, Illinois 60189. All rights reserved.

Scripture quotations are taken from the *Holy Bible*, New International Version®. NIV®. Copyright © 1973, 1978, 1984 by International Bible Society. Used by permission of Zondervan Publishing House. All rights reserved.

Scripture taken from *THE MESSAGE*. Copyright © 1993, 1994, 1995, 1996, 2000, 2001, 2002. Used by permission of NavPress Publishing Group.

This novel is a work of fiction. Names, characters, places, and incidents are either the product of the author's imagination or are used fictitiously. Any resemblance to actual events, locales, organizations, or persons, living or dead, is entirely coincidental and beyond the intent of either the author or publisher.

**Library of Congress Cataloging-in-Publication Data**

Martinusen, Cindy McCormick, date.
   The salt garden / Cindy McCormick Martinusen.
      p. cm.
   ISBN 0-8423-7364-0
   1. Women journalists—Fiction.   2. Survival after airplane accidents, shipwrecks, etc.—Fiction.
3. Loss (Psychology)—Fiction.   4. Female friendship—Fiction.   5. Women novelists—Fiction.
6. Shipwrecks—Fiction.   I. Title.
PS3563.A737S25 2004
813'.6—dc22                                                                              2003024485

Printed in the United States of America

09  08  07  06  05  04
 9   8   7   6   5   4   3   2   1

You will know if it's for you.

———————◈———————

I write as a pilgrim,
qualified only by my craving for grace.
—Philip Yancey

U-Turns

# Sophia Fleming

*There are places within us we do not often share,*
*And sometimes do not know so well ourselves.*
*Places of longing and love,*
*of near-forgotten dreams and secrets we cannot speak.*
*These places are sometimes found by others, and once glimpsed,*
*there is no turning away.*

———————✦———————

I found something today.

One of those somethings you imagine finding, then wonder what to do once you have it.

I paused before plunging my hand into the cold seawater, the first of three attempts to reach the object. Water always teases perceptions. I nearly missed it. And how that would have changed today and perhaps my tomorrows also.

A slight flash of sunlight magnified within the water caught my eye as I walked along the tidal pools. Square objects don't abide with the rolled and worn shapes of the sea, so I knew it was made by human hands. A small metal box, perhaps, or a piece of wood with something reflective attached. I made the guesses as I approached.

When I found it, a sense of a dream enclosed around me. There are plenty of dreams I've wished for, or even better, desired the real-life experience instead of the dream. Perhaps this is why I am drawn to put words upon the page, to attempt to capture what I cannot have in reality. Be it some moment of elation or love or reconciliation. Some moment so perfect that it must be captured in writing or in a moving picture. A moment with background music, maybe the sound track to *Casablanca*. The scent of the sea and the touch of wind upon my face would give me a look of eternity, and dare I dream, of beauty, even at my age. Perhaps I'm overly dramatic, but it isn't often that I find a true treasure along my sea walk.

My, how the water was cold and the tidal pool deeper than it appeared as I carefully bent along the craggy crevice. A woman of my age must be careful along those wet rocks; I'm not the youngster I once was, and some days it feels as if I've always been old. That icy salt water chilled me to the bone, all the way up to my pushed-up sleeve. The surge in and out of waves soaked my walking boots. Just as I thought to pull away, my fingers touched something that reflected in a tangle among the seaweed and rock. A spider starfish observed my quest from a few inches away. The wind whispered in my hair that the scent of weather was in its touch, but no movie music filled the spaces.

The treasure—for all beach litter is a treasure, even the old boot I found decades ago, which now serves as a geranium planter—was nearly more sea than civilization. A book with a metal cover plate. It was so tarnished and dented that the lock had rusted shut.

My walking stick (some call it a cane; I prefer walking stick) back in my right hand and the ocean's treasure burning a hole in the pocket of my raincoat, I shortened my usual route and high-stepped it toward the cottage.

The outside is clean now, at least from seaweed and the sludge of the deep. Rubbing my hands together, it feels as if I've found the Holy Grail. I stare closely, then attempt to break the lock with a steak knife. I try several times before it opens with a click. Barely lifting the cover, I see pages glued together in a solid soaked mess, and I fear they'll disintegrate at a touch. It's a miracle paper could survive in all that salt, but recalling images from other shipwrecks, I know it's possible.

It's surely from that shipwreck.

The *Josephine* made Orion Point a historic landmark. That stormiest of nights back in 1905 became emblazoned upon my mother's memory as she scoured the shoreline with her family in search of survivors.

What was this book's journey before the wreck that plunged it to the bottom of the sea? Whose hands once turned the pages? Were any creatures from the deep inspired by the message inside? That's my foolish thinking, yet I savor such fanciful thoughts.

For over fifty years I've kept myself here on Orion Point. My wide world shrunk to these eighty pine-covered acres of West Coast woodland with one dog and one neighbor as companions. Orion Point may never be the same after today. I must think and pray.

It feels as if life-changing capacities are held within this book I found. I know it's God's nudge that I've tried to ignore for a while now. He's opened a door. I've seen many seasons cycle around me during my seventy-odd years, changing me as they've gone. This feels like the first cold breezes of a monumental storm. Maybe it's all my imagination.

Somehow I think—and fear—it's not imagination but truth.

My old dog yawns at my feet as we warm ourselves beside the fire.

An artifact should be sent to a museum or the archaeological society for examination. A team of scientists has been diving and probing the ocean floor for the past week at the shipwreck site; surely they'd want this relic of the sea. It may be their probing that brought it to me.

I know these things, but tonight as it sits in a strainer on my kitchen counter, and as I sit beside the fire warming the chill from my old bones, I cannot help but want to keep it.

Somewhere I have a very old newspaper article my mother kept, telling of objects found from the wrecked *Josephine*. Clipping such stories was a hobby of my mother's, though as I now think back, it was more of an obsession. As a young girl living in the new stone house on the Point, she'd been here that night of howling wind and fierce water. She met the storm, carrying a kerosene lantern behind her parents as they brought blankets and searched for survivors. In her older age, she recalled the slow dawn that revealed the choppy waves filled with debris and the pale twisted bodies washed ashore.

The stories from childhood return to me now, stories of the ship's demise off the rocky shore that became my play yard and later my sea walk. Mostly, thoughts of the stormy crash never entered my mind full of youthful musings. Other times it was with adventure and danger that I replayed my own fictive illusions of what had happened.

As I rock in this old chair, I can nearly touch those days gone by. I can hear Phillip and Helen, just children then, shouting out a welcome, coming to the Point to play. We'd inevitably find our way to the rocky piece of shoreline within view of where the schooner floundered.

"Let's get Ben," Phillip said so often, standing atop a rock where the crisp wind tickled his cheeks, and his brown hair fluttered up as if to sweep him away. I first loved him in those days, seeing the essence of life that filled him and overflowed upon us all. People were always taken by Phillip, from childhood until his death. There was something of the eternal in him, I believe. Something that reminded of things beyond the moment, and it drew people to him. Few felt it as strongly as we did—his sister, Helen; Ben; and I.

"Let's save Ben from his father," Phillip would say.

Our feet would rush along the path to the lighthouse. Ben would have too many chores, his stern father staring at us as if we were intruders from an invading land. Within an hour, we'd pick the nets clean, rake the stalls, stack the firewood, and polish the glass on the lighthouse tower until it gleamed in the sunlight—dismissing every excuse his father could think of to keep Ben from frolicking. The chores completed, we'd head for the forested trails beyond view of the lighthouse. Ben would be ours.

"Let's be pirates fighting upon the rocks as the *Josephine* is sinking behind us," Phillip shouted more to the sea than to us.

Ben needed a few minutes to shed the coat of his father's tyranny. Then suddenly he'd raise a piece of driftwood like a sword saying, "We'll kidnap the girls and take them to the South Seas."

"No way." Helen's hands fisted on her hips. "Girls can be pirates too."

Their voices remain with me tonight. I wonder if Ben remembers them while he sits before his fire in that same lighthouse, just a quarter of a mile away. Does he remember our losses and find longing in the days of youth?

How have so many years passed us by? Every year amazes me more, and yet the feeling of a journey's end rises as an eventual destination through the fog of future.

An emblem from the *Josephine* came to me today as if delivered from the past. I've picked it up a dozen times, imagining what words could be written inside. What if it belonged to that woman, the one the ship was named after, the one my mother recalled when they found her barely alive that frigid morning?

When Ben comes by, I'll show him the book. Speculating on what is hidden within its pages reminds me of the days of yesterday, but these memories comfort me without inflicting the usual pain. Such comfort feels good to these old bones. Surely the scientists searching the wreckage would like to see it.

But for now, it is mine.

### THE TIDAL POST
Your local paper serving Harper's Bay since 1882

**ROAD CLOSURE FOR WINTER MONTHS**

Scheduled delays on the reconstruction of Wilson Bridge have brought the project into the dreaded winter season. For the next several months old Highway 7 will be closed.

Harper's Bay will be inaccessible by road to the residents of Orion Point. Ben Wilson, lighthouse curator and resident of the Point, responded with a hearty chuckle when interviewed. "I always come to town by boat anyway."

Reclusive author Sophia T. Fleming, the other resident of Orion Point, was unavailable for comment.

## Claire O'Rourke

I'm stranded.

This truth has taken ten distinct minutes to fully sink in. I'm stranded along a coastal road with the dense woodlands turning dark around me, and no one will be coming this way tonight. The road is closed.

Technology is worthless. At least when your car breaks down on a deserted highway and the little receptor bars on your cell phone announce there is no way it can find its home antenna.

Vaguely I recall the orange signs some miles back that I didn't read in my haste to get out of Harper's Bay before the town tightened like a boa's embrace to keep me from leaving.

*"Claire O'Rourke, no one can abandon their hometown."* Those would be my mother's words from earlier this afternoon. I think

she says them, or some similar version, every visit. I'm not trying to abandon my hometown, only put some distance between it and me. I know where I'm supposed to be going, and it's not to Harper's Bay.

I tabulate the sixteen miles to town, the growing darkness, and the ominous clouds overhead. As a bird flies, Orion Point holds the closest residence. But a bird flies over the thick, deep forest and over the bridge detour that engineers blocked off. Even as a girl walks, Orion Point holds the closest home, but the driveway is long and hard to find in its nearly overgrown state (at least it was overgrown last time I saw it in high school; it might be completely eaten by woods now). And I've never actually been to the house of S. T. Fleming. It's somewhere near the northern edge of the densely forested peninsula. Strange that such a mysterious place is within miles of where I grew up, and I've never seen it.

Of course, almost every citizen of Harper's Bay is curious about S. T. Fleming. Every year daring high school students make a trek toward the Point with ominous tales of why she shuts herself away from the world. Aliens and UFOs are mentioned or, of course, ghosts. No one ever comes near the house. Mrs. Fleming, she knows to lock the huge iron security gate.

Locked security gate—that could be another obstacle toward reaching help.

Ben Wilson lives in the lighthouse at the very tip of Orion Point, but I'm not sure of the way to that either, except that it's beyond Mrs. Fleming's place.

It's strange to be here when I should be cruising down Highway 101, excited to be driving a fuel-efficient car with low miles I bought at a great price and listening to a book on CD over my stereo (Dickens's *Great Expectations,* since it's been a while since I read it). Strange too, as I headed off just half an hour earlier, I wondered, *Perhaps I'm not supposed to be on this road out of town.* That quick thought was followed by turning a corner in the road and spotting cement blockades in my path. As I braked abruptly, there came a sudden lurch and pop beneath the hood. Voilà! Stranded.

I toss my cell phone onto my seat and try to recall any place along this mountainous, old Highway 7 that receives phone service without walking miles. The hood is up on my politically correct vehicle (which means it gets over 30 mph). The cold is coming off the sea, and I can barely hear the waves half hidden by thick foliage and the coming darkness of night. Looking beneath the hood into the labyrinth of hoses and shiny metal parts, I try finding a resemblance to the Willy's Jeep engine I helped my father work on in junior high. A whole world of differences separate a '47 Willy's and a 1998 Honda beneath the hood, like comparing the intestines of a wall clock to those of a computer.

A large, moss-covered rock beside the road provides a hard seat as I stare at my broken-down, new-to-me car—the kind that doesn't have a warranty. Suddenly the thought returns that I again brush away like the raindrop that splatters upon my jacket sleeve.

*Maybe I'm supposed to stay.*

Today my mother told me about a great job at the local paper. Her definition of a great job pretty much means it's located within a twenty-mile radius of home. My journalism degree would put me on top of the application stack, she's sure of it. I could move into the bungalow at the back property—Dad's inventor's studio that went awry and now is shamefully used for storage—such a cute little apartment it could be.

Earlier I was leaving town. With the road before me, I was escaping little tinges of my hometown's seduction. The quaint life that conjures thoughts of a forest called Walden, my parents close by (which I would actually enjoy), and sleep (oh, how I sleep with the sound of the sea around me) begins to stir up a yearning I quickly beat away. Once I'm home in San Francisco, I'll wipe my brow in relief for escaping again. I always do.

San Francisco reminds me of all I need to accomplish. I missed
an important meeting on Friday, needing the day to come here to
pick up my car. A friend on her way to Seattle dropped me off, and
Friday was the only day she could go. My supervisor at the *San
Francisco News & Review* said it'd be fine to miss the day, but talk
was circulating about changes, new roles, promotions. And then at
church a meeting is set for tomorrow—the singles group is planning a trip to Mexico. A missions trip might also help me connect
with a few other singles. With so many people in the group and my
busy life of dreams to realize, I've gotten to know very few.

Alone next to my car, I realize that I've made few connections
since moving to the city after college. My list of acquaintances is
long, but only a few have slid over into friendships.

"Are you dating anyone?" Mom asked earlier, as if she doesn't
ask me on our weekly phone calls, or perhaps she thinks I'll suddenly confess a secret love life because we're together in person.

"No, Mom, no one." My mother once would ask if I was dating
anyone "special," and now she just asks if I'm dating. Her two
best friends have been grandmothers for some time now, and
every time I visit she tells me how they share grandchildren pictures and funny stories while she has none.

"There's no one at all?"

I could share the stories of the three men I've dated in the last
year. Hancock and I dated for three months, though I don't
think we completed a single meal without a long line of food getting stuck in his teeth. I'm not talking about once in a while or
a little speck of food. For several weeks, I thought he was testing
me or something. We'd eat, say a scone at Starbucks, and as Hancock explained about the seminary class he'd attended that day,
he'd smile or grimace, depending upon the class—eschatology
always produced a grimace—and there they'd be. The blueberries
or cinnamon or just scone stuck between gum and teeth.

I lost five pounds dating Hancock. What's worse, he dumped

me. He said his studies were making it too difficult to build a relationship. I'd wanted to quit after the first date, but his sister, who was a friend from church, kept saying sometimes it takes time to recognize the person God has for us, even when they've been before our eyes all along. Hancock was definitely before my eyes; I was just disgusted by what I saw.

Tayler was definitely the best-looking guy I've ever dated, which really helped my confidence level after Hancock's rejection. One of those heart-stopping kind of guys, the kind you wouldn't really want to marry 'cause most single women on the planet would be looking at him with wonder and you in critique. But it was nice to be the reflection in his eyes, even for only a month. He knew I was a Christian from the beginning; we met at the church singles group. But I guess he'd never dated a Christian who really meant it. Once he discovered that things such as casual kissing in the choir room weren't an option, he pretty much moved on. I think he was rather accustomed to being the downfall of women's convictions. He left me at a restaurant with the dinner bill. Should I tell this to Mom?

Mark, an intern at work, took me to lunch. Well, kind of. Our department was supposed to have a get-together, but we were the only ones who showed up. He did pick up the bill, so does that count? Mom would say it did, but I didn't want to actually date Mark anyway. He picks at his ears when he works on the computer. So that might make me sound a little shallow and/or immature, but if a guy's idiosyncrasies are my pet peeves, what's the use in considering forever with him?

"Mom, life's too short to spend seeking some elusive guy."

"You could spend a little time seeking him."

"What if it's not my calling in life to get married and have kids?"

"I know it's my calling to be a grandma, and my calling hinges on you."

"Oh, brother."

"Yeah, I've given up on him, your brother. He'll probably become a professional mountain man before I see him near the altar."

"Mom, I think he is a professional mountain man, not that a mountain man won't find a mountain gal."

"I think he's married to a tree."

She has a point. My brother, Conner, grew up reading books like *Tom Sawyer, Huckleberry Finn, Surviving in the Wilderness,* and *My Side of the Mountain.* He's had a tough time separating adulthood from childhood forays into the wooded areas of our youth. One Christmas he showed up at my parents' doorstep looking like Bigfoot—I hardly recognized him until he showered, shaved, and pulled his hair into a ponytail. Conner and I stayed up until 3 A.M. telling each other stories—mine of San Francisco and his of adventures along the Pacific Coast trail and working odd jobs from outfitter to assistant biologist. If Conner settled down, worked banker's hours, wore a tie, and drove a minivan, I'd lose all faith in a world of individuality.

The rain that started like a spit-wad match is now pelting me back into my car.

The door slams and here I sit in this compact space. Suddenly I realize that I'll have to sleep in my car. No one is coming down this road tonight—the bridge is under construction and the whole town knows it. I have to quit thinking about serial killers, werewolves, and bears. *Hey, killers and werewolves and bears, oh my!* Great, now I'm making *Wizard of Oz* jokes with myself. What's that a sign of—hypothermia? But I'm not cold—not yet.

This was simply an overnight trip to buy a car. My mom's old boss had the Honda for sale at a steal, and Dad checked the engine. It was worth the trip home a few weeks before Thanksgiving. Or so I thought.

"*A good attitude is a choice.*" My father's words, and ones I don't want at this point. I know that God is right here even in my trouble—especially in my troubles. And I have some supplies. Just before I pulled from the driveway, Mom carried out a new blanket she'd bought for me. A supersoft chenille that's quite warm. Dad had filled my red Starbucks thermos with coffee—the special Holiday Blend. And on a whim, I had stopped by Old American Bakery on my way out of town. Even living in San Francisco with its famous bakeries, this is my favorite. Perhaps because I worked there for several years in high school, and the owner, Martha Washington (a descendant from the original she claims), always adds a dozen sticky buns to my order of sourdough and honey wheat breads.

Blanket, coffee, food. Guess I could stay trapped a week and survive. Perish the thought.

Diving back into the sputtering rain, I glance toward the thick growth of ferns, bushes, and pines that could hide almost anything, then quickly open the trunk and pull out what not so long ago were goodies and treats. The loaf of sticky buns and a jug filled with Harper's Bay pure H2O are now "provisions." The chill turns quickly toward cold as icy fingers creep along the collar of my jacket and the edges of my ears. Unzipping my suitcase, I gather extra socks for my hands and feet, sweats to pull over my jeans, and several shirts in case my coat and blanket aren't enough.

Images of lions and tigers and bears—or killers and werewolves (I recently watched an old werewolf movie)—are beginning to eat away at my fearless resolve. My faith has been like that lately, a little tattered on the edges, though I only notice during moments of forced reflection. God is with me and I should listen, but sometimes it's hard to hear over life's distractions.

Mom's mention of that job returns. *The Tidal Post,* the local weekly newspaper, has a circulation of several thousand and consists of local news and once in a blue moon the mention of a newsworthy item beyond the Del Norte County borders. *The Tidal*

*Post* is humorous reading for me when I visit. Since I began working at the *San Fran News & Review* two years ago, I've seen the humor of small-town headlines. In the city, you don't read headlines like

```
FISHING TOURNAMENT LANDS SOME WHOPPERS
CITY COUNCIL TO MEET AT EDDIE'S GRILL
ANNUAL YARD SALE EXCEEDS PREVIOUS TURNOUT
```

This makes me think of next week's possible headlines at *The Tidal Post:*

```
STRANDED GIRL SPENDS THE NIGHT IN CAR
MISSED BY NO ONE
```

And it's true. No one will miss me tonight. Or tomorrow. Or really the next day, even though I should be at work on Monday. How long will it take for anyone to wonder?

It's going to be a long night.

# The Memoir of Josephine Vanderook

## October 1933

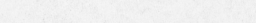

I would have followed him to the end of the world.

Some would say that I did.

Yet one night at sea after so many others upon the water, one night of wind and rain, one night destroyed our lives, and it was I who would return to Boston alone.

It is a night that has haunted my days.

Despite these years between that life and this one I've lived without him, the words between us have not left me. I trusted him with myself, gave him my very being. The having and losing of him opened a void within me that I have yet to fill. He was neither the beginning nor the end of me; nevertheless he was explicitly essential.

The story herein is mine. The writings of Josephine Vanderook. I am writing at the request of the Harper's Bay Historical Society as a shipwreck survivor and woman of this early century. These pages will record the memories and the thoughts I've gathered as the years have passed. Yet I write them for Eduard, first of all, who left me in that lonely land of the western seas, who gave me something that I continue to claim as mine alone. I write for my children also as a tale of caution or as a guide, though I have yet to discover exactly how my story can change another life. And I write for the understanding of a generation. Perhaps the retelling of events will finally settle this loss within me, and I too may be free of it, even after so many years.

Regardless, I begin. I begin with Eduard.

I first saw you in my father's library, surrounded by books. It was the eighteenth day of April. My father had invited a gathering of community members, and I saw you as you entered. Even though we spoke and you asked my name, I did not believe you truly saw me, for mine was not the only name you asked as you met others in the room. Certainly I did not expect you to remember me. I could not know that you would change my life in such profound ways.

But that would be some time later. . . .

**BRIDGE DEBATE CONTINUES**

Should old Wilson Bridge be demolished once the new sprawling bridge is completed nearly 100 feet above the original? That topic has been hotly debated, sparking anger, protests, and division in the community.

While state officials hope to attract tourists to the state park and Harper's Bay, giving a much needed boost to the economy, many locals want the smaller historic bridge to remain and fear that the bridge construction will change the small-town atmosphere of Harper's Bay. . . .

# *Claire*

---

The inevitable. Even though comfort is not a commodity, at least I'm finally warm beneath my pile of coats and clothing, with every conceivable draft tucked and closed. Then it happens. I need a ladies' room or rather a ladies' tree. Try as I might to deny it, the body does not obey the mind in such matters.

My father told me to stop for a flashlight before I left town. In fact, he reminded me twice. So this is what I get, stumbling along in the dark and cold because I didn't obey. Dad always worries about me and alleviates that worry by checking my oil, the air pressure in my tires, replacing the old flares in the roadside emergency kit he bought me one Christmas. He'll sure be irritated when he discovers my breakdown without a flashlight.

I make my way around the hood of my car, the rain pattering steadily on my black umbrella. I'm so often motivated by what-ifs, considering the many scenarios of a young woman stranded in the dark on a deserted road with only an umbrella as protection. I hurry toward the side of the road, wanting to get back to my car as quickly as possible.

Struggling with the umbrella in my left hand, my right hand searching for the big rock that should be nearby, I hear a sound beyond the rain.

A car. Headlights erupt far down the road, bobbing against the trees and the sharp mountain cliff. Help is on the way. I'd be cheering if my pants weren't tangled. Quickly I try getting back to the road when the headlights shut off, but the car doesn't stop. An involuntary reflex makes me duck and scurry toward the trees. My umbrella catches in the vines and brush; I get it closed and find a wet but somewhat secluded spot just as the car stops behind mine. The engine is killed, but a faint reflection distinguishes both vehicles in the night.

Doors open; interior light pops on and off.

"It looks abandoned," the driver says in a loud whisper.

"You better hope."

"What if someone's here?"

"Shut up!"

Flashlight beams fling like searchlights across my car and around the ground. Doors slam shut—one, two.

"Could you be any louder?" speaks a crass female voice.

"Yes, I could," the male voice shouts, the ricochet echoing up the canyon walls. "No one's down here. The hood is even cold. Maybe one of the workers broke down—looks like a disaster inside. You're paranoid."

"Let's just hurry and get out of here."

Frozen with fear, terrified I'll move and reveal myself, I stay hidden. A trembling rolls over me. My teeth chatter until I hold my cheeks with my hands. The footsteps and flashlight beams continue down the road toward the bridge construction. Seconds later they're out of my view. Maybe they left the keys inside their car. Should I run to it and try to escape? or stay here? scream for help?

Every suspense flick I knew to never watch now returns in flashes across my mind. The rain soaks through the back of my jeans. And then I hear them return.

I remain still, frozen.

"I'll drive this time," the female voice states.

"What's wrong with my driving?"

"Well, turning off the headlights and nearly crashing the car—and you have to ask."

After the car doors open and close, the engine roars loudly to life. I try to read the license plate, but the car takes off too quickly.

I wait until the sound of their vehicle disappears. The sharp cold brings me back to my car. With my teeth still chattering and the eerie feeling I can't shake, I stare down where the darkness has swallowed the road and the visitors who could conceivably come back.

Alone again.

Somehow it's worse the second time around.

Hours have surely passed. The temperature is mostly bearable, but the aches are getting to me. Finally I turn the key and push the radio on. How I wish for the music I forgot to grab on my trip north. The tuner scatters static through the car speakers as I search for a station.

I turn the static low, wanting to perceive any outside noises—those night visitors have heightened my anxiety. What were they doing here? Was I truly in danger, or was it my imagination? Maybe it was just an engineer or the bridge architect checking on the bridge. I could be drinking coffee at my parents' house or sleeping in my old bed. Maybe the overactive what-ifs were getting the best of me.

Finally a channel comes in, and it sounds like a hard-rock station. I run through FM and AM but still find only the steely guitar sounds of a big-hair band. Yet silence is worse. And so the seconds and minutes pass with the screams and shouts of hard-rock American music. I begin to laugh when a mellow love song with electric guitar comes on.

I'm stranded in my car, on old Highway 7, bundled beneath blankets and clothing as "Love Bleeds" plays over my stereo.

Who can guess what life will hold? Oh, for the ironies.

*Love hates, love bleeds.*
*Love ends. It's full of lies.*
*But love is what I need.*

My life is filled with doing things, reaching for goals, seeking to accomplish and be things for other people. I have love in my life, I do. But something of love, something I can't quite grasp, is missing. That comes to me suddenly as the disc jockey interrupts my reverie, a voice in the darkness who knows nothing of a stranded girl on a lonely road.

What could be missing?

# The Memoir of Josephine Vanderook

He named the ship for me.

The memory of that day still overcomes me. How proud my husband appeared at the shipyard as he pulled the blindfold from my eyes. And there was my name painted in fresh red letters across the gleaming wooden hull. Until that moment, I had hoped Eduard's and his brother's newest venture to expand the family shipbuilding company to the Pacific would eventually dissipate, and we would remain in the city I loved.

"This **Josephine** will take us to the great Northwest," he said with an enthusiasm that successfully destroyed my many hopes. For months, he kept the surprise from me. During those same months I humored his thoughts and plans as fleeting fancy.

When the revelation was exposed that a ship had been named for me, my sister by marriage, Karen, was filled with the jealous anger I had merely glimpsed since my marriage to Eduard, for it was only upon necessary occasion that I found myself in her company. Karen carried a stern expression even in her smile, and disapproval came quickly to her countenance, but this dark anger shaded her face with an ugliness I nearly feared. Eduard and John had built four ships, and not one sailed the sea with her name upon the stern.

"It's bad luck to sail on a ship that bears your own name," Karen said to me on the day of our voyage. They were spiteful, jealous words. And upon the day of our departure, Karen had the most evident look of satisfaction upon her face. Yet her words bore deep into my thoughts . . . like a bewitching curse. I watched my beloved Boston grow smaller and smaller behind me and felt a foreboding that crushed any courage and enthusiasm for the trip ahead. I spent that first night in our cabin with my head turned to the wall and Eduard believing that the seasickness had already begun its work.

God forgive me, but at times such superstitions had a power over my faith and logical thought. They were words Karen would later repeat as if savoring the fate of her husband's brother and the love between us that she would never have in her own life. How I fought with hatred toward that cruel woman until we finally found peace with one another in the months before her slow death.

The years have discarded the superstition, and my faith has found not only sustenance but evidence and beauty and truth. Yet, during the time that began the descent of our old life, Karen's words would whisper through my being again and again.

THE TIDAL POST

WEATHER FORECAST
  Saturday: High 45 Low 28

RESEARCH TEAM STRUGGLES IN COLD WEATHER
  Due to recent low evening temperatures, researchers for
the History Network have slowed progress on their expedition. They are seeking evidence for their documentary on
what happened the fateful night the *Josephine* sank. Most
believe it was the storm that drove the ship to the rocks
off Orion Point. However, one surviving crewman claimed
there was trouble in the wheelhouse that night. Another
crew member, James T. Roan, went to his death silent,
never willing to testify.

# Claire

---

Coffee.

I'm sick of sugary treats and would pay fifty dollars for another
cup of coffee, maybe more. Sometime in the night I finished the
last drops in the thermos, one of those horrifying moments when
you realize you should've been rationing. Wonder if pioneers ever
did that with water while crossing the desert—guess this isn't quite
the same, but it sort of feels like it.

The chill has finally found its way through my layers of clothing and coats and blankets. Morning leaks like blue ink into the
dark sky to the east. Gazing above the sleeping mountains, I
watch the slow color that will create a new day. I attempt to
stretch the kinks from my neck without moving; movement

allows the cold to seep further into the nest of clothing I've encased myself in. Wish I could turn on the heater for just a few minutes, but the engine won't even turn over despite my repeated attempts—I think the starter has received about two hundred tries since last night. *Maybe this time. Maybe it was flooded before. Oh, please Lord. Come on, baby car!* It doesn't work.

The coldest hour comes right before dawn; clichéd, yes, but how true both literally and figuratively. If it were not Sunday, I'd hope for construction crews, my orange-outfitted heroes, arriving in pickup trucks and carrying lunch boxes and hard hats. But alas, this damsel must be her own heroine, as usual.

A night of anxiety in my car has dissipated any inhibitions over approaching the home of S. T. Fleming, locked gate or not. Fear gathers perspective and casts away lesser worries. My imagination could try on the idea of what it's like to sleep in my car all alone, in deep darkness, with a slight storm (but storm nonetheless) shaking and tapping against the glass and metal hood and roof. But reality is much worse.

Time, which slips through my hands every day and which I never have enough of, stands still. Weariness presses around me like a heavy wool coat, itchy and suffocating, yet keeping me from sleep. The seat, which felt so comfortable when I test-drove the car, quickly begins to knot my spinal column from skull to tailbone, even in a reclining position, and nothing would relieve it. Headrest pulled out, reclining all the way down to the backseat, fetal position; head against steering wheel, body stretched over front bucket seats; trying the backseat with legs in every possible position. This car was not made for prolonged occupation.

Who would've thought economy-sized seats should gain status in the Museum of Torture Implements?

I thought dawn would never come.

Am I now afraid to show up at the home of S. T. Fleming? Ha! Last night cemented my resolve to return to my parents for a hot shower and sleep in my comfortable old bed. The car will be towed and I'll get back to San Francisco somehow.

Maybe Ben Wilson or S. T. Fleming has coffee.

With that, I kick off the jackets and clothing cocooned around me, and with a push on the door, it opens. I'm slapped in the face by the stinging cold. But I'm up and out of the car, doors are locked (I'm not sure why), and I'm climbing the barricade that blocks the detour down near the creek bed, across a temporary bridge that might soon be underwater if those storms continue spouting. This road will get me home.

*Orion Point, here I come.*

# Sophia

*I remember the first day we met,*
*though you may not remember.*

---

There are things unsaid between us.

We do not mention them, yet both feel their presence and know their depths.

It lingers in the spaces as we sip our tea with milk and sugar from dainty cups, and I think as always how small and fragile the handle appears within the grasp of large, callused fingers.

He loves me.

For over thirty years he has come to my door, carrying a bag of groceries from town and sometimes his own fresh fish wrapped in a paper sack and tied with twine. I thank him and invite him in for tea. In cold weather, we sit before the warmth of flame, and in the milder months we sit on the patio while our gazes meander the flowered pathways to the sea. We talk about the weather, the fish in his nets, our old dogs, my discoveries at the seashore—once I found a wallet that belonged to a missing fisherman, and there's the old boot he still teases me about.

After the sun falls from its noon height and dives toward the grasp of the sea, he rises from his chair, with knees creaking and back stretching, to pick up his hat and call his dog. I send along flowers cut from stems and bushes, flowers that bloom almost all year long. He smells them and smiles. There was a time or two—though years ago now—when he would pluck a flower and, to my embarrassment, pull each petal slowly, watching me all the while as he softly said, "She loves me; she loves me not." When it ended with *not*, he'd hold up the stem and announce with a smile, "She loves me." I'd slap his shoulder and shoo him on home.

It was our joke but not really funny. There were painful truths behind it.

"My son wants me to sell the boat and move inland," Ben says, leaning back in the chair now.

I chuckle at how little his son knows about him. Ben could never leave the sea. "Was he disappointed in your answer?"

"I haven't given one."

My teacup shudders in my hand as if my arm were the San Andreas Fault. "Why not?"

"I'm old." His eyes examine my reactions.

I can't deny that; we're both old and years past trying to say we aren't. Silence between us is nothing uncommon or unwelcome, but now the unspoken words move within me: *You can't leave. What would I do without you?*

"You'd leave the lighthouse, the boat, the Point?" What I'm really asking is whether he'd leave me, yet I don't know if he understands. I'm never convinced that he understands such nuances in our conversations. Perhaps I'm not granting him enough credit. It could seem I never really have. After sharing memories since childhood, we should understand everything about one another. We've lived as neighbors for decades. Ben loved my Phillip with a bond not even I could share—as only boys who've grown up together and shared foxholes in foreign lands can. It was the two of us mourning for Phillip, and later Helen, that grew this affection toward greater depths.

"It wouldn't be easy. Not saying it would. But I need to think about it. This body is decaying right out from under me." He tries to make light of it now, smiles a bit, his blue eyes twinkling. He's not fooling me.

"Come see something," I say. There's a moment of hesitancy, perhaps irritation that grips Ben, then slips away. Does he want me to plead, beg him to stay? Would it change anything? Would he stay if I asked?

I don't ask and instead rise from my chair in that crickety way age and osteoporosis require. "Yesterday morning on my sea walk, I discovered something."

"Is this a real something or just a somethun'?"

This makes me laugh since Ben knows how excited I get at any unique find along my shoreline walks. My treasures are anything from shells, crab skeletons, unique driftwood to actual human-made finds. The items are story fodder that amuse Ben. From the discovery of that boot, I tell the daring adventure of a sailor plunging overboard to save his love who had tried to reach him by coming out in a small motorboat during a rainstorm—no, a monsoon—after her father refused their marriage. No, they aren't all this frivolous and uncreative, only on days I really wish to see Ben's eyes rolling.

To the boot story, Ben replied, "Maybe a fisherman left his boots on deck and then accidentally knocked one overboard."

I chastise all such common sense. Orion Point only beckons treasures with a story attached, I chide.

Last night I put the book in my kitchen strainer so air could circulate around as much as possible and the water could drain.

"Come see," I say, eager for his reaction. "This one is a genuine treasure."

"Let me guess: a message in a bottle?"

"Close," I say.

The book is actually a ship's log of some sort. I discovered this once I gained the courage to carefully lift the metal cover and peek inside. I used tweezers, just to assure any future archaeologists once they discovered that I'd displaced, cleaned, then opened an archaeological artifact that I'd been careful. Oh, well,

I had to know. The front cover has someone's name etched into the metal, but rust and age and my worn-out corneas make it impossible to decipher. The pages are swollen and ruffled like the edges of kitchen curtains. I had barely glanced inside when the edge tore from the tweezers, causing me to set them aside.

"So, what is it?" Ben asks, coming up beside me and winking. "Where's this genuine treasure?"

I pull a faded dish towel from the stainless-steel strainer as if I'm a magician's assistant. "Ta-da!" I say and peer down as our faces draw close together. The book sure doesn't look museum-worthy, sitting inside a kitchen strainer. The metal cover is all corroded with a barnacle attached to the outside.

"Sure looks more interesting than that old fisherman's boot."

Ben's excitement further heightens my own. "A book. Can you believe it? Surely from the *Josephine* wreck, don't you think?"

Our faces lean in close and Ben's mind is clicking. "Where'd you find it exactly?"

"The tidal pools on the north side of the Point."

"That wreck's only a few hundred yards off and straight down from that side. Might be from the *Josephine,* just might be. A book of some kind, eh? That team was out diving again today." His thick finger taps the metal covering and barely lifts it.

I smile, then say, "I'm worried about the pages when they all dry out. Do you think they'll disintegrate?"

"Maybe. We should get this in to those scientists—"

Suddenly, my dog jumps from his spot by the woodstove. The hair on his neck bristles with his nose poised and frozen toward the door.

"Hello?" we hear someone call out.

In five decades I've had few welcome visitors to my place here on the Point. During the summer months I'll sometimes get the curious tourist sleuthing through the forest or by motorboat after hearing the story of a reclusive writer as if I'm some anomaly of the woods. Over the years it has happened less and less. A gated driveway has helped, even though the security system is broken and you can push right inside, but my seventy-pound yellow Lab, who responds to the name of Holiday or Cujo, has helped maintain my privacy. During autumn and winter and spring I haven't worried about visitors in years. So who could this be?

"Anybody home?" The call comes again.

Ben and I weave around my furniture to the front window. Out by the front picket fence I see a young lady leaning against the gate, her eyes darting around the yard.

"I'll go," Ben says, always protective and knowing.

"Thanks."

From my cautious view behind the drapes, I watch. Ben says hello as the front door closes; he makes careful steps down the porch. The girl, a pretty thing, appears a bit frazzled as she runs her hands over her hair, then motions down my driveway and toward the freeway. It's strange to see her here—she's out of place, like maybe a book washed ashore. An oversized purse sags on her shoulder, her blonde hair seems a bit tousled, her jeans and brown coat are smudged with dirt, her brown boots caked with mud. Dozens of story lines play through my mind as I study her.

Within minutes, Ben trudges back to the front door and comes inside. I see the young lady watch him, then gaze curiously around the property, pausing for a moment at the window. It seems our eyes meet, although I know she can't see me.

"She broke down on old Highway 7, spent the night in her car." Ben chuckles a little.

"It was cold last night," I say, shivering at the thought.

"Industrious little lady. Daughter of Mary Lou and Bill O'Rourke. They're good folks." Ben glances at the door. "Her name's Claire. She was heading back to the city."

"You sure got a lot out of that short conversation."

"Think she was pretty glad to see a person after the night she's had. I'll take her to town in the Evinrude."

"Should I have her come inside, make her some tea?" I ask, anxiety fluttering through me. I find a wad of drapes clenched in my hands. Ben is the only visitor who has been inside my home since my parents' passing long ago. Yet how cowardly to not invite this girl inside; I try to squash the thought of the Good Samaritan.

"I'll make her something at the lighthouse before taking her across. Her family may be worried." He nods good-bye and picks up his hat from the chair.

"Ben. Thank you." He knows how great a toll a visitor would be on me.

"I'll try to come round later about that book you found. Maybe there'll be some homemade crumb cake for a poor ol' fella like me."

"There just might, if he's a lucky poor ol' fella."

"*Old* is certainly the accurate word." And I see something cloud through his thoughts that I wish to know. Then another thought takes over and he says while opening the door, "It might interest you that the historical society received the memoir of Josephine Vanderook, the wife of the shipbuilder. She was a survivor, but her husband perished in the wreck. They're hoping to get some answers about what happened that night."

A flurry of questions arises with this.

"But I better save the little damsel. Good day, Sophia."

"Good day, Ben."

SHIPWRECK SUBJECT TO DOCUMENTARY

A century has passed and still the questions remain. The wreckage of the *Josephine* on November 17, 1905, resulted in the deaths of 62 people with only 23 survivors. Those who were willing to speak of the event produced varied accounts of what happened that night.

This week a team from the History Network has been combing the seafloor at the wreck site for any clues to the real story. Divers and a miniature submarine are part of the equipment being used. The cable television network plans to air a one-hour documentary about the shipwreck within the next few months.

# Claire

---

I feel as if I'm nine and I've been playing too long in the winter woods until my hands are stiff with frostbite (surely frostbite, since they hurt and sting so), my nose is running, and my socks and shoes are soaked from the tiny seasonal creek marking the back acre. I love that sudden switch from fun to deep chill, then the incredible warmth after a bath, hot beverage, and the comforting crackle of a fire.

Home.

Pajamas, clean hair with new leave-in conditioner (Mom bought it for my Christmas stocking but after such a horrifying night gave it to me early) blown dry until silky soft, and slippers that are tiny masseurs to the blisters and aching places on my feet. This house has a familiar scent, some indistinct combination that has settled in from the sea and the deep surrounding woods, along with the antiques, my mother's vanilla candles, the new rugs, and the clean lace curtains. Is it a scent or a cumulative feeling that creates such soothing warmth?

"Some tea made the English way?" Mom asks as the teakettle whines in the kitchen. Ever since she had tea at an English-woman's house, she now drinks only PG Tips tea (the Lipton of England, she was told) with milk and sugar—*white* being the proper term. I've come to like it nearly as much as my coffee.

"Sure, Mom." Suddenly I feel a pervading nervousness. I think I've become like a seduced frog in the pan of water. First I hop in thinking I've found paradise, the water warming like a Palm Springs spa. But before I can jump out, my legs are sitting on someone's plate as the main course.

The water's warming around me, and I'm starting to justify why I shouldn't jump. Maybe this is where I'm supposed to be.

After we stopped at the lighthouse for gasoline and a thermos full of coffee (I pray God's blessings on that man), Ben Wilson gave me a ride, or tour actually, of the tip of Orion Point and the half-moon cut from land that is Orion Bay. Ben indicated the rocky outcroppings that are hidden during high tide, the reason for the ship's demise so long ago. There was a large fishing boat anchored near the rocks; Ben explained that a team of scientists is researching the site for a documentary. We waved to the men on board, who waved nonchalantly back.

Ben was a wealth of information, pointing out types of trees, giving a lighthouse history, naming beaches; and as we approached Harper's Bay, he gestured to my parents' house located in the hills above the town. If I hadn't spent the night in my car and had a total of one hour of sleep, the tour would have been one of the most interesting things I've ever done. How strange to see the place where you've spent the majority of your life from a completely different angle. Harper's Bay from the sea appeared as unique as if I'd seen it from the sky.

Meanwhile back at the O'Rourke house, my parents were leaving for church when they received my phone call from the lighthouse. Mom was frantic at the thought of her daughter stranded with no one knowing it. "I was sleeping in my warm bed last night, and my girl was cold and alone," I heard her say in the background after my father took the phone. They were waiting at the docks when I arrived with Ben.

My car is now at Kenny's Auto where, so far, he can't find anything wrong. I've slept and taken a very long, hot, soothing shower and now must consider what to do—I'm supposed to be at work tomorrow morning.

"I was so worried." Creases cut into Mom's forehead as she pours hot water into cups for late-afternoon tea.

"We weren't worried until Claire was okay," Dad reminds Mom as he pulls up a chair and drops his work boots to the floor.

"Which is an even greater travesty. Our only daughter, trapped alone, sleeping all night in the cold—who knows who could've come along on that dark, deserted road. . . . My word, it's like a Dean Koontz movie!"

"Or novel," I say wryly.

"Exactly."

"Mary Lou," my father says softly, though he's really saying, "Don't be overly dramatic. Your baby daughter is a grown woman and has a life of her own."

To which my mother harrumphs in irritation while acknowledging this truth. This gets a raised eyebrow from my father as he sits at a kitchen chair to put on his boots. I can't withhold my smile.

"I still can't believe you didn't have a flashlight," Dad says. "I'll pick up one in town."

At this moment I decide against telling them of the arrival of those mysterious people in the car last night. Sometimes events are more traumatizing after the fact than during. Survival mode, denial, prayer—they help during the moment, but afterward the what-ifs come like a marching band, tooting their horns, high-stepping in rhythm at how easily my comfortable world could be shaken.

"So what did it look like?" Mom asks while stirring sugar into her tea. Curiosity is in the turn of her chin when she looks up at me.

I smile, knowing my entire experience has an exciting note. I've seen S. T. Fleming's house. "Well, *quaint* would be the word. Cute, kept up, kind of Irish cottage-looking. It reminded me of something you'd picture on a calendar of the old country—ocean barely seen through the back." My mind tries to recall every detail. "The house was made of those round stones. Vines grew up the sides, and the vine leaves were autumn red. It had a stone fence and archway with a white gate beneath the arch. Now I wish I'd had time to explore or remember it all."

"But you didn't see her?"

"I thought I saw the curtains ruffle, like she was watching."

"What a strange one, that ol' bird."

"She's not that strange at all," my father says, tying the laces on his boots.

"Of course she is. Hiding away for decades, hardly speaking to a soul."

Dad crosses his arms like he always does. "Well, when I talked to her, I found her to be right friendly."

"You talked to her?" Mom and I ask simultaneously.

"Sure. I've helped her a few times down at the docks, loading the boat with supplies after Ben had that shoulder surgery last year. A right fine lady."

"What . . . when . . . how come you never said anything before?" Mom sputters.

"Because it's foolishness how people carry on about her. She likes her solitude—there's no crime there. And it wasn't any big deal. I just carried some groceries for her and Ben. We chatted 'bout the weather and some new boat that had come in from the South Pacific. Nice lady."

"Well, I'll be," my mom says, scratching her head.

"And I'll be off to take a look at the bungalow back there." Dad quirks an eyebrow as if to send me a message.

"Why?" I look at one, then the other.

"Your mom suddenly thinks it'd be a fine time to clean it all out."

"It's been a mess for years," she says with a shrug. "And you never know—maybe we'll rent it out for a little extra income. It'd make a nice studio apartment. Just going to waste back there and such cute possibilities."

I open my mouth to speak, then let it go. Why get flustered and irritated that my mom misses me and wants me home? Yet inside I think, *Run!*

The day disappears in a blink as I shuffle around the house in recuperation mode and wash my clothing that served as blankets, but I don't accomplish much. How often I find time rumbling at my side like we're racing one another. Time, however, finds no need for rest so I'm left gasping on the sidelines.

Dad and Mom have nested down in the living room for their Sunday evening favorite reruns. I hear Squiggy's high-pitched voice from *Laverne & Shirley* and a few chuckles drifting into the kitchen, where I'm calling from their rotary telephone—yes, one of those actual relics that take time to dial. Drives me crazy. If for one year you added the additional waiting as each number cycles around, you'd have time to read a novel or sew a quilt or invent a cure for the common cold (as I've told my parents on numerous occasions).

My car should be fixed by morning, or rather it should be fully examined. Dad checked on the progress, but Kenny still can't find anything wrong—seems to be running great now. I'll definitely need tomorrow off; I needed to use some sick days before the year ended anyway. I'm making the slow process of dialing home; it's finally ringing. My roommate, Susan, is usually home now. Sunday evenings she frantically does laundry so she'll have clothes for the week ahead.

I nearly hang up as the answering machine picks up but then catch a new message—Susan's never changed our message in the year we've shared an apartment. "You've reached Claire O'Rourke's place, but I'm not Claire. I'm her ex-roommate, who is leaving on Saturday night for Reno to not gamble . . . well, actually some might call it that, but I'm doing the other most popular Reno event—getting married! So good-bye, single world and hello, marital bliss. And . . . um . . . Claire, if you happen to call and hear this before you get my note, sorry for the shocker. I'll be back in a week for my things. Guess this is my notice. You can call me on my cell on Monday. The phone is off until then—bet you can guess why. Oh, and everyone other than Claire, leave a message and she'll call you back 'cause she's responsible and—"

There's a beep and I'm left holding the phone to my ear, leaving a message of stunned silence on our machine. Surely something is wrong with my ears. I go through the series of numbers once again and hear what I couldn't quite comprehend the first time.

Susan's tone is filled with all the energy of a sweepstakes prize-winner. Is she crazy? I've asked myself that a million times and now know it's true, true, true. Susan's boyfriend, now most likely husband, is one of those would've-made-a-great-pro-athlete guys if he'd had talent but became sort of sad living off his parents' wealth (they pay his rent, gas, insurance) while he critiques what the pros do wrong. I had expected this to be another phase in Susan's quest for where she fits in the world.

If I hadn't needed a roommate so desperately when my last

one got married, Susan would've never been my choice. She keeps me up late, pays me to grocery shop for both of us, thinks I'm her therapist (though she ignores all the advice she seeks and seems to agree with), and claims I'm her confidante, even though once I heard her blabbing her deep, dark secrets to the guy who fixed our leaky sink. I am her friend—when her other friends are busy or her boyfriend is at a sports bar. I am her laundry advisor ("So you're sure my dry-clean–only slacks can't be washed with my white sweater?"). And I'm her spiritual mentor ("Now, what is it you believe again?").

I don't have a roommate.

Laughter mocks from the other room. The theme song to *Laverne & Shirley* seems like the sound track to my life.

# The Memoir of Josephine Vanderook

---

I recall our arrival into San Francisco Harbor like a grand entrance into a celestial port. The gates of the Bay were rounded mountains decorated green with spring splendor, and the morning had yawned and fully awakened by the time we came toward the long docks to port. My feet so yearned for earth beneath them that I held my breath impatiently, nearly racing without propriety from the deck. Of course, as the wife of the shipowner, I maintained my proper graces, though the handkerchief in my hand fared none too well. Finally, Eduard completed all manner of business and could escort me like a lady into California society, at least for a few days until we again headed north toward our new home in Seattle.

The Palace Hotel appeared to me like the first oasis in a wide desert. The luxury of rolled-out carpets, gleaming chandeliers, sheets and towels without any hint of a musty ship smell, and a call button that brought staff to the door—heaven would be like this, I thought. Only a year later, I would read of the great earthquake that nearly destroyed the city and ruined this grand hotel. It would be rebuilt, brick by brick. By then, I too had survived something akin to an earthquake.

Upon our arrival in 1905, there was an anticipation in me that was not in Eduard. No longer was laughter quickly found in him. His thoughts were not of me and this lush room, nor even of a new beginning only weeks away in the unpredictable land of the Northwest. Eduard was never good at hiding worry from me. Lines cut into his forehead and around his eyes as we walked through the crowds.

Simply minutes after our arrival into the room, after I'd explored the luxuries and planned for a long bath, Eduard announced his imminent return to the ship. I tried to persuade him otherwise, first with a loving embrace and soon with annoyed disapproval, but he could not be reckoned with and promised to return for supper. My inquiries revealed only that a cargo was arriving that he found important to supervise, although I knew it was a decision of spontaneity. What shipment, he would not explain. Why we were taking more cargo when we'd reached capacity with the additional passengers joining us, he would not answer. Why no one else could supervise, he left without saying.

My worry was great, and yet I was the wife. My mother's many reprimands came to me then, and a look in Eduard's face extolled my obedience—an expression I recognized from the men of Boston that had excluded Eduard until now.

I attempted civility after his departure, taking a hot, gluttonous bath. All of my clothing, washed upon a ship for the past several months, felt unbefitting a dinner in this golden city. My blue dress suit was chosen and others set aside to be cleaned by proper hands in the several days of our stay. How I wished this was our destination and rued the ideas of my brother-in-law, who bespoke of the great northern cities of Portland and Seattle, saying that 'Frisco was already too established. Established sounded marvelous to me.

The hours of afternoon wore by as I busied myself with dividing our clothing to be cleaned, working my hair into a stylish coiffure, even attempting some reading, though my restlessness kept me from concentration. The window coverings endured my constant fidgeting as I sought the street below for the approach of my husband.

Supper was long over when at last I heard his arrival, my hunger turning to sickness from worry. There was no explanation and from his expression I did not need to ask. We went to sleep that night with few words between us. The next morning Eduard was gone early, and I spent the day shopping with Mrs. Worthington.

San Francisco extended her hand to us, offering promises and excitement after so many months upon that ship and stopping in strange, foreign cities, but the shadow of Eduard's worries slapped away that offering.

From the day we arrived in that city until that terrible night of the storm, I knew something was wrong. However, I did not know how wrong it would become.

# Claire

---

This morning, after dealing with the rotary phone again, I receive a second bit of news. I've lost my job. There have been layoffs at the *San Fran News & Review,* most recent employees going first, effective immediately ("Didn't you get the memo Friday?"). In one weekend I have no roommate or job, and I'm getting more than just inklings that I should return to my hometown, which I vowed to never do.

Everything seemed to be going great in my life—*seemed* now being the operative word. Reflecting on the past tense is not really helping, but I'm doing it anyway because I'm unable to believe that things have changed so quickly. I lived in a small, cute place in the city I loved, worked a job with great potential. My roommate was working out for the most part, and I was involved at a nice church, while taking steps toward the goals I believed God had placed within my five-year plan. How strange that those goals, aptly held within a mission statement, are suddenly like helium balloons taking flight.

*God, what is happening?*

So Mom and I are kneading bread dough. Probably every woman in Harper's Bay has a bread machine by now, my mother included. She uses hers on occasion, but some of those favorite, tedious routines are tough to change. I must admit, her home-made bread puts the machine to shame.

"Why not stop by the newspaper and see what happens? It wouldn't hurt to just stop by." Mom says this without knowing I've lost my job. Haven't had the heart to admit it even to myself yet. *Oh yes, it could hurt to just stop by,* I think. Kneading bread dough is a better workout than I remember, as I look to see we have three more minutes of this.

"Mom, sorry to change the subject, but—"

"Sure you are." She tosses a smile my way and nods for me to keep kneading.

"Anyway, I was wondering about Sophia Fleming. What's the real story behind her?"

"The real story behind Sophia Fleming . . . well, that's the mystery. She grew up out on the Point; I think her family's been there for a few generations. From what I recall, it was in the fifties that she came back from New York. I remember people saying she'd been to Europe too. Because so few people had traveled that much when I was a child—anything outside Harper's Bay was travel—you can imagine the buzz over Europe and New York. By then, she'd written her second book. No one knows for sure why, but her second book got bad reviews, and that always sounded a little strange."

"When did her parents die?"

"Her parents died some years after she moved home, I think. Seems they died within a year of one another. I remember her parents at church when I was young. At her father's funeral was one of the few times I saw Sophia Fleming."

"It's funny how we all call her either Sophia Fleming or S. T. Fleming or Mrs. Fleming, not Sophia."

In fourth grade, our class wrote letters to Sophia Fleming, and we were thrilled to receive individual responses. Somewhere in Mom's collection of school memorabilia is that letter. Maybe I'll go looking for it.

"I never thought of that, but yes, everyone calls her by her full name—maybe 'cause she's a sort of celebrity or legend or quack, depending on who you talk to."

What would it be like to spend decade after decade in such a small space? What would drive someone to such a life after living in New York and traveling to Europe?

"Here, add some more flour."

I hadn't noticed the dough sticking to the board while my thoughts were wandering to the little stone cottage on the Point.

The phone rings.

"You get it. I'm not sure your bread's going to make it anyway."

I shake off dough and flour from my fingers and grab the phone. My hello brings a pause and then, "Claire?"

"Yes?"

"Hey, this is Griffin. Griffin Anderson."

Time warp to high school and my old friend, then ex-friend. "Griffin, how are you?" I know Griffin's stayed in the area, but I haven't talked to him in years.

"Good, very good. Are you here on a visit?"

"Sort of. It's a long story, but I'll probably be heading home tomorrow."

"Home as in San Francisco?"

"That's right." It's strange hearing his voice; it sounds different, and a million memories are attached to it. The first is of Griffin at Sunday school, the kid who always beat me at the Bible race. Just before I'd find the verse, he'd shout out, "Found it" every time. He shared his prize Tootsie Rolls when he realized how mad I got at losing. "And what have you been doing?"

"A lot, I guess, when you consider it's been . . . what? . . . six years since we last talked."

"Yeah, how do you sum up six years?" I say this thinking of my own life, college, internships, then a real job, and now that real job I don't have. But Griffin had stayed in Harper's Bay, so what long list could there be for him? He's probably either still working on his dad's fishing boat or at the lumber mill or as a youth pastor—the list could go on but not far with the employment possibilities in this community.

"Maybe if you stick around we can meet for coffee sometime. There's a few more from school who'd love to see you, I'm sure. I see Tamara Kazowski off and on. She's waitressing and has two great kids."

"That'd be fun. I'll give you a call sometime. But you probably weren't calling me."

"Your mom actually."

"Okay." That's strange. Griffin keeps in touch with my mom? I glance over and see she's cleaned her hands off and her ball of dough is resting neatly in a bowl, while mine is kind of sticky and rugged on the cutting board. "Here she is."

I return to my bread pile and add more flour, determined that a ball of ingredients isn't going to get the best of me.

"Griffin, how are you, hon?" Mom's cheerfulness reflects that this isn't a rare phone call. "It is? . . . Great. When can I pick it up? . . . You will? . . . That'll sure be helpful. . . . How'd it turn out? . . . Really? . . . Wonderful. He's going to love it."

My hands aren't doing their job again as I try to figure out this conversation. The bread dough appears a little better. But what is my mother talking about? The phone cord stretched across my chest and extending to Mom isn't helping. I decide right then to buy them a cordless phone, even if just for my visits.

"Sounds good. I'll distract him—take him for a drive or to lunch. Or, I know, we'll go to the flea market. . . . True, that would spark suspicion. . . . Ah, perfect. We'll see you then. And thanks, Griffin. Really."

She twists the cord around me and hangs up, then starts straightening the kitchen.

"Well?" I say.

"Well, what?"

"The phone call."

"Oh, that." She turns on the faucet, and the rush of water fills dirty bowls and measuring cups.

"Is there something you don't want me to know?" I say over the whoosh of water.

"Huh? No, I mean, you'll probably think it's silly anyway. But guess you'll see it next time you're here so—"

"Mom, what are you talking about?"

After turning the water off, she wipes her hands on her apron. "Well, you haven't seen Rooftop Road, so it's hard to explain."

"Where and what is Rooftop Road?"

"It's new . . . well . . . in its official capacity. Griffin revitalized a whole street to such an extent that the city council changed the name from Fourth Street to Rooftop Road. It was quite the conversation piece last summer. The paper ran some stories and letters to the editor. Got worse when they debated changing the street name—you know how Harper's Bay doesn't like any change; just look at the mess with that bridge. But since it was such an average name anyway—"

"Wait, wait, wait. What does a street changing its name have to do with Griffin? Did he reroof all the houses on a street or something?" After living several years in the more civilized part of California, the part people think of when they hear the name of the state, I've developed an impatience for the slow, meandering trail of conversation in the rural places like my hometown. My tongue must have scars from holding back an irritated tone that wants to spout, "Get to the point."

"No, he didn't reroof the houses . . . well, I guess he did in a way. The things you don't know about your old boyfriend."

"Mom, he wasn't my boyfriend."

"Well, you dated during the Winter Dance. I still have the clipping from the paper."

"Mom, I think age is taking your memory—no offense." That newspaper photo started the rumor, I recall with chagrin. Our photo in the local-scene section turned our sort-of friendship into a suddenly serious relationship—much to our surprise and horror, especially since we weren't speaking to one another.

"A little offense taken, missy." Mom frowns a little warning my way.

"Could you just tell me what Griffin has to do with Rooftop Road or Fourth Street?" I ask in a more respectful tone.

"Oh, yes. His art. Griffin does this quirky—I think that's the word for it—art. Sculptures are what they are. They're made from old scrap metal and household appliances. Doesn't sound appealing, but he makes these amazing creations like this giant spider, inspired by Tolkien, made out of tractor parts with antique clocks for eyes. He put a sculpture on his roof at Christmas one year, and all these people stopped by. So after that, he made this superman holding up a giant earth. Then his neighbor diagonal from him wanted one on her roof, and that started it."

"Started what?"

"Rooftop Road. Something like ten houses down that street have Griffin's roof sculptures on them—'course not everyone on the street has been pleased. But the travel magazines got ahold of it, and now Rooftop Road is a tourist route along the California coastline. Money to a community soothes a lot of debates."

"How come I've never heard of this?"

"You aren't around for long when you visit." Mom gazes out the window toward the back lawn. "You know, if you have questions about Sophia Fleming, you should ask Griffin."

"And why?"

"Griffin's best friend is Ben Wilson. They meet every Monday for some sort of Bible study at Blondie's Diner."

"Griffin's best friend is Ben Wilson?" The image of Griffin Anderson hanging out with someone fifty or so years older is quite stunning. How did something like that happen?

"And, of course, Ben Wilson is the only person close to Sophia Fleming."

My hands are still in the dough when Mom leans over me and says, "Give it up, sweetie. We'll only need one loaf for dinner."

I mold the lumpy dough into a ball and drop it into the greased bowl Mom prepared for it earlier. Without a word, I place a dish towel over the top, my sign of triumph over that mass of ingredients.

I have decisions to make.

And that dough better rise.

# The Memoir of Josephine Vanderook

I can never remember exactly when the storm arrived.

Better if it had come before San Francisco, before so many lives joined the voyage north; then the loss would not have been so great. And yet the storm arrived.

The decline came like a whisper that grows into speech, inconspicuous second by second until the chill and winds became an established, relentless reality. First the dip in the morning temperatures, my wool, knit shawl unable to keep the coldness from reaching my arms as I walked from hull to stern and back. The clouds gathered in dark discussion, and the dishes at lunch began to shiver and quake upon the wooden table. Gusts of Pacific wind that had traveled from Alaskan glaciers, passing the Sound and dipping down like migratory geese, whipped upon the sails.

Perhaps the forces of weather modeled their patterns after the tensions upon the ship. For days, I had recited prayers and Scriptures to make it through each day, so intense were my worry and claustrophobia. If my cabin had not contained the dank sea smell that reminded me of the pneumonia that had cluttered my lungs as a child, I would have spent those remaining days and nights hidden away.

It was a new life the adventurers sought in the West, and I had seen the vision in Eduard's eyes. Of course we knew the fables about nugget-laced rivers and fields of lush farmland. Eduard and I would laugh and expound upon them as we walked parkways in Boston. The rivers became pure gold, and every tree dipped from the bounty of fruit on its branches—Eden returned. We humored ourselves this way, without my perception that my husband had fallen in love with a place he needed to see and conquer.

If only he'd known that it would be himself who would be conquered.

Dearest Eduard, even now after all these years and through the choices that cost so many lives, even now, I miss you with every breath.

**MEMOIR MAY CONTAIN ANSWERS TO SHIPWRECK MYSTERY**
The words of shipwreck survivor Josephine Vanderook will be reexamined this week by scientists associated with the History Network. Josephine Vanderook, for whom the doomed ship was named, was the wife of shipbuilder Eduard Vanderook, who died with 61 other travelers in the 1905 wreck off Orion Point.

Although written in 1933 at the request of the Harper's Bay Historical Society for the survivor testimonials, the memoir was never delivered until this month when the History Network obtained it from the family of Josephine Vanderook. Researchers hope to discover the cause of the ship's demise in the waters off Orion Point.

# Claire

❧

*Of* course, Mom's bread rose nicely; my loaf did something, and though minimal, enough of something for me to bake it. For a time I felt as if my whole life depended on that lump in the bowl. Mom once again remarked how nice the bungalow would be to live in. I needed some air.

I borrowed the family Oldsmobile to check on my car. Kenny's Auto consists of Kenny and his dog in a large double garage beside his house and is nearly impossible to contact unless you stop by. Neither house nor garage has a telephone except for his cell phone, which gets very bad reception. My dad wouldn't let anyone else so much as gaze into the innards of his vehicles. Dad calls him "Dr. Kenny."

The gravel driveway kicks up a bit of dust as I pull toward the shop. Kenny comes sliding from beneath a bright yellow Camaro that I recognize as my cousin's car.

"It must run in the family," I say, wondering about my cousin Ty, who usually works out of town.

"It always does. Seems when one car goes, the whole family ends up here." I've often tried to estimate Kenny's age, but the grease, full head of dark hair, and weathered skin make me guess anywhere between late forties to early sixties. He's slim and tall with an Adam's apple that likes to exercise.

"So what's 'er damage?" I ask, quickly falling into Harper's Bay lingo. I need to stop that.

"Nothing for now," he says, snagging a ragged towel from the top of a rolling box of tools. "I checked her out, and she's running just fine. If you weren't Bill's daughter, I might guess you didn't know how to turn over an engine."

"I tried everything I could think of. The connections on the battery looked good, and it was running fine when I left."

"Guess this one doesn't want to live in that big ol' city."

"Guess." His words are troubling in light of the past two days' events. But how can a car determine such things? It can't, for pete's sake—oh, more hometown talk. I need to get outta here. "I'll pick the car up when my dad gets home tonight."

"Sounds like a plan, Stan. Good seeing you, little lady. You've been gone too long—yer pop misses you. That city living gets old anyway."

"How do you know? You've lived here your entire life."

"Exactly. Some people are smart enough to know things without having any trial and error." With that he winks, which makes me laugh. "Really now, sometimes you gotta return to things if you want to start anew."

"What does that mean?" I ask. Kenny's never shown his philosophical side before.

"Means you might find more than you think in your hometown if you give it a chance. Might get you where you want to go even more than by running away."

"I wasn't running away."

"Sure about that? There's all kinds of ways to run."

On my approach back to town, I see Harper's Bay as a stranger would view it. It hits me how easily you could drive through—just pass right by without ever really seeing it. The small harbor and docks, where boats rock on their moorings; the gas stations and harbor shops with miniature lights in the windows; three traveler accommodations (Best Western, Holiday Inn Express, and Sea Lion Motel); the elementary school; five churches (Catholic, Baptist, Four-Square, Community, Latter-Day Saints); McDonald's; and the new Taco Bell.

My hometown clings to the winding Pacific Highway 101, where drivers cruise north to Oregon's rocky coastline or south to better known Californian destinations like the wine country and farther south to San Francisco. Some may stop for gas, a bite to eat, a bed for the night, or a glance at the charming harbor as they continue on. It's strange to pull away from the knowledge of lives lived here, of the inside of shops, back-alley shortcuts, docking areas of the harbor—to imagine the people as strangers and see the town as the tiny dot of existence that it is.

Why have I become a tourist to the places of my past? And what would it mean to become a resident once again?

*"There's all kinds of ways to run."*

Could my haste to achieve actually be running from something? Can people try to run from themselves?

The questions seem to wait before me, and my old answers sound like excuses to my ears.

# Sophia

*I find this to be my way to speak what must be told.*

————◇————

The door makes a high-pitched complaint as I push it open, sending invisible wisps of dust and memory to wander the spaces of air and light. The bedroom, once occupied by my parents, I had converted into a library of sorts until the books overwhelmed and kicked me out. Now they live here, and I come for social visits from time to time, take one of them into my space, and leave them to their own discussions. Dickens and Dostoyevsky surely confer over the political and religious aspects of their times. Austen and Brontë sip tea and debate love, passion, and whether there should ever be happy endings. Tolstoy and Greene ponder if faith is relevant within the common moments of time.

A sneeze erupts as I begin to meander through the stacks that appear like the random, staggered spires of a castle. Ben volunteered to build revolving bookcases, but somehow the books wanted to be stacked. Ben just shakes his head at that. Against the northern wall where the big walnut bed used to be, I find the stack I'm looking for. All day, the thought nagged me that I might have information of interest within the confines of my own library.

There it is. Piled among other nonfiction works like *Birds of Northern California, Coastal Best-Kept Secrets,* and *Crustaceans of the Pacific* is *Lighthouses of the West and Their Mysteries.* The dust brings another sneeze; I really need to take a week and clean this room.

The fire crackles as if greeting my return to the reading chair. Interesting how solitude creates personification of the many things around me—the wind can be a whisper, the fire a friend, my chair a companion.

I settle in and browse through the book, finding several pages of interest. Ben's lighthouse and the shipwreck have elicited enough mystery to be recorded. I read the usual details—the disagreements of what happened, a possible ghost ship, an argument in the wheelhouse—and then find a list of survivors written with exaggerated slant to evoke more mystery than actual truth allowed.

> Margery Falkner died one year later on the exact date of the shipwreck's fateful demise. One report claims her face whitened as she gasped her last words, "They finally have me."

Farther down the page I read another:

> Reed Harrington never fully recovered from his injuries. He died twenty years later in an insane asylum.

There are only fifteen survivors listed. Only what can be construed as scandalous or suspicious in their lives has been included. The author scoured and sought any sensational line to create a "mystery," even when none existed. Margery Falkner's last words could have a myriad of meanings, with reasonable explanations if included, but the writing conjures up intrigue. What audacity to assume that Reed Harrington died in an insane asylum because of surviving a shipwreck twenty years earlier.

Down the list, I find Josephine Vanderook. This woman has a connection with me. I haven't thought of it in years; some things are so long attached you nearly forget their presence. Though my mother rarely spoke of the shipwreck, in her older age, she told how her parents discovered Mrs. Eduard Vanderook on the rocky shore that stormy morning. The woman, barely alive but with a haunting beauty, left an impression on my young mother. Some of what I read in this ridiculous book I already know, but the dates are of particular interest.

> Josephine Vanderook, wife of shipbuilder, returned to Boston. After remarrying, she had two children and died February 22, 1934. However, she never changed her first married name and had arranged to be laid to rest with her parents instead of her deceased second husband. Her inscription read "Together again at last," though her second husband had died only the year before. Many believed she never got over the tragic loss of her first husband. She went to her death knowing the truth of the shipwreck. The mystery continues.

How strange we humans are to always long for the ghosts and skeletons of other people's lives. Reading between the exaggeration, I think of Josephine and her return to Boston. How long did it take her after the shipwreck? How did she walk those streets where once she'd fallen in love and married and then said goodbye, believing a new life awaited in the great Northwest? What kind of defeat consumed her to return empty and alone? And yet she married and had children and lived a life, though her later days would return that secret love she'd harbored all those years.

Looking at the dates, I realize our lives overlapped. I was a child upon her death, living here on the Point. What was I doing on the day her life passed from this world to the next? Perhaps I was playing with Ben, Phillip, and Helen that day, bundled up tight against the winter cold. Did I pause for even a moment as if a whisper of this woman's life were spoken to me? Fascinating how lives are brought together at different points and places, the obstinate power of connections reigning even over time itself.

My eyes are pulled into the dance of flames in the fireplace. The warmth touches my cheeks as I wonder about Josephine Vanderook. The book from the wreck could be hers, or she could have seen it, read from it. How strange to have such connections beyond my own life.

I put the book of fabricated mysteries aside and think about my afternoon prayers. Is it possible to pray for a life that is already gone by? My life of prayer brings such unusual and inventive questions. Can prayer travel through time? Logic refutes such a thing, but I wonder about God and his ways. Somewhere I seem to recall St. Augustine, who questioned time and its origin. Something about how it came from the future that didn't yet exist, into the present that had no duration, and journeyed to the past that had ceased to exist. Such are the ponderings of an old woman.

I have time to ponder and pray.

My special place beckons. No specific reason; this just happens at times. I've put a routine into this life of mine—a routine of waking, praying, eating, gardening or cleaning, and praying some more. Ben's visits interject into the routine a welcome divergence from rigidity. Sometimes a nudge comes from within, and over the years I've tried to listen.

As I kneel, my knees creak nearly as loudly as the old chair—our hinges aren't what they used to be. Beside my cozy chair, my knees upon a folded rug that I've replaced many times over the years, I find the tiny place where my heart opens like arms spread wide and all that is within me is humbled before my God. The fire crackles and burns as if speaking its own requests. Holiday sighs beside me and wags his tail. And here I find my purpose.

My life of solitude has not been unfruitful. The outside world has speculated on why I've hidden away so long. One other person knows the true catalyst that began this journey. Maybe it's expected that I've spent these quiet decades writing masses of fiction that will be turned into something after my death. Annually, I receive a letter from a publishing house inquiring if I am still among the living and whether there's anything remaining to be printed in my name. My stories didn't go away with my self-confinement. I have notebooks filled with them. The stories are my friends, my enemies, and the beauty and evil I have seen.

But much more than the stories have been my prayers. Many

more notebooks are filled with names and concerns, losses and loves, sorrows and joys. What began as my own desperate need upon my knees extended and grew to afternoons in prayer; some days my prayers have lasted until night has fallen deep and dark. Sometimes it seems I can acutely feel the pain and tears of the whole world—they reach for me and find me here. And so I pray.

That, perhaps, is my calling upon this earth. It wasn't to write great works but to change this world a little by the prayers of my heart. Prayer can feel so insignificant, so miniscule, so imaginative. I talk to the Lord about that and ask him why he can't make it more magnificent. Why not flames dancing above, mountains truly and physically moved, or a great show of who he is? Are my discussions and questionings more like Satan's words when he tempted Jesus in the wilderness? Why not leap from this height? Why not turn the stones to bread? My words can border on such things. My reasoning sounds so reasonable.

Such have been the days of wrestling with him. I see Jesus in such different ways than when I first returned here. The Jesus who came to be a human, to understand our deepest pains and heartbreaks, who lived to die so I can live in death. I found him here. It took getting down, down to a depth I didn't think I'd survive, and there I found the true him. Not the flannel-board cutout Jesus, the bearded man in the frame on the wall, or the broken body on the crucifix, but the one who would let those he loved murder and mock him. The one who finds me here, all alone on the Point. It seems too fantastic at times, too unbelievable. And yet I walk my sea walk, I pray my prayers, and God is in such intricate daily details all around me. He's woven the fabric of a reclusive woman's life.

Often I begin my prayers with Scripture, praying those words back toward heaven. Some days there is no format, just my pleas. Sometimes it's conversation, though I try to listen more than I used to.

*Josephine Vanderook, Lord. She's gone from this earth now, but still her name comes upon my heart. And that girl yesterday, the stranded one who came to my doorstep and I lost the courage to greet . . .*

And so I pray.

And my Lord is faithful to remind me that he hears. It's in the silence that I hear him. It's in the wind, a flower, or a song that reminds me to let all pass away for a few moments.

*Turn your eyes upon Jesus,*
*Look full in His wonderful face,*
*And the things of earth will grow strangely dim*
*In the light of His glory and grace.*

How the world does fall away from me now. How I wish to remain here, where the things of earth have grown strangely dim and I breathe comfort and peace and love. I can give something to my Lord; I can pour my prayers and the needs of the world like rich perfume at his feet.

Alas, so slowly the world comes back. My knees begin to ache and life waits to be lived. My time is not over here, though I often wonder what meaning my reclusive life has. The prayers, I tell myself. I'm here to pray for those who do not pray. I'm here for those who need more than they ask for. Yet today I add an extra wondering prayer for myself. Things are unraveling around me; I feel it and am hopeless to stop it. It is a divine unraveling. Fearful that I am of it, I trust in it.

There is a mystery in prayer. It doesn't make sense to our common sense. Even after decades of faithful devotion throughout the day, even seeing its results, I still do not understand it. Why did God create a need for it both within us and within himself? He who created and snapped together the intricacies also molded a need that we be linked with him, but so often we dismiss it and live with the silent scream of yearning.

I am drawn to the mystery, desiring to understand its ways.

Throughout my prayers, I give time to listen. Sometimes I'm sure that the quiet voice within is not my own and is certainly the Lord's; other times I'm not so sure and must pray all the more.

*That girl, that girl.* No longer is Josephine Vanderook in my thoughts. Instead, my inner hearing gets focused on that girl. She's on a journey of some sort . . . well, we all are. But she needs my prayers on it.

She was brought into my life for a purpose. I know this. Yet I also fear it.

# THE TIDAL POST

LETTERS TO THE EDITOR
Dear Editor,

I am the saboteur of the construction crew's equipment on the Wilson Bridge on Saturday night. I confess that proudly and did it to rally the community to help me fight the influctiveness of our government into our small-town life.

We didn't want the new bridge, and now they want to destroy the old one instead of keeping it as a landmark to our historical past. This is not acceptable, and I will do whatever I can to stop it.

Sincerely,
Adversary of Change


Dear Adversary of Change,

Do you really think you can stop change? Try as you might, fight as you will, change wins every time. You can sabotage the bridge, protest against it, and write letters to the editor, but the new bridge will be completed. Did you read the engineer's reports explaining the necessity of building the new bridge after the old one sustained structural damage in the 1999 quake?

Though the fate of the old bridge remains unclear, it will not be used for usual traffic again, of which I say, thank you. Accept the change and put your energies into more serviceable issues. And what does *influctiveness* mean? If you're proud to confess your crime, why not include your name?

Sincerely,
Rob McGee
Editor

# Claire

My internship at the *San Fran News & Review* had immersed me in an exciting, whirling information mechanism. Reporters, photographers, copy editors, editorial assistants, researchers—people are the bytes and RAM of the newspaper machine. A high-rise building holds the offices and cubicles, coffeemakers and walnut desks, framed photos and tap of computer keyboards.

I loved the hum of movement, voices, and words in creation. I arrived each morning by the public transit BART, parking being impossible in downtown 'Frisco.

Pulling into an empty parking space (there are several right in front) at the offices of *The Tidal Post,* I hesitate to pick up my résumé in the file folder—the résumé, though several years old, that had still been on my mom's computer. That paper seems to wait there on the passenger seat like a plane ticket about to take me to Kansas City instead of to some Mediterranean village as I'd expected.

I've struggled with this before. Gut reaction is not always God's path. What feels right at the moment has nearly led me down some wrong avenues. I know this as truth even when that wildness bubbles within me and I want to succumb to instinct alone. It can feel right to drive fast or to run away to some island and write for months on end. It feels right to leave Harper's Bay behind.

Just then I see Loretta Preston, staff writer at the paper, waving awkwardly from the sidewalk as she balances a carrier with four thirty-two-ounce Pepsis, white straws poking from the lids. Loretta has been my mother's friend for years, but I'm a little surprised to see her dressed as usual in her Wrangler jeans, Western shirt, and hair in a long braid during work hours. *Guess the professional attire is pretty lax,* I think as I glance at my gray skirt and white blouse.

"You made it," she says when I exit my car, reluctantly picking up my résumé and locking the doors, though I don't really need to lock them.

"I sure did."

"Wonderful. Hey, I put in a good word for you, and Rob sounded real interested." Funny, she says it like *innerested.*

She put in a good word for a job I hope I don't get. Such irony. This feels like jury duty—I'm required to show up, but I really want to blow my chances of being picked. Wish I'd say something like, "I really have strong opinions that tend to come out in my work." But I won't. I'm a chicken.

*The Tidal Post* is not the *San Fran News & Review*. Of course, I know this. But it's nearly laughable as I enter the double-glass doors to what feels more like a public-records office. A long counter stretches in an *L* shape with a view of a few desks and some cubicles along the adjacent wall. The usual office smells of carpet, metal, and machines are missing. There's a scent of newspaper (ink and recycled paper perhaps?) from the stack at the end of the counter, but then I think I smell popcorn. The sounds of *The Tidal Post* remind me of my high school yearbook club, muted and confined: hums from computers, a staticky police scanner, a voice on the telephone.

My hope was to drop off the résumé to an anonymous secretary and later receive a call that at this time the position had been filled, I was overqualified, or budget cuts wouldn't allow another employee as first hoped.

"I'm so glad I saw you pull up—perfect timing," Loretta says as she sets the Pepsis on the counter. "Rob should be here; he's been working right through lunch the last few days. I'll introduce you—might help cut some red tape, get you that extra in." Her voice drops as if we're conspiring to get my application pushed through to the CIA. "Let me take that and don't move."

"I'll be right here," I say, thinking I could make it to the door in 3.5 seconds.

Not a minute later, Loretta peers from the cracked doorway of the lone isolated office she just disappeared into. She's waving me toward her and giving the thumbs-up signal. I glance at the front doors and then the clock. What am I doing?

Then I'm sitting before editor/publisher Rob McGee, shaking hands, making small introductions to the fifty-something man with disheveled, peppery gray hair and bloodshot eyes.

"We're not usually this crazy," he says, rubbing his forehead and eyes, then sighs heavily.

I gaze out his office window, following his line of sight, and see four employees in various duties—he thinks this is crazy? If only he'd spend a day at the *News & Review*.

Rob takes a gulp of coffee, then returns the cup to the dried stain on his desk. Stacks of papers and files clutter the desk except for the cleared area in front of him. He opens my file folder and peruses my résumé. "You know we don't pay much, right?"

"Yes, so I've heard."

"You'd be sort of a sweep-up person at first—various duties from taking photos, copyediting, reporting."

"Reporting?" I say. This bit is *inneresting*.

"Until Margie retires. Then you'd be a full-time staff writer."

It does sound intriguing—can't deny it. My internship and then low-level position at the *San Fran News & Review* evidenced the stark reality of the rough-and-tumble newspaper world in a metropolis. But a small-town paper shot me straight from coffee, copyediting, and research assistant (otherwise known as grunt) to reporter.

"Could you start right away?" Rob rubs his face again and looks at me with tired eyes.

"Well . . . yeah, sure."

"How's now?"

"Now?"

"Sorry, we're just shorthanded with Margie taking time off and Burke down with the flu. But of course, you couldn't start today. Guess that's asking a bit much. So when would you like to come in?"

*What am I doing?* "I guess I could start now. Can't think why not except that . . ."

"It'll give us both a few trial days. Then we'll go over everything and see if you'd like to stay."

And so I have a new job. Just like that, in one of those bizarre twists that change life so completely from what it was a week earlier, or in this case, five minutes ago. How quickly my plans and focus are turned from the long-studied and pursued course of action. I feel as if I've been warped into the life I would've had if I'd stayed six years ago. It might seem like what I've worked so long for is gone, and I could've stayed and been standing in this same spot regardless. I don't want to think of that.

Loretta is thrilled, jumping up and down and giving me the tour while squeezing my arm occasionally. "Do you want me to pinch you? Can you believe it? Isn't this the greatest?"

The tour consists of showing me the small rooms in back: the darkroom, which is the size of a large closet and used only for developing film—a photo printer does the actual printing; the archives; one tiny bathroom; and the break area, containing a table, an ancient coffeepot, a shelf of goodies—including cookies left over from last Easter, several metal chairs, and a refrigerator.

"Of course, you'll want to look over this week's paper. Do you have a subscription sent down to you in the city?"

"Uh . . . no," I say, taking the paper from her.

"A lot of folks who move from the area like to keep in the know with Harper's Bay. We even have a guy in High Desert Prison who sends in for a subscription. Funny, huh?"

How can I admit that I've rarely, if ever, read the entire paper? I decide against it. I gaze down at the thin weekly paper, thinking how this encompasses these people's lives and now my own. With the closest news station a few towns away, most of the local news comes from this source. Then a headline catches my attention:

WILSON BRIDGE SABOTAGED

Scanning the words I say, "Last Saturday? Wilson Bridge? I saw this."

"What?" Loretta asks as I open the paper.

"My car broke down at the bridge last Saturday night. A car drove up, and some people went down to it."

"You saw the Adversary of Change?"

"The what?"

"Oh my, Rob! Claire was at the bridge the night that person sabotaged it."

And thus begins a commotion of questions and Rob calling his buddy at the police station, Deputy Avery. I'm surprised at the ruckus it creates, especially when I have little information of value. No license-plate number or make and model of the car. No visuals or descriptions of the suspects. My contribution: there were two people in a car, possibly a male and a female who seemed older (I don't know why I think this, but as I talk to the deputy that impression arises), and they went toward the bridge with flashlights, returning about five to ten minutes later.

Loretta is already working on the story for next week's release:

```
POST REPORTER EYEWITNESS IN SABOTAGE CASE
  Claire O'Rourke, the newest addition to The Tidal
Post's reporting staff, was an eyewitness the night
of the Wilson Bridge sabotage. Police say she's given
important details that will help in the investiga-
tion.
```

"I told you it couldn't hurt to stop by," Mom said when I arrived home. Loretta had already called to tell her.

Mom is none too thrilled about my omission of the mysterious visitors on the night I was stranded. It kind of slipped out while I retold the events of the day and nearly squelched her enthusiasm for my new job. Nearly but not quite.

Night falls early in November. As I slide beneath the covers on my old bed, I marvel at the monumental changes in my life. Then comes the strongest sense that the changes have only just begun.

# Sophia

*What we've shared is not conventional; it is not well understood.*
*We should keep it in the ways that we can, because it is rare.*
*And it is ours. Ours alone.*

---

My sea walk.

Such is this path. In some places, my feet have smoothed even the rocky edges by the steady plod of footsteps for fifty consecutive years, not counting the years of my youth or my mother's steps before me.

Today it is not the wearing of age that I so often perceive; there is a feeling of newness that chills me. Something has disturbed the circuit of my footfalls: a book brought from the sea, like a prophet spit from the water and back onto land, so stunned and confused and changed. That is it—change. An object from the sea has brought change, so I will remember it on every future sea walk. I too often find myself staring at that water-soaked book, willing it to dry so I can discover what's inside.

I pause along the trail. The sun warms my face as the ever-constant breeze carries the freshness of miles and miles of ocean travel. Grasses sun-bleached white bend away from the waters, and the waves crack and sigh against the rocks and tidal pools. At this elbow of land before the knobby north end of the Point, I recall the object shining from beneath the tidal pool. Just that little change in my sea walk creates ripples into other changes, echoing, moving, expanding outward from my sheltered existence. Change becomes a wild storm brandishing its powers against my small cottage walls. I cannot deny my fear of change. And yet it has come.

The questions rise up again as I squint to gaze at the boat of those scientists bobbing like a buoy a quarter of a mile out. Their teams ask the same questions I have. What secrets does the sea hold? Will enough prodding convince the waters to reveal them? Has it longed for someone to listen?

Between that boat and this rocky shore, sixty-two lives were lost upon those gray waters. I can nearly hear their cries as the wind gusts through the cracks and hollows of the boulders and rocks of the Point. I'd mostly forgotten that until yesterday.

Holiday's blond tail pops up like a periscope from a thick gathering of grass.

"Come on, boy," I say.

He bounds forward as if to say, "It's about time."

With careful steps, I continue much slower and less hurried than in years gone by when this was simply the first leg of my morning exercise. The years have shortened the course to my favorite paths from my cottage to the end of the Point and back through the woods. In younger days, I'd continue around the Point, passing Ben's lighthouse, where I'd pet his old husky, Matilda, and think of him out on the waters, fishing the morning away. Then on to the edge of the state park, sometimes even venturing those paths in the seasons when the tourists had all gone home.

An unusual amount of debris has come from the churning water in the last few days. Perhaps the divers and their mini-submarine are breaking the wreckage apart in their disturbance of the ship graveyard. As I peruse the stony pools, I spy the unfamiliar. The rocks are slippery in places; every step must be calculated, Ben scolds, wishing I would stay on my path when he is not with me. A group of broken seashells caught in the hollow of black rock—this is my first guess. But no, it is glass. White jagged pieces, sea tarnished with a visible pattern of blue flowers in places. I pick up each piece, finding a teacup's handle and then the rim of what appears to be a plate. Eight pieces swept from the sea and dropped upon my shore. Suddenly I don't know if these offerings from the sea are gifts or if these remnants from ages gone and lives lost are like hauntings I'll soon hope to forget.

Their cold wetness soaks through the fabric of my jacket. But I take them home anyway.

Ben picks up the pieces, trying to connect a pattern as I did earlier. Two pieces do come together, portions of a small plate. The others are a mismatched group with only the cup handle revealing its origin. Yet the pattern is obvious now that I've cleaned them—bone white china with small blue flowers and green vines.

"You know where these should go," he says, looking over his glasses that have fallen low on his nose. "Especially that book. It could provide valuable information in the research they're doing. And it's probably illegal to keep it."

"I'm just holding on to it for now," I say. My kitchen is beginning to look like a science lab. "Come see—the pages are drying, too slowly though. It doesn't appear to be a book, maybe a ledger with handwriting inside. Hopefully in a few days I should be able to read something."

"Incredible. I mean, this is really a great find, Sophia. It might take some time for the pages to dry, and when they do, they might fall apart." I know the historian in Ben is dying to get this to experts, but I just can't part with it yet. "It's tormenting you, isn't it? A writer who can't read what someone else has written. A professional could figure it out for you."

"If we turn it in, people will be scouring my shore every day. And then the scavengers and tourists will arrive in droves. The Point will never be the same."

"You mean your solitude will never be the same."

"Both are accurate," I reason. "The tourists hardly bother me anymore. And you've established a good system with the lighthouse. You think your scheduled summer tours would work once such news broke? We'd have tour boats loaded with people and cameras, and explorers marching all over our pathways and gardens, knocking on our windows, pulling up every rock in hopes of treasure, interrupting our—"

"Okay, okay, you've really taken this to the worst-case scenario, haven't you?"

"Worst case often happens."

"Guess there's no real harm in keeping this to ourselves for now. And me the local historian. I'm a disgrace, hiding historical evidence." He pulls off his glasses and shakes his head slightly.

"It's fun being accomplices though," I say with a wicked grin that makes him chuckle. "However, before the historian hat is completely destroyed, tell me what you know about the shipwreck."

"I am an encyclopedia at your disposal." Ben spreads his arms wide, then adds, "But some tea and a foot massage would make the pages open a bit faster."

"Tea, yes; foot massage, no."

"Ah, compromise, my best friend."

Turning on the faucet, I enjoy the sound of water rushing and filling my metal teapot. It's the same sound when I fill my silver watering can outside. As I remember why I love this sound, the memory of a little Alpine village in Europe returns: the old man filling a metal watering can before he shuffled around the graves, watering the flowers planted upon them. There was such tenderness in his movements. Why do I think of that now as my kettle overflows and I just watch the water tumble and bubble out and down the drain?

"Whoa there; need some help?" Ben asks, his gray eyebrows scrunched together as he comes beside me.

I turn off the water and respond with a smile.

"Reminiscing, I suppose," he says as I turn toward the stove.

My thoughts struggle to remain in the present, to not attempt to reclaim those days of youth. Europe with its lonely and melancholy journey despite the whirl of a book tour. My ulterior motive was to understand Phillip and his war years on that same continent, the place that changed him. Phillip . . . it always came back to Phillip.

"So anyway, guess new information has been found about the wreck."

The past fades away, and I turn toward Ben, who is at the pantry reaching for the tea. Already he's set out the sugar dish and our cups on my mother's wooden tray.

"What new information? And I want to hear more about Josephine Vanderook's memoir."

"The things I must do to pull you back," he says with irritation in his tone as he brings a canister of Earl Grey to the tray.

"We're old people; what do we have if not the past?" I lean back against the counter and watch him.

"We have today's tea, and hopefully we have tomorrow's." Ben continues the activities that I usually do. After dipping the loose-leaf tea from the canister and placing it in the diffuser, he pulls down a porcelain teapot from my shelf. I notice he passes over the older ones and lifts the newest, one he bought several Christmases ago. It's more modern in style than the others, clay brown and artisan made. My teapots range from classic Victorian and elegant, to cute and country, to unique and contemporary—a teapot for every mood.

"The past is stretched out behind us more than the tomorrows ahead of us," I say, wondering why I don't change to a new topic, like this new information Ben was about to reveal.

Ben stops suddenly, his hand falling to the counter. "That is one of the saddest things you've ever said. You really believe that we have less ahead of us than behind us?"

"Well, no, of course not." Now I'm stumbling a bit. "There's the eternal living ahead. I just mean, in this life we have so many memories to grapple with, and not a lot that's really going to happen until we reach the other. Not much has changed in decades for either of us."

"See, see this is exactly what is wrong. And speak for yourself. My life is not contained on Orion Point. I have changed a lot in the past decades, and I'm looking ahead. The future doesn't stretch like the same ol' day for years and years to come."

"This is the life that chose me; I didn't choose it." The defensiveness rises in me as the teakettle begins a low whistle. Even as I say this, I wonder of its truth. My return began in guilt and sorrow, but that excuse has long since settled and now I cannot say why I remain. Once a hermit, how do I reenter the outside world? And would I want to?

"Maybe in the beginning it chose you. But you chose this life, Sophia. And regardless of whether it's the purpose for you or not, it's not over yet. Life is not over yet."

We stare at one another for a moment, trying to decide if an argument is worth continuing. We've hurt each other in the past, forgiven, and moved on. But this is different and his words, in their proximity, sting.

"You know, if you don't mind, I'll skip tea today. We need a few changes."

Before I respond, he has his coat, hat, and boots on. Ben leaves softly, not with hard footsteps or a slammed door. And with a last glance back, he calms my sudden anxiety. "I'll see you tomorrow, Sophia."

The teakettle shrills from the stove, and I let it bellow steam into the air. The broken china and book on the side counter draw my attention as I force myself not to go after Ben. Yet should I not go after him?

Instead I go to the objects and pick them up one by one. It's as if such lost emblems arriving in my life are invoking the fears I've kept like buried skeletons. Fears that faith and prayer have kept away. Fears of change and unrest. Fears I've never put into words.

# The Memoir of Josephine Vanderook

Just days into our journey north along the Pacific coast, the tension aboard turned thick and stolid. Eduard became not only distracted and uncommunicative toward the crew and myself, he continually met with Mr. Lendon in his cabin.

After our time in San Francisco, I made no attempt to intercept my husband and turned instead to my prayer book, which had not been opened since those harrowing days in Central America. Most assuredly I was a disappointment to Father God, a shameful fact that often kept me from my prayers and reading. However, the plummets of need, indignation, and humility brought me to my knees. What a wayward child I was and still can be. Perhaps much of what would come was punishment. Punishment for what Eduard had done. Punishment for my unfaithfulness to God. Punishment for lives ignobly ignorant.

What would be our last day together would consist of two shared meals and rare glimpses of each other, although Eduard seemed blind to my presence. If there had been a woman of beauty upon the ship, my suspicions would have aroused. Instead I felt competition with a ship that bore my own name.

Years have passed now, years of contemplating and scouring memory for factual conclusions. How I wish to answer the many questions. The constable at Harper's Bay told of an account of another ship in the water that night and asked if I knew of any argument between Eduard and anyone else, of which I knew of none. Once the storm attacked at full gale, I was sequestered in my cabin, where I stayed until the crash. Second Mate Lance found me there and surely saved my life by taking me to the lifeboats.

Why did Eduard not come for me? Where was he as the lifeboats were dropped in mayhem—some capsizing immediately, others floating away from the lights of the ship where the darkness engulfed us, as the boat did that I was in. People screaming and dying. The frigid water and flailing bodies. The blackness and roar of the storm. Hell upon the water. And somewhere in the cacophony of terror, I lost my Eduard. The mouth opened and swallowed him up along with so many others, the innocent others.

Many times, I wished to believe what I clung to in those first months after the storm—that my husband was another innocent victim of nature's fury. I wished to never know the truth I later discovered, the truth of dear Eduard's portion in the tragedy. Somehow my survival and my husband's mistakes have been a guilt I've found hard to relinquish.

That storm lingers upon my memory.

# Sophia

*Do you think of me? Do you still want to know me?*

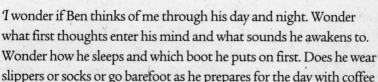

*I* wonder if Ben thinks of me through his day and night. Wonder what first thoughts enter his mind and what sounds he awakens to. Wonder how he sleeps and which boot he puts on first. Does he wear slippers or socks or go barefoot as he prepares for the day with coffee and a fire, patting Matilda's head and talking to her softly? When he stands at the top of the lighthouse and peers out into the evening sea, does he wish for things or only long for what is already gone?

Why must we live with lost loves?

Morning brings these thoughts, awakening me, tapping at my subconscious like a child waking a parent. Rising from the warmth of my thick covers, I walk to the kitchen and glance out my window at the first glow of dawn.

Yeast takes its time to rise; there is no hurrying it. Several hours later hot cinnamon rolls, drizzled with a glaze of powdered sugar, butter, and vanilla, are working their fragrant magic. As I open the door to Ben's knock, feeling both an unnerving flutter and a settled relief at his arrival, his solemn expression turns to a smile as he breathes in the aroma.

"You're forgiven," he says as he comes inside, placing each boot in the horn to pull them off.

"I'm forgiven?" I say tartly, my hands landing on my hips.

"Yesterday I didn't tell you about the new information, did I?" he says, and I can accept his forgiveness or continue to behave as if I'm not asking.

"No, you didn't, and I was left wondering all evening about it." Though I was mostly thinking of him all night. "Will a cinnamon roll help?"

We settle at the table, cups of tea in place and dainty plates nearly overwhelmed by the puffy rolls. Glaze drips like a lazy yawn onto the table. Even with linen napkins on our laps, we choose to lick our fingers clean.

"So the memoir. In the twenties, Doc Harper decided to compile a historical record of area events and people. He contacted survivors of the tidal wave and the shipwreck, along with men who worked on the railroad, some fishermen, Native Americans, and old gold miners who'd come during the gold rush. It's called *A Local History of a New Era* and has been in the museum all these years. I knew about it, of course, but I guess Josephine Vanderook never sent in the story of her life. The History Network contacted as many relatives of the survivors as they could find and discovered the memoir. Her family gave it to the museum. They're hoping for some clue into the ship's wreck."

"Remarkable," I say, imagining what such a memoir might contain. Perhaps Josephine Vanderook's thoughts and feelings . . . or would it be more fact and detail than emotive description?

"And . . ." He takes a large bite, and I have to wait until he's finished. "Guess the divers believe they've located the main cabin section of the ship, broke through some debris that blocked passage right before that little storm last weekend. They had to wait to continue searching, and one guy said they were afraid the storm waters might have cleaned out some of the artifacts."

"So that might be how the book and china pieces came to my shore?" I ask with hesitation.

"That'd be my very educated guess." Ben takes another bite. "This must be the best batch you've ever made, Soph." He licks his fingers again after another engulfing bite. Funny how such words fill the spirit—why is that? A simple compliment and my early morning rising becomes fully justified.

"Wish we had my mother's and her parents' version of that night," I say, more to myself as thoughts of the wreck return. "It was a subject my mother rarely spoke about. But then, that's her generation."

"I'd rather have people speak of things than have it all buried, but that's just the historian in me." Ben leans back in his chair and rubs his stomach.

"Not everything has to be said."

"It would be nice if some things were." And the way he looks at me, I believe Ben is talking about us again.

"My mother saw Josephine Vanderook that morning after the storm," I say, deflecting the subject back to the wreck. "Did I ever tell you that?"

"I think you might have, some time ago. But pretty amazing when you think of it all. Wonder if they were interviewed during the investigation."

"What investigation?" I ask. His expression shows surprise. "I can't know everything."

"That's shocking." Ben winks and reaches for another roll. "The Harper's Bay constable investigated the crash; perhaps the high loss of life and the amount of the cargo the ship carried led to the courts. I've heard that the accusing finger pointed all around to the captain, even though he was dead, to there being another ship in the water, and even to my father, who was the lighthouse curator at the time. There was never enough evidence to pin charges on anyone, so the storm kept the blame."

"Do you think we could get a copy of the memoir?"

"Whoa, now." Ben squints, hands held up in protest. "A copy

of the memoir would be tough to wrangle from the clutches of the historical society. You aren't exactly Mrs. Crow's favorite citizen."

"But you are."

"You'd force me into shameless flirting?"

"Maybe just a little."

Ben shakes his head with a humored smile. "It sure would help if you'd come out of your turtle shell instead of sending me on a million errands."

"You want to know what happened as much as I do."

"Not quite as much."

But I do feel a little guilty asking Ben to traipse around town on extra errands, flirting, no less, to get the memoir without Mrs. Crow knowing it's for me. Her complaints against me are long and not altogether unjustified. The fact that I refused to contribute to her museum display began her aggravation years ago. She designed a "display of honor for author S. T. Fleming, whose best-selling novel, considered a modern classic and made into several feature films, put Harper's Bay on the map." But I wasn't ready to be a product or to have my life exacted like some dead historical figure. Shouldn't I be in the ground at least a few years before such a prospect?

Without my consent, Hilda Crow summoned my life and contribution to the world and displayed it in some obscure area of the museum. Her ulterior motive wasn't honor but to draw tourists to her tiny museum.

Another complaint against me, gathered from a myriad of old spinsters and widows, is my clutch on Ben Wilson. The two of us have joked excessively about it.

"We'll make a deal," I say, looking for a way to assuage some guilt. "You get the information, and I'll do all the sorting and trying to get answers. How's that?"

"Still think I'm getting the short end of the stick."

"And I'll make corned beef and cabbage for us on Sunday afternoon. After your usual post-church musings, we'll enjoy a nice meal and some shipwreck info."

"With red potatoes and that Irish soda bread you made last St. Paddy's Day?"

"You'll have to pick up some groceries."

"Deal." We shake with sticky fingers. "But what's this about my post-church musings?"

"You are kidding, right?" By his expression, I believe he isn't. "After church every week, you share the theme of the message and the happenings of church; then you invariably start mulling over the oddities or ironies of your Christian community."

"I do not."

"You do so."

"No, I don't."

"Yes, you do."

"We haven't advanced past third grade very far," Ben says, and neither of us can stop the chuckle of memory: a miniature Ben in flannel shirt and overalls, weighing around sixty pounds; me in a dress with too much lace. Arguing over whose turn it is on the tire swing at recess or who put the frog in Bartholomew Winston III's lunch pail when we both were conspirators in the deed. Our chronicles of "did not, did so" could fill a volume.

"Anyway. Corned beef, cabbage, red potatoes, and Irish soda bread."

"Fine."

The contract negotiations finalized, I pour us another cup of tea and carefully lift a third cinnamon roll onto Ben's plate. Ben pulls from his mental histories what he knows of the wreck. At first I think it's a rehash of what I already know, but slowly, interesting details seep out and a burgeoning picture emerges.

The ship en route to Seattle never should have been that close to Orion Point unless it was coming into port at Harper's Bay.

Ship records in San Francisco indicated a course set from city to city without any scheduled stops.

The lighthouse was in operation that night, and the ship passed by it before hitting the rocks, where it floundered and sank within a half hour. No survivor, even the ship's officers, could ever remember seeing the captain or Eduard Vanderook, the shipbuilder, after the ship hit the rocks.

I've known there was a mystery attached to the shipwreck. But many questions still haunt the wreck:

Why was the ship coming into port at Harper's Bay?

Where were the captain and shipbuilder when the ship was sinking?

Was there another ship in the waters that night?

What was the cause of the wreck?

Was there gold on board?

"Gold?" I ask once Ben reaches this part of the story.

"More rumor perhaps." With a long sigh, Ben stands, stretches, and pats his stomach in satisfaction, all indications that we've sat too long and he's ready for a walk. Suddenly that sounds quite nice.

"Do we dare leave this mess?" His expression makes me laugh as he stares in mock horror at the plates and cups, the drips of glaze on the table. That Ben can make the funniest expressions. "What next—running off to Las Vegas to elope?"

"Once the decline begins, who can tell."

He holds out my thick red slicker, and I slide in one arm, then the other. I button it up as he wraps the scarf over my head and gently around my neck. Then he takes his own camel-colored coat and slips it on. Our tall hiking boots wait in the front mudroom.

"You should wear your gloves," Ben says. "The wind has a bite today."

After pushing my fingers into the gloves, I follow Ben out the patio door. From the sound of it, the surf is high today.

"My son called again this morning."

"Wasn't that nice of him." I notice my voice sounds overly cheerful, fakelike cheerful.

"Once he gets something in his head, the wheels of planning start churning."

"Bradley needs a hobby."

"He thinks I'd like it better in Redding. You know how I complain of the cold in my bones come winter."

I stare toward the windswept path ahead, where the tall pale grasses bend to follow the angle of the waves. "Do you suppose anything else has washed ashore? Maybe something more from the main cabin?"

"Soph." His hand holds my arm before I walk ahead on the narrow path.

"What?" But what I really want to do is quickly walk down the path and chat about the weather and the story of an old shipwreck before returning for another cup of steaming tea.

"Bradley is serious, and I have to think about it seriously. Not only am I not getting any younger, but I'm getting mail now addressed to 'elderly recipient.'"

"Well, you have to do what you have to do."

"For such an intelligent woman, sometimes you can sure act ridiculous."

"What's that supposed to mean?"

"Why do you always do this? I want your feelings on this."

Shaking my head, I look toward the ground at our matching boots. His, so large, and mine, smaller versions of his. "I don't know, Ben. Why do things have to change? Why must these decisions be made?"

"Because they do. Soph, you know they do. All your work to shut out the world can't keep it from happening. The seasons go so fast. You can't hang on to 'em or stop 'em. That's for God to deal with. Just give me your opinion, your thoughts."

It's my chance. Now I should pour out the mess of feelings I have for him. Confess how I await his daily visits, practice in my thoughts the things I'll share with him. I should tell about the times he's gone inland to visit his son for only a few days, or when he stayed in town after his shoulder surgery, how I missed him so deeply the Point felt more like a prison than my secluded castle.

"If I could, I would tell you."

"This reclusive life has ruined your skills of adaptation."

"Don't be mean to me, Ben." I study his face, wondering what he sees when he looks at mine. He takes my hand and the sea air whirls around us, creeping in and chilling me deeply. "This is your decision. You have to decide what's best for you. If you want this, don't let me hold you back. I'll hire someone from town to bring me groceries and such. Holiday and I can get along just fine."

He releases my hand and turns away. "You need me. Why can't you admit it?"

We could go on playing this game forever, until death do us part or until he moved away and we both died alone. I know I've kept him from other things; there've been sacrifices he's made for me and my silent repose. He deserves much more.

"I need you," I say softly.

A look of revelation, then suspicion, crosses his face.

"Really, Ben. Of course I need you. I'm sorry it only comes up in Christmas and birthday cards. I need you very much, and if you left . . . well, it'd never be the same."

"Of course it wouldn't."

We chuckle for a moment, both knowing that the words *it'll never be the same* are on our list of phrases to ridicule, phrases that are obvious and yet said anyway.

"It's good to hear you say it. What a man has to do for some affectionate words."

I realize how the novelist, the wordsmith, has kept my words inside me. How easily they get tangled in the folds of stories and never make it to my own lips. Almost every story I've worked on in the last twenty years has in some way included Ben or my feelings for him. But in the realm of the real, I find these emotions impossible to express.

"So that settles it."

"No, Ben. I want us to pray about this. Your son is giving you a very gracious offer. I can't be responsible for taking that away. You have a grandson who should know his grandfather. A son who has been too busy making it in his career but now wants to know you. Not many people get that chance."

I say all of this, but inside I believe he will stay and that, really, he should. This place is Ben. I can't conceive of him anywhere else. But what if I'm wrong? "But for now, let's turn back. I make a mean cup of tea."

"That's for sure. And I bet those cinnamon rolls taste just as good cold."

Ah, my respite. If only it would remain.

# Claire

---

I never expected my first actual assignment as a reporter to begin at Brothers Harbor.

The docks of the harbor exist as an intriguing realm all their own. I open my car door to the smell of it—salt, wet wood, fish, and weather.

Stepping from the car, I feel smaller and in need of my father's thick fingers encompassing my own. Have I ever been here without him? Dozens of memories unfold of my father; brother, Conner; and me arriving at these docks to watch the boats come in. Dad's friends would greet us loudly, all red-cheeked, weathered, weary, and eternally happy to be men of the sea. We'd hop onto a boat, get a peek into the hold while pinching our noses against the pungency of those limp silver corpses.

Billy Cotter captained the *Hurricane Maker;* it was our favorite boat to discover at dock. Billy would pull us aboard and bring out steaming cups of cocoa or coffee, if cocoa wasn't to be found.

"There be some things moms just don't need to know," he'd say with a grin that revealed two missing bottom teeth. Billy would pull his biggest catches from the fish well, slapping them onto the deck. "This beaut is a ling. Ain't she ugly? And still there's something of beaut in her too."

I'd never seen anyone kiss a fish until Billy Cotter did, and he'd kiss them often, picking up their slippery bodies and staring into their black sightless eyes. "Oh, you pretty fish, thanks for coming to my boat." Then a sweet smack on the side of the slimy gills or onto those wet puckered lips. Conner and I would stare in cringing wonder.

A few years after I moved to the city, Dad called with news of Billy Cotter. His boat was lost in a storm off the Oregon coast; they found Billy's body after days of the townsfolk's believing the old codger would pull a miracle as he'd done several times before. The name of William "Billy" Cotter joined the host of other seamen on the memorial rocks at the tip of the harbor point. Even now I gaze where the fishing boats pass every morning and night, toward those engraved stones, the reminder of what the sea gives and takes away.

Coming here is like returning to something old.

I dressed for the occasion as I did as a girl, finding in my dresser at the house a down jacket, jeans, a wool fisherman's knit sweater, a scarf, and gloves. Suddenly I remember my camera case and hat in the passenger seat and dash back to get them. The case carries all my reporter gear: notebook, pencils, camera, lenses, film, and handheld tape recorder. When I put the hat on, my straight hair tangles over my eyes for a moment. *All ready now,* I tell myself with a slight flutter, finding it humorous and irritating that coming here sheds all the professional dignity I thought I'd gained over the years.

The stairs wobble beneath my feet with the groan of wood and water—the wavy steps remind me of Conner and me running up and down the docks feeling like a water-bed mattress beneath our feet. I long to see Billy Cotter hold up a percolating pot from the cabin of the *Hurricane Maker*.

The boats should seem smaller the way so many things of childhood do when one becomes an adult, but I feel dwarfed following the line of them rocking on both sides of me. Reading names as I go, I recall only a few. It's been a long while since I've come here with my father.

Then I spot the *Melinda Rose*. She's a larger fishing boat with wooden sides and appears to have needed a fresh coat of paint about a decade ago. Yet she sits high and proud in the water. As I approach starboard, the deck appears scrubbed, and the metal casting lines shine like new.

"Hello?" I call in a tentative voice, again missing my father's presence among the world of fishermen.

I hear rumbling down the cabin stairs. Something drops, a few gruff profanities, and then a head of wild white hair appears up the stairwell. The man shakes his hand in the air and wipes it off on his pants. "Scared the life outta me. You early or somethun'?"

"No. I thought we were meeting at 7 A.M. It's 6:58 by my watch," I say in apology.

"Yep, you is early. No mind, just some spilled espresso."

*Espresso*—was he serious?

"You must be Bill O'Rourke's daughter. Pleased to meet ya." He extends a wet callused hand, and I notice a red scald along the top.

"And you are Charles Kent. Nice to meet you."

"Round these parts I'm Cap Charlie. Only my old mam calls me Charles."

"Okay, Cap Charlie. Are you ready to show me the site?"

"That's why I'm paid the big bucks, now that I'm supposed to be retired from the fisher ways."

"A fisherman never retires; that's what my dad says."

Cap Charlie laughs, his head thrown back and white hair bobbing in the air like the rise and fall of a plastic bag in the wind. "You got one smart pop. Before we head out, you be needing anything 'forehand?"

"No, I'm fine," I say, setting my camera case on a wooden bench with bolted holders for fishing poles.

"What 'bout an espresso? I can make a latte too, but I'm outta chocolate for a mocha."

I pause, trying to gauge if he's speaking the truth or not. Hesitantly, expecting a mocking laugh, I say, "A latte sounds good."

"Come on down the galley."

And then we're heading down the stairs, camera bag back on my shoulder. The galley fits the rest of the boat—tired paint, worn cushions around a square table, charts and jackets tossed carelessly on a shelf and coatrack, the musty scent of a sea boat. But then the surprise: a shining, stainless-steel espresso machine.

Cap Charlie moves around the machine like a Starbucks barista and smiles at the whirl and *whoosh* of steaming milk. He talks weather and fishing news as he works, although the machine drowns out much of his musings. From a hook above the stove, he pulls down two cappuccino cups from a mismatched arrangement of coffee mugs. I notice another cup by the stairs that he must have dropped when I called out earlier.

"There you go, ma'am," he says after sprinkling a dash of cinnamon on top of the white froth.

"How long have you been drinking espresso?" I ask as he pours a shot into a cup.

"Few years now. Went visiting my sister in the city and came back with my own machine. Took me a while to perfect it."

The tiniest sip of the steaming brew brings a smile to my face. He has perfected it.

"We better get ya out there. I have some guys coming after lunch for a little chartering service. They stayed too late at Rusty's last night. Otherwise they'd be coming with us now."

I'm suddenly grateful for Rusty's—the favorite pub of Harper's Bay.

We return to the deck; then Cap Charlie climbs up another set of stairs to the wheelhouse. A moment later the boat rumbles to life. I find a seat on the port side, sipping my latte.

"Toss the fore and aft lines, will ya?" he calls. "You know how?"

"Sure," I call back, setting my cup in a holder attached to the bench, a bit exhilarated at being accepted as a seawoman by Cap Charlie. I hop over the railing onto the dock and rush to the front of the boat. The thick knot comes away, and I toss the spiny rope onto the bow then hurry to unleash the aft lines as the transmission whines into reverse. Cap Charlie doesn't look to see if I make it back onto the boat. Evidently he's sure that an O'Rourke kid will be back aboard, sure that sea legs return like riding a bike.

From the *Melinda Rose,* I watch the dock slide away while Charlie turns us around and toward the harbor gateway of buoys and lines.

And for the second time this week, I am upon the water.

The breeze curls around my face and lifts my hair from my shoulders. A plume of smoke rises from the wheelhouse, where I see a wooden pipe poke from Charlie's mouth as he salutes another fisherman. Gulls call their lonesome cry, and another fisherman gives a solemn wave when we pass the outer docks toward the bay. After a few gulps of Cap Charlie's perfect latte, I pull out the camera and begin to click away, deciding to buy this first roll for myself. It's a gray harbor morning, a morning of hazy clouds, light silver waters, and fog drifting like ghosts over the sea.

The waves jar beneath the hull as the boat accelerates past the last buoys and breakwaters. Farther from shore and toward the horizon line we go. How have I forgotten what it feels like to be upon the sea, a minute breath in a universe of water? Waves to gunwale, the shudder of billions of tons of movement and energy beneath me.

"Come on up 'ere," Cap Charlie calls, rising to see me.

I gather my belongings and climb the stairs.

"You be wanting another latte there?" he asks as I carefully take a seat beside him, looking over the instruments—CB radio, autopilot, and other gauges and buttons.

"Love one," I say, watching a wide crooked smile spread over his creased features.

"Soon as we anchor out at the Point."

"So what do you know about this expedition?" I ask, pulling out my notepad and tapping it with my pencil. This to remind myself to be a reporter.

Steering with one hand, he keeps his eyes forward as we jostle upon the waves. "Not much. They's city folk and don't much congregate with us locals. A few of 'em have, but they're pretty closemouthed about the whole deal. Guess in that world you gotta keep quiet or the surprise gets ruined. I know they've been diving and using sonar, brought out that miniature submarine for a few days—now that was inneresting to see. I brought out a few buddies, and we watched that little capsule dive down. Looked like a sci-fi movie or something."

I flip through the notepad I bought just for the occasion, thinking that soon it'd be full of notes and worn-looking like a good reporter's notebook. Before leaving the office yesterday, I jotted down the basic facts of the shipwreck and read over the reports of the team from the History Network. Looking over my notes, I repeat a few things and get Cap Charlie's nodding acquiescence. My hope for some surprising new detail quickly fades.

We bounce our way across the bay and toward the open waters, and I begin to recognize some of the rocky shoreline Ben Wilson and I rolled along in his small boat just days ago. Orion Point consists of acres of forest and rock in a jutting peninsula from the south edge of the bay. Offshore a large white boat dips and sways on the waves, growing larger as we approach—the team of scientists, Cap Charlie explains.

A hundred yards from the boat of the History Network, he shuts down the engine. With a splash and clanging rumble, the hydraulics lower the anchor and chain down to the seafloor, though the boat continues to rock from side to side and turn on its mooring.

My fully automatic camera slides easily through a roll of film. Another roll winds in, and I try to capture through the view-finder the width and breadth of this wild Point, where the waves dash themselves angrily against the shore and black porous rocks erupt from the waters. A few members of the History Network team wave at my camera, then return to their work, dropping several divers into the churning world below us. I gather all I can, taking photos of the Point, the divers, Cap Charlie while he drinks from a cup at the helm of our fishing boat. My cheeks are ice and my hair whips around my face, yet it's invigorating. The wildness of it all.

And then, as if my thoughts are the wind changing course, I consider the scene upon which we've come to hover above. I wonder of the lives that in one dark night were swallowed to the seafloor, breath extinguished, possessions torn and scattered, promises and dreams easily drowned.

Somehow this thought confronts my own self-focus. It sends reminders of mortality that usually inspire my feet to keep mov-ing, to do something with the time God's granted me on earth, to make a difference while I can. Today it is different. I pause at this railing, in a boat so tiny against the sea, beside a grizzled seaman. I pause and consider the questions I rarely allow myself time to ask.

What's it all for? Once my body falls beneath the earth, what will remain? What does God truly want from us?

A flutter of movement on the rocking shoreline pulls me from my thoughts. Someone is walking along a sandy path dotted with sea grasses. I watch a red coat move away with the occasional wag of a dog's yellow tail following behind. It's her. In an instant, I know it's S. T. Fleming.

I point my camera, zoom in, and click a few photos. She seems to perceive my eyes looking her way, because she turns for just a moment. I capture her profile, but it's too distant and hard to distinguish her features. When she turns fully, the camera lowers as if of its own accord. Can she see me? Does she know I was at her doorstep only days before? What does she think about during her long days and years of solitude?

It seems our eyes connect across the distance, though my logic reminds me that she most likely sees merely people on boats, not individuals, not me and only me. Yet it feels as if we've connected; it feels as if she knows I'm here. Foolishness, but I can't shake these feelings. In my entire life, I've never seen S. T. Fleming until now, yet I suddenly think she could give me something of value, something essential.

"I've met her a few times," Cap Charlie says as he delivers a steaming cup to me. I hadn't even noticed he'd gone down or heard the staticky sound of steaming milk. "Years ago now—and I mean years—I picked her up from the airport in the city back when it was a big shebang to fly in an airplane. Was her chauffeur—is that what it's called?—driving her all the way up here."

The red coat disappears into the pines.

"They made a big ol' fuss about her returning for that class reunion, and I got the honor of driving her up, me being in student council back when my pop tried to keep me from the sea. He made me try all kinds of stuff in school—French class, woodshop, drama."

I'm not sure what part intrigues me most, the idea of Cap Charlie in student council and French class or the details of his meeting S. T. Fleming. "So she was having a class reunion, or you were?"

"She was, 'course. She's ten years older, I guess, since it was her ten-year reunion and me still being a senior. Everyone was making a hype over it, her being famous and all, and the first famous person from Harper's Bay."

"The *only* famous person from Harper's Bay. So what was she like?"

"Really nice, acted like everybody else. She seemed real innerested in me, didn't sit in the backseat like I 'spected when we made the drive. Even bought me a pop when we stopped for gasoline. Think she was really excited about coming home and seeing her friends. Sad what happened, a real shame."

"What do you mean?"

Cap Charlie leans against the rigging, the top of his white hair rising and falling in the wind. "The big town fire—clock tower burned down. The reunion canceled after only one night with that guy dying in the fire and all. Bad business it was, real sad time for the town."

"What guy died?"

"Can't remember his name now, war hero, though. He was there for the reunion too. That fire put the town in chaos like no one had seen since the tidal wave so many years before. A messy time."

The boat continues its rocking and turns against the prevailing winds. I can glimpse Sophia Fleming's house through the trees, the cottage roof and a corner of a wooden deck.

She is the story I want to investigate. Somehow I'm drawn to her and the reasons behind her seclusion.

Sophia Fleming has stories to tell.

# Sophia

*God who brought us together,*
*cannot he also show us the pathway for tomorrow?*

◦──◦◦◦──◦

*H*ow remarkable to see that girl again. Surely she saw me; how could she not in this tomato red raincoat?

After watching the science crew ready for a dive and the arrival of another fishing vessel, the aches of being out too long sent me back toward the cottage. My search of the tidal pools revealed no new discoveries, and the winds carry the scent of a storm upon their fingers. And there is one cinnamon roll left in the pan.

Casting one final look at the water, I see not only the fisherman but a girl with her face turned my way.

For a moment I'm lost in the vision of her standing there at the railing of the boat. I visualize Josephine Vanderook upon the deck of the *Josephine,* that ghost ship upon the seafloor. I envision a girl upon that water, a girl seeking and dreaming and yearning for things she hoped a new land might bring. Perhaps she was already searching for them with words that would someday return to this place in her memoir years later.

In a moment the girl on the boat is no longer Josephine Vanderook. Her hair frolics in the wind, like fairies at play. I wonder about her, a girl of today upon the waters of yesterday. And then I know her, that same stranded girl who appeared upon my doorstep and had entered my thoughts during my hours of prayer.

Once within the thicket of forest and safe from view, I pause to look back. These eyes don't see like they used to. So maybe it was all my own invention. Regardless, when Ben comes later, I'll ask about that girl. He'll know something; after all, he gave her a ride to town. Why is she here again? A tinge of suspicion rises within me, but curiosity beats it down. It could just be a coincidence, except I don't believe in coincidence. All encounters have a purpose, even when that purpose remains hidden from us. It's not always for us to know.

But, somehow, I think this one will be revealed.

# Discoveries

THE TIDAL POST

**NEW EXHIBIT FOCUSES ON SHIPWRECK**
  The Harper's Bay Museum will feature an exhibit on the
*Josephine*. Recovered items, photographs, timeline, and
testimonies of shipwreck survivors can be found in the new
permanent displays. Mrs. Hilda Crow, museum curator, said
the historical society worked with the History Network to
include current information on the shipwreck. "We're most
enthusiastical to have the memoir of Josephine Vanderook
arrive in time for the exhibit," said Mrs. Crow.

# Claire

The scanner crackles and speaks from time to time, the only
noise in the office of *The Tidal Post*. The staff has traversed to different locations, working on stories or eating out. In my newly
acquired cubicle, I arrange my belongings and gaze for a moment
around the room at an old-time newspaper in the midst of creation—articles cut and pasted onto the layout sheets on the light
table, wastepaper baskets filled with crumpled paper and the cut
edges of stories and photographs as they're sized to fit within the
layout sheets, coffee mugs, and large Pepsi cups on cluttered
desks. Even though the paper is not high-tech, there seems to be
a deep attachment to stories cut and pasted and arranged.

   Turning to the computer, I decide to write my first article.
After the trip out to sea and a basket of fish-and-chips from
Brothers Harbor Café (somehow boats and greasy food go hand

in hand), I'm launched into this role of staff writer. The blinking cursor on the screen impatiently awaits the words that will turn my new position into reality. Writers require words. My notes wait beside the keyboard, but all my opening lines and headline ideas have been abruptly deleted as I try and try again.

Twirling around in the office chair, I focus on Margie's side of the cubicle. Curiously, there are no framed photos or personal doodads like on the other desks and cubicles. Perfect organization. A notepad in the corner that appears brand-new, pen and pencil beside it. Nameplate says *Margie Stinton*. I wonder if I'll get a nameplate, then wonder if I want one. A little cheesy, and yet I might like it.

The phone rings, making me jump. No one told me to answer so I'm not sure if I should. Finally, I push the blinking button and pick up the line. *"Tidal Post,* Claire O'Rourke speaking."

"Ah, yeah, I was looking for Rob McGee; he around?"

"No, he's not in his office at the moment. Can I take a message?"

"Naw, I'll give him a ring later. Oh, actually, maybe if you see him, remind him that he's picking up Chuck for the game tonight."

"Chuck, okay. And does he have your number?"

"Yes, ma'am."

I get off the phone and scribble the note on a Post-it, then take it to Rob's office. I stick it in sequence with the line of others on the rim of his cluttered desk. Meandering back through desks at obscure angles, the fax machine, the long wooden drafting board with paper organized in collated spaces below it, I think about my former coworkers and their activities at the *San Fran News & Review*. It feels so far away from this quiet place.

On a table by the archive door, I spot a Mr. Coffee machine that looks like the one my parents had when I was a kid. That's what I need—a muse of black brew. In the break room I search the cupboard and find a red can of Folgers among the odds and ends of crackers, coffee filters, tea bags, and a package of Halloween candy. A dark ring circumvents the inside of the glass coffeepot after I dump the old coffee down the sink. Overzealous suddenly, I scrub the entire appliance inside and out, then fill it with clean water, a filter, and fresh coffee—at least the aroma still rises when I open the plastic coffee lid, indicating it's not outdated.

Within minutes, I hear the slight sizzles and pops from the newly cleaned coffeemaker. Back at my desk I attempt a few sentences, a headline, then another and another.

It's only *The Tidal Post,* I tell myself. It's a local weekly paper in Harper's Bay—a dot of human existence found on a map and only a California map. What's so tough about writing a little article?

But my thoughts return to the sway and bend of Cap Charlie's boat, the sound of his creaking "gal," as he called the *Melinda Rose.* I think of S. T. Fleming in her red raincoat. But the story should be facts and information about the divers at the wreck site. I realize my data is limited to my own emotions, nothing journalistic about that. The crew from the History Network and the scientists involved are essential; I need to interview them. I scribble that on my notepad and hear the jingle of the bell as someone enters the office.

"Coffee? Can it be true that I smell coffee?"

"It's almost ready," I say, glancing at the coffeepot and then at Leonard, the sportswriter.

"You the only one here?" he asks, dropping his camera bag on the receptionist's desk.

"Yes, for now."

In the whirl of beginning my new job and meeting the other staff, I recall Leonard by my jaded observations—balding, halitosis-ridden, a sportswriter who doesn't even know sports. That sounds judgmental, I remind myself. He seemed like a nice guy even with the waves of bad breath that made me blink in surprise when he shook my hand at that first meeting. Maybe he'd had garlic for lunch that day.

"Any trouble on the article?" he says, leaning into my cubicle and slapping me with a wave of pungency. *Maybe he has garlic every day,* I think.

"It's going fine." I page down to a blank space when he peers toward the computer screen.

"Off to the darkroom for me. Two rolls of track and field—people jumping, running, tossing things, twisting over bars for some reason—it's a mystery to me. Anyone show you how to develop a roll of film?"

"Not yet, and I have two rolls from the expedition site."

"Perfectamundo. Sure glad you got that assignment—I start feeding the fish about five minutes out to sea. Just watching the waves makes me seasick. The annual rowing and yachting tournaments are dreaded days for me."

"Sounds like it." Sometimes visual images are not good things. "How long have you worked here?"

"'bout two years. I'm getting that itch to move again. Three years is the longest I've lived anywhere."

"You're a wanderer, I guess."

"That'd be me. Luckily these hometown papers seem in need of staff writers, so when I get the inkling I check locations around the country. You really get to know a community by working at the paper. Nothing like it. Wouldn't trade it for any other job in the world . . . well, except for the job of lazy millionaire."

"Yes, there's always that."

He picks up his camera case and walks toward the back room. "Now don't get worried about me trying any funny business with you in the darkroom."

"Uh . . . okay." I'm confused by this offhanded remark, so I'm not sure how to react.

"I'll keep all my instructions out here and then let you go on in and try it out. We'll get you a trial roll in case something goes wrong in there."

Waves of Leonard breath roll over me as he describes the developing process, showing me the instruments to pop off the cap of the film canister. He instructs me to reenact each step in the development process until he's confident I can do it alone in the dark. I'm sufficiently sick to my stomach by the end.

I take a few steps away from Leonard toward the rows of bookcases that line the walls. "Are those all the archives?"

"Yes, those boxes hold every single paper that's been produced in town."

"How far back do they go?" I ask.

"It's on the cover of every paper. Since 1882."

I'm intrigued, realizing somewhere within those boxes are surely records of S. T. Fleming's life, success, and return to town. It will also include details of the shipwreck that I need to keep focused on. I long to start digging into those boxes, but Leonard and his halitosis wait near the darkroom.

"Ready for a test try?" he says, holding up a roll of film.

After lunch, the staff returns. The phone rings with Katt, the receptionist, sending the lines to Rob's desk or one of the cubicles. I've been working on my article for an hour with little success when I remember an excuse to get out of my chair.

"Rob, I left a message on your desk," I say at his office door.

Rob scans the row of Post-its and picks up mine.

"Chuck needs you to pick him up tonight."

"Great, thanks. I almost forgot that." He crumples the note and makes a basket in the trash can. "How's the article coming?"

"Okay. Leonard taught me how to develop the film, and I'm ready for Loretta to print the photos. Hopefully there will be some good shots. I'm supposed to meet with some researchers tomorrow."

"Sounds like you've got it bagged."

"I think so."

"And you like all this so far?"

I pause and consider what to say when suddenly I realize that I do. "Yes. I really like this so far."

"Don't sound so shocked."

"Uh, yeah, sorry."

"Anyway, we'll get you started on all the little machines around here and get you a key in case you ever need in after hours. And this week you'll see how we put the paper to bed." Rob pauses. "I'm sure you know what that means."

"The paper goes off to the printer."

"You got it. Some weeks we're scrambling to find good stories, but other times we're overwhelmed. There's never a dull moment in the paper business."

I nod. How strange to find this rather fascinating. Who would've imagined all that a small-town press could offer? "And the archives. Is it okay to look through them?"

"Sure. And if you come across an interesting historical story, let me know. We're always digging around for old stories. Everyone loves that section of the paper."

"Great."

By the end of my first week at *The Tidal Post*, I've been a staff writer, photographer, copy editor, paste-up girl, and coffee maker, and I have complete access to the archives of Harper's Bay. It's as if a buried treasure is waiting for me to dig it up.

# The Memoir of Josephine Vanderook

Lost to me are the days and nights that I spent in the tiny village of
Harper's Bay. An elderly couple, Mr. and Mrs. Wilkins, took me in, the
survivors from the wreck being divided and nurtured by local families.
I wavered to and fro between hope and sorrow. My feet would carry
me along the shore, where wreckage from our boat was sometimes
found. I asked to be allowed upon the searching vessel but was denied,
my being a female of delicate constitution, especially after surviving
the wreck.

I continued my walks along the beach, taking hours to follow the trails
that led from the village toward Orion Point, where the ship had floundered, and near that stone cottage I was first taken to. Upon the return
from such a walk, I perceived the approach of the town constable and
knew something was amiss.

My Eduard had been found. I could not believe it until arriving at the
hospital basement where the bodies awaited names and burial. His black
suit had turned tattered and gray beneath the pummel of rock and
waves. It could not be Eduard.

I insisted on seeing his face. The man at the table, whom I cannot
remember in detail now, tried to deny my insistence. How I now wish
I had listened. Forever is that mockery etched into my memory. It is a
mockery of life and love and memory. My beloved appeared like a mon-
ster from the darkest dream. If not for his widow's peak and the deep
scar upon his hand where a barbed fish had cut him when on the seas of
South America, I would not have believed it. The scar reminded me of

his prideful smile at the great catch, despite the wound it extracted. I could hardly believe this was the same man.

It seemed another wrong to bury Eduard in that cold and windy land that felt a stranger and fiend to me. And yet that is where my husband's body will rest forever.

God had forsaken us, I believed.

When the time was spent—weeks perhaps—and the other survivors were beginning to find their way to destinations far and near, the good Mrs. Wilkins sat with me and invited me to stay with them. Such a generous and kindhearted woman I have never known before or since. However, it was not my home, and I could not live my days in the shadow of death.

Instead I journeyed to the home in Seattle that Eduard had purchased. I refused passage on a ship. Yet the stage was much more wearisome than one could imagine. My arrival in the port city of Seattle was not met with pleasure; I desired only rest and a decent meal. The new household help awaited my arrival. I daresay my eyes barely beheld them, such was my state from the travels and the realization that this house in this new city would have been Eduard's and my home.

After a few days, I began to reawaken to my surroundings, questioning the objects furnishing the house, wondering about the city and the servants, even picking up a newspaper to glimpse the world beyond. It was then that I noticed the trunks waiting in the parlor.

What I found inside changed all I believed.

LETTERS TO THE EDITOR
Dear Editor,

This is the Adversary of Change. At this time I am unable to reveal my identity because of the importance of my cause. We must preserve our heritage and stop the change that will turn our town into a carbon copy of others.

You asked what *influctiveness* means. Get a dictionary; you edit a paper.

Sincerely,
Adversary

Dear Adversary,

I have a dictionary; that's why I asked. It's not a word.

Sincerely,
Rob McGee
Editor

# Claire

I think Mom had an ulterior motive when she asked me to drop off a check to Griffin Anderson. She had been married and expecting her first child at my age, so any available guy is an option for me right now. Mom reminded me that I'm in town today and Griffin would be several blocks down at Harry's Hardware, where he works part-time.

I decide to walk to Harry's Hardware during my lunch hour. I discovered that the end of the week is busy at *The Tidal Post*.

Loretta said that they've fallen into some procrastination at the beginning of the week, then cramming toward the end. The office is full today, with everyone intent on their computers and phones. A walk sounded like a great way to escape.

The newspaper is on the quaint Front Street of Harper's Bay. Both sides of the street are lined with shops that sell knick-knacks, handcrafted toys, clothing, antiques, books; business offices; an espresso café; and a few restaurants. It's been too long since I browsed through the array of shops, so they are especially inviting as I walk to Harry's Hardware.

Harry's sign proudly asserts: Established 1875 and Survived Tidal Wave. Few buildings and businesses in this section of Harper's Bay can make such a claim. The tidal wave of 1925 pushed most of this downtown section into one heap, right at the doorstep of Harry's Hardware. Even with the arrival of Wal-Mart in neighboring Crescent City, which everyone expected to cause the doom of small businesses, Harry's will forever thrive. It's a local hangout, especially with Willy's Barbershop next door. A barber and hardware store—a male mecca in this town.

A bell jingles as I pull open the glass door.

"I'll be right with you," a male voice says from the faucet aisle. Even though his back is toward me, I immediately recognize Griffin Anderson from his frame and the casual slouch to his back, the thickness of his hair (though it's cut differently), the jeans a little baggy with speckles of different-colored paint.

He's never left Harper's Bay. People who remain in their small towns remind me of those who only dream of getting married and having kids. It's like they're on some multileveled conveyor belt of birth, growth, reproduction, retirement, death. Their children and parents are on belt-line conveyers above or below, all carbon copies of one another, living such similar lives that from afar they seem to be sharing the exact life with the same journey toward death.

I shouldn't be so opinionated. Seeing Griffin is probably

another of God's instructions for my life, for my judgment on people who stay in small towns. I'll probably discover all kinds of amazing things about Griffin and all the others I graduated with who never ventured from the meager city limits and discovered what the real world is like—

Oops, there I go again.

"Now who is putting this in for you?" Griffin asks the elderly woman he is assisting in choosing a faucet.

I wait near the front counter. Harry's Hardware doesn't appear to have changed at all since I was a child. Maybe some updated tools and products, but the same tall rows with faded signs hanging from the ceiling that list the contents: Nuts & Bolts, PVC, Electrical Supplies, Home & Garden. . . .

"Les said he could do it," the woman responds.

"You know, why don't I stop by and put it in? It's got this tricky seal that can give you trouble if you don't get it right."

"We can't afford a house call, especially with Les's new medicines."

"Why not the barter system, Mrs. Henry? If you'd make me some of those oatmeal chocolate-chip cookies, I think I might owe you."

Mrs. Henry laughs and slaps Griffin's arm. "You have a deal, young man."

"I'll get everything together and bring it out with me, say around . . . 4:30?"

"That would be perfect. They'll be hot out of the oven," Mrs. Henry says, her voice quivering as it does so often in elders.

Mrs. Henry bids good day and shuffles past me, smiling as she goes. I watch Griffin carry some supplies to the back.

I hear him say, "Pete, I'm going to lunch after this next customer. That okay with you?"

"Sure, man, just stay away from the chili at Blondie's today. Ouch." Pete's chuckle follows Griffin, who is grinning and looking down as he comes back up the aisle.

"Sorry 'bout that. Can I help you?" He's squinting as the light from the doors behind me floods his eyes.

"Hi, Griffin," I say, suddenly bashful, though I'm not sure why.

"Claire?" And then a wide smile. "How are you?"

"Good . . . well . . . yeah, good. My mom asked me to drop a check off to you."

"Great, but she could've paid me later. No hurry."

"She seems to think artists have empty refrigerators."

"She's actually not too far off there," he says.

I'm struck by the blue of his eyes, lined with dark lashes—when did Griffin Anderson become handsome? And yet, I also instantly see him as a second grader with Bible in hand, shouting out, "Psalm 119, I got it!"

"So what are you still doing in town?"

"Actually, it looks like I'm staying for at least a while. I started working at *The Tidal Post*—I'm on my lunch break."

Griffin appears slighted by the update of my life. "That's a big change from a few days ago. Are you okay about it?"

I smile, thinking that no one has even asked that. "Not really, but I hope to be soon. It's temporary anyway."

"Hey, I'm starving. Want to have a quick lunch and catch up a bit?"

"Okay," I say.

We cross the street and walk down a block, talking about the changes and nonchanges of downtown Harper's Bay. Green lawns and ornamental flower beds surround the courthouse and tall clock tower. Seeing the tower reminds me of the fire that took the first one, and again I'm curious about that night and any possible link to Sophia Fleming.

Griffin holds open the door at Blondie's, and I enter the fifties-style diner that replaced a steak house back when I was in college. "Hound Dog" is playing, and the waitress—a tall, brassy blonde in her forties, I'd guess—approaches wearing a pink-and-white uniform. On the walls are old 45 records and framed posters of the movie *Grease*, Elvis, and of course, Marilyn Monroe, whom the restaurant honors most.

"The usual spot, eh, Griffin?" the waitress says while chewing a wad of gum. Her name tag actually reads *Flo*, which I can't help but wonder about.

"That'd be great, Flo."

Flo gives me a smile. I feel like she's very interested in who I am and why I'm having lunch with Griffin. We slide into a booth, and I notice a miniature jukebox on the table surrounded by condiments.

"Special is Mel's chili," Flo says, then glances toward the kitchen and lowers her voice, "but I'd avoid it at all costs."

"Thanks," we say at the same time.

Flo leaves to get coffee and water, popping her gum as she goes.

"I've only been here a few times with my parents." I gaze around at the overblown attempt to capture an era gone by: black-and-white tile floor, Formica tables, and a long bar with round barstools.

"I come here much too often for my own good." I've noticed that Griffin hasn't opened his menu. "But anyway, we were talking about you. So, how are you?"

"I'm fine."

Small talk kills me. I always want to skip right through it and get to what people really want to say. Why can't we? Who developed small-talk etiquette—a device as frivolous as pristine table settings, not just for some fancy-schmancy dinner party but for those regular nights of meat loaf and chicken salad. I wish to sweep past it and jump in and say—

Griffin interrupts my thoughts. "Are you dying to get out of town first chance you get?"

His sudden directness throws me off. Despite my irritation toward small talk, I guess I'm more accustomed to its presence than I'd like to admit. "Maybe a little. Maybe a little more than a little."

"Do you wonder how people stay here, never get out and see the world?"

I shift in my seat. *Guilty* is probably emblazoned across my face.

"It's okay. I understand. Believe me, I never intended to stay. But sometimes God has other plans, and now I love this place as I never have before. I think travel helps me when I get that restless bug."

"My mom mentioned that you've traveled," I say as Flo sets down our drinks, steam rising and twirling from the coffee cups.

"I was inspired a long time ago."

"Inspired?"

"By you actually. When you'd go off on those trips—church-building in Mexico, that student-exchange summer in England—sharing your photos and stories. It made me want to see a bit of the world."

This surprises me. I never realized he noticed me much beyond being his rival in Sunday school competition and then our fateful prom night gone awry.

"My mom made it sound like you've seen more than a bit."

He shrugs, and I realize how our eyes lock so easily. I find it hard to look away.

"I've found it addictive."

"And I haven't been out of the country since that England trip."

"But you did get out of here like you wanted."

"What do you mean?" This is true, but I can't believe he'd say it in such a way, as if Harper's Bay was some trashy neighborhood and I dreamed of Beverly Hills.

"They quoted you in the yearbook with something like 'Leaving for bigger and better things.'"

I'm a little embarrassed that this was the quote I'll be remembered by. "Who remembers what they wrote in the yearbook?"

He smiles. "That sounded pathetic. I actually pulled mine out last week. A guy from the year behind us died in a wreck and for the life of me I couldn't remember what he looked like. Then I did the inevitable perusing of old times. Read your quote and thought how you'd really done exactly what you said."

"And then I come back."

"Nothing wrong with that."

"What was your quote?"

"Can't remember," he says too quickly.

"Sure you do. I can dust off my old yearbooks and look it up, so you might as well just tell me."

He smiles and lowers his eyes, almost like he's suddenly shy. "It sure showed my age back then—the immaturity of an eighteen-year-old."

"What was it?"

"My quote, the words I decided to leave as my epitaph to my public school education . . . are you ready for this?"

"Very." I'm chuckling already.

"'Born to be wild.'"

"No, you didn't."

"Yep."

Our laughter infects one another, and I notice an older couple from another table looking our way.

"Yours wasn't exactly original either," Griffin says.

"But it's not 'Born to be wild.'"

"Okay, I knew I shouldn't have confessed." He's still laughing as he says this.

I lean back and reach for a creamer and packet of sugar. "Blue Suede Shoes" plays now, and I get the hint that Elvis is on the listening menu today. "Isn't it strange to be a real adult? Coming home always makes me feel like I'm twelve years old."

"It sometimes feels that way for us who stayed here too."

"Yeah, guess it would. What's your favorite place you've traveled to?"

"That's a tough one. I like places in South America a lot, but then there's this amazing village in Austria that I wanted to live in for a while. I've been wanting to explore Croatia next."

Flo comes by for our orders, and then we continue talking about places in the world. I feel as if we're there suddenly, walking narrow passages, looking into the eyes of children who don't speak English, tasting foreign cuisine, and crossing borders. It seems like only minutes before our food arrives—Griffin's grilled cheese and fries and my French dip sandwich.

"I'm reading this book about travel," he continues. "One quote said something like 'We love the vision of a horizon, of what is just beyond our eyes, the next turn, the next face, the adventure just beyond our grasp. And so we travel to find it.' Guess I don't have a favorite place yet . . . well, except for home. But I do enjoy imagining those adventures just beyond my grasp."

"Tell me about your work, these sculptures. My mom is very excited to get Dad's." Mom's enthusiasm for Griffin's art has given me an image of little country-style characters made out of household scraps—something I'd find cute but not really remarkable. But his expression intrigues me. In his eyes I see that his work is very much his love—it's him.

"It started as a hobby. I went through this Salvador Dalí stage. Do you know who he is?"

"Uh, yeah." I'm surprised that someone, *anyone* in Harper's Bay would know who Dalí was. His surrealist paintings and sculptures, though quite bizarre, somehow appeal to me. Perhaps it's his melting clocks—*The Persistence of Memory* one is called—that connect with my interest with time and memory and how they melt from our conscious grasp. Something like that.

"Not many people around here do, or if they see one of my books about him they think I'm nuts because Dalí can be pretty weird. But there's something about his work, the way he's attempting to capture the dream or the conjugation of dreams and visions onto a single image, that interests me."

He leans back with his elbows resting on the back cushion. His thoughts seem to be perusing the pages of those images as he talks. "I started dabbling with things in the yard. You probably don't remember how my dad was a collector of . . . well . . . junk. He'd bring home the strangest things—the top of a horse trailer, the driveline of a Buick, old railroad lanterns, even if the glass was broken out. He taught me to weld when I was young, so one day I walked out to his workshop and started welding things together. Sounds odd, I know, but it just kept developing. Before long I had some hideous creations around the place that I'd take apart and weld in a different way."

Now he leans forward earnestly, and I'm moved by his intensity for his work. "Then for Christmas, I stuck one on my roof. It was my first Christmas without my dad, and I was feeling down. As I was driving home, all these houses were covered in decorations. I decided to do some decorating, something to kind of celebrate my dad's life—I don't know—but I needed to do something. The only thing I had around was this sculpture. Sure, it was a sight. And that's how it started."

"I hear you have one on your lawn too." His energy over his art intrigues me to no end. I want to rush over and see what these sculptures are all about, though I'm a little afraid of not liking them. What if they're cheesy and I have to pretend they're not?

"Yeah, I was working on my superhero guy around that same Christmas, and when I finished, I mounted him to the lawn. An impulse really. Then people started driving by, stopping, coming up to my door. And the neighbors, except for a few, asked me to make sculptures for them."

"I haven't even seen them yet."

"You should come over sometime." He takes a bite of his grilled cheese, then says, "Man, I'm terrible. I never talk this much. Sorry 'bout that. I wanted to hear all about you, life in 'Frisco, everything."

As I tell him, it strikes me how few people have listened to me in the last few years. Sure, I've been around tons of people—coworkers, friends from church, roommates. But everyone's been busy, myself included. The closeness and intimacy of real friendship have been lacking. Relationships have been filled with goals and destinations in mind much more than taking the time to hear or be listened to.

Griffin leans in, nods, comments, and seems as if he'll actually remember some of the things I'm saying. Then I realize it's five minutes past my lunch hour. We could've talked for hours longer.

After work, I drive to Rooftop Road. It's one of those tree-lined streets with neat lawns and flower beds adorning the yards of small older homes. The change comes from Griffin's sculptures. On the lawn of 1017 Rooftop Road is an enormous superhero holding up a red-and-black world. I pull to a stop in front of Griffin's house, knowing it's his by a sign in the driveway that reads Artist, with a large arrow pointing toward the backyard, where neat piles of scrap metal are barely visible.

I'd planned to take a quick drive by the sculptures, but as soon as I see the first one, I pull over and get out of my car, then stand beneath the fifteen-foot superhero. He looks down upon the red-and-black globe that I think was once a wrecking ball. It's a mixture of brilliance, quirkiness, and imagination. Across the street, on the roof of a yellow-and-white, cottage-style house is a beetle with wings outstretched.

I walk the sidewalk, searching for houses with Griffin's works, finding a cobalt blue airplane that appears to have crashed through a roof, a butler driving a tractor along a gutter, a character holding an umbrella as if flying away like Mary Poppins.

I realize a smile hasn't left my face. What inspired Griffin? His pieces of art are the most intriguing things I've seen in Harper's Bay, probably in my entire life. After twenty minutes of strolling up one side of the street and down the other and realizing I could spend even more time dissecting the objects used to make the sculptures, I finally return to my car. Griffin doesn't appear to be home, and I'm not sure I want to see him—it's all just a little too strange.

Turning from Rooftop Road, I drive toward my parents' house, my house. Meeting Griffin has knocked me a little off-kilter, I admit. I know I have this judgmental side that I'm often fighting against. But today I recognized the depths of my assumptions about people. What I envision is nothing remotely similar to the reality. Humility hurts.

Coming home is disturbing me. It's easy to live an anonymous life in another city—refreshing even. There are many traits you can avoid admitting about yourself, traits that people who know you would identify. I've been on the fast track toward living a big life for God—or so I've told myself these past years. But in that hurry to achieve, I've left little time for self-reflection. And I'm not sure I'm ready for it.

# Sophia

*Will you share your dreams with me?*

---

Scissors, plastic gloves, tweezers—it looked like surgery on my kitchen counter. The waterlogged book was dry enough to inspect the first section of pages, and I couldn't wait any longer.

As I waited all morning for Ben's arrival, I tried to decide whether or not to tell him what I discovered. One part is dying to tell, but another part wants to read everything and then show him. Perhaps I know it'll need to be turned in to the researchers once Ben sees what the book really is.

Sundays often keep Ben in town all day with church service and occasional deacons meetings and activities of one kind or another. Today, not long after lunch, Holiday raises his head when we hear Ben's footsteps. As Ben takes off his boots, I launch into his attempts to get Josephine Vanderook's memoir, which he was planning to do on Monday, not today, as he reminds me. He's not his jovial self.

"So how was church?" I ask, glancing toward the counter where all evidence of the earlier surgical procedure has been erased, the book placed in my bedroom.

"Church was great, really good message. But why does Stephen King get hate mail from Christians?"

Ben drops me these questions as faithfully as U.S. postal deliveries. I usually nod and let him work through his own annoyance. Once in the middle of one such discussion, I tossed out, "Why are you a Christian, Ben?"

"Because of Christ, of course." He didn't even hesitate, which sort of amazed me, but I'm not sure why. Perhaps because it flowed so easily from him, as if his being is saturated with what he believes. I recall his awkward gaze, the kind that seems confused as to why I'd ask—did I really think he'd lost his faith?

"My questions are not about Jesus. Not anymore. Long ago I wrestled with him. Is he really the Son of God? Why would God plan it out like that? Why would God take Phillip when he was one of the best men on earth and then Helen? All the questions that I've come to peace about. Now I'm going through an examination of the depths of Christianity."

Ben warms his hands by the fire while discussing with himself how he should write Stephen King a letter apologizing for all the hate mail he's received and telling him that God loves him despite what people who claim to follow Christ do and say. I try not to chuckle at all of this.

"And on this same subject, why do people so often complain about doing business with Christians?"

"Where did this come from, Ben?"

"I was at the docks talking to Popeye Pete. Guess he reads Stephen King, and then he started ranting about this client who chartered the boat for a men's Bible study fishing trip. They brought the boat back trashed, with chairs damaged and food crushed into the carpet in the cabin. Pete was ticked, said they left several of those Christian tracts on the boat as if that'd change Pete's life. What would really make him take notice would be to have a clean, undamaged boat. Drives me crazy!"

"Another of those questions we can't find answers for."

"Pete was cussing about those guys, saying, 'Them Christians are the worst to do business with. I won't do it again.' Then he remembers it's me he's talking to and is all apologetic."

"Only thing I can say is that we Christians are still people—full of faults and easily blinded."

"I know; it's just frustrating. Griffin and I always go back to the same simple truths. God wants us to love him and love others. If we simply do that, the world would change."

"Wish I had advice for you, but I'm just an old hermit."

Ben sits at the kitchen table with a sigh and rubs his brow. He looks my way, then toward the window. "Bradley is coming next week."

I don't even pause in pouring the water for tea, though my heart skips a beat at the progression of events. "Well, that's nice. When was the last time he was out? Seems like quite some time."

"Think it must have been '89 or so. He never was much for the sea."

"Isn't that the strangest thing?" I say, thinking how the sea is as much Ben as the blood in his veins and air in his lungs. How did it not extend into the fabric of his son? Ben told me about Bradley's getting horribly seasick the last time they took a short tour of the bay. Just watching the waves turned his stomach. "Does he know the road is closed?"

"He got a prescription for the seasickness patch."

"That will hopefully help." I keep my voice cheerful and hope I'm fooling Ben, which is never easy to do.

"I think he's coming to convince me."

"Maybe instead it will convince him that you belong here."

"Maybe. Should I bring him over?"

This further surprises me. I've never met Ben's son. Why now? Perhaps so much talk of change has led him to believe that I'd welcome visitors. I want to say no, please no. But this is his son, Ben's only child.

"All right. Bring him after my walk, if that will work with your itinerary."

Ben's smile makes me feel guilty for the attitude that's creeping into me. The idea of Bradley's arrival rubs me wrong, like a pair of unbroken shoes—the rubbing that eventually leaves you raw. Bradley barely knows his father if he thinks Ben could survive away from the ocean he loves. Whose best interests are in mind here?

I try to picture Ben in slacks and a golf shirt, going to McDonald's for coffee every morning, watching his grandchildren swing at a playground. The image seems lonely to me; I find him content but missing something.

I'm startled to think of his missing me. More startled to think of how I'd miss him. Could I really exist here without Ben Wilson? Could I ever get over the loss of him?

Why can't I tell him? And if I did, would it matter? Sometimes you have to let people go. You do it because you love them more than you love yourself. But I don't think I could live without him.

"Soph, are you okay?" Ben is staring at me, and I've lost all sense of time for a moment.

"Fine. Just fine."

"I don't have to bring him over. That wouldn't be a problem."

"No, bring him. I should've met your son years ago, years and years ago."

"Well, should-haves aren't much good, are they? You'll meet him next week."

That makes me smile. How easily I fall into regret, and there are a million behind me. But as Ben reminded, what good are they now?

WINTER PREPARATION CLASSES OFFERED
  Don't let winter storms catch you unaware! Classes are
being offered to help you winterize your home and vehicles
before the damaging storms arrive. This year *The Farmer's
Almanac* predicts a troublesome winter starting early in
the season.

# Claire

*Home.*

I'm rediscovering what that means.

What an odd word it can be. Over a week ago, I was calling my miniature apartment and the city of San Francisco home.

The last few days have been jammed with details. My first week at the paper I learned how the edited articles, photographs, ads, and news are pasted onto the layout sheets for every page. After the paper was put to bed on Saturday, I drove down to the city. Time to make the arrangements I've been avoiding, the finale it seems.

Between the packing details, I had lunch with a church friend, which made everything worse. She lamented my departure, claiming she'd die in a small town and said, "People are just backwards there."

By Sunday night, I'd left that home behind after sorting and packing, making calls, giving notice to my landlord, and driving until exhaustion had nearly taken me captive.

My car packed full of boxes, with another trip or so needed to complete the move, I arrive back in Harper's Bay and realize that this is my home. Again. For now. And yet it has also always been. Over the years, whenever I'd drive north for a visit, I'd say, "I'm going home for the weekend." Then while leaving my parents' house, checking the time to avoid any rush hours, my thoughts were, *Gotta get home before the traffic. Are the Giants playing tonight? When will the spectators invade the roadways?"*

So where is home, anyway?

Too many thoughts swirl as I pull into my parents' driveway. They've left the porch light on. My dad, worried about such a long trip, wanted to come with me. I promised to stay another night if too weary, but I needed to get out before sorrow overtook me. Why can't I adapt more easily to change? Why are crossroads and old paths the places I stumble and want to just collapse, going no farther? I don't want to be here. I don't want to be there, not after this week. I'd like to be the person I was before my car broke down on that lonely road. Yet in life, there's no going back. You can return, but it's a return unlike a first visitation. For the good or the bad, everything moves on like a steady, continuous river that's futile to fight against.

My head against the steering wheel, I could fall asleep right here. Somehow, now that I'm home—this home—the decision decided, the arrangements arranged, and the realization fully realized, I feel something I don't expect.

Relief.

Like an ache that suddenly disappears.

I look forward to the richness of the silent mornings. As much as I love the pulse of the city, I'd created a warfare I'd grown accustomed to. My life had become about "making a difference"—the catchphrase I'd inherited from others and fully converted to. But, oh, to rest awhile. To have life simple and unruffled. There is a drawing toward such an idea.

I leave the boxes in my car and carry in my purse and keys,

yearning for a hot bath and my pillow. The door is unlocked, which makes me smile. On the table by the door is an oversized brownie waiting for me. Beside the plate, I find a piece of paper with a list of phone calls—so much for the simple life. My old roommate, Susan, from Vegas; Rob at *The Post*; my uncle, who missed me at church. My mom's handwriting says they're at the movies and not to wait up.

It feels like midnight, but it's only 9:30. I want to take this night to myself, a rarity in San Francisco with my roommate's frenetic life intruding on the few nights of quiet I might have had. Now that I'm inside, I'm too wound up for sleep. What sounds great: a candlelit bath, the chance to finally start *Brothers Karamazov*, or maybe seek a DVD from my parents' collection, though my glance reveals mainly John Wayne Westerns. But they must be watched with my father for full enjoyment as he points out facts like names of minor characters and what other movies they were in.

As I'm reading the back of the DVD *Pork Chop Hill*, an old war flick, headlights sweep through the miniblinds. The rumble of a diesel motor vibrates through the windows—a big-rig truck in our driveway? I hear a door open and then shut. Before I can peek through the closed blinds, the truck backs up, headlights illuminate the room, and footsteps come up on the porch.

A moment later, someone knocks. With the porch light still on, I can see the outline of a man through the entry window. I recognize something in the way he steps away and gazes across the porch. At once I know who has been dropped on my parents' doorstep.

"Conner," I shout with the door swinging open.

My brother jumps back, and suddenly someone—a little some-one—is crying. There's a child with him, whom I've just scared nearly to death.

I say, "It's okay. I'm so sorry. Are you okay? Come inside. Can I get her something?"

The little girl now resides in my brother's arms. She stops crying slowly as they come inside the house. Her tears draw lines of dirt down rosy cheeks, and I notice the tangles in her dark hair.

"What are you doing here?" Conner says in a voice that holds hours of weariness. He has several days' growth of beard on his face, and his hair is cut short compared to the ponytail he had the last time I saw him.

"What am I doing here? What are *you* doing here? And who is this?"

The girl buries her face in Conner's neck.

"Long story, very long. Man, I haven't seen my little sis in what, two years?"

"Has it been?" I recall the Christmas two years ago and how we've missed one another when Conner has visited since. "Yeah, I guess so."

"This is Alisia. Alisia, *el ist* Aunt Claire. My Spanish is hideous. Thankfully, Alisia speaks pretty decent English."

"Hello, Alisia, or should I say *hola?*" I'm not sure whether to put out a hand to shake or pat her back. My eyes dart from the little girl to my brother. "Did you say Aunt Claire? And does that mean . . . ?"

"Well, yeah, it's a long story. . . ."

In such situations I usually look back and wish I could withhold my reaction. This will be another such time. My mouth is gaping and my mind is telling it to shut, but I can't seem to move anything. Does he really mean that this is his daughter? My brother has a child? My brother has a child who must be three or four or eight—I'm not the best with kids. The idea of my brother and this child pulses through me instead of the oxygen I will soon need before I literally faint, further harming the situation.

My brother is a father. He's been a father for some time.

"Do Mom and Dad know about this . . . I mean, her? Who, what, when did this happen? How old is she?"

"She's four," he says, and I realize he doesn't want to say too much in front of Alisia.

"Four," I repeat and notice Alisia tugging on Conner's sleeve.

"I think she needs to use the bathroom," he says.

"Oh, of course. Should I make some coffee? Are you hungry?"

"Yes for both." He sighs heavily.

"Okay," I say, stunted and awkward as they move down the hall.

The refrigerator holds such variety, yet I find myself locked in front of the yawning door with cold air leaking all over me. *Food—they need food,* I think, forcing myself to function and not demand answers.

"Hey—" my brother leans in through the doorway—"I'm going to lay her down. I'll explain as soon as she's asleep."

After taking a jar of homemade jam from the fridge, I'm drawn to the noises in the living room. Conner carries a doll he pulled from the backpack by the door. I never saw the backpack, such was the chaotic nature of our reunion. Then he picks up Alisia from the couch and takes her to the recliner, where he begins gently rocking. The lights already turned low, Alisia blinks long and slow within the warmth of my brother's arms. Her little rag doll is nestled against her chest.

They don't see me as Conner gazes at his daughter (such an amazing thought) and sighs while the weight of travels unknown to me rise from his shoulders. I think for a moment that he too may fall asleep when Alisia's eyes close and her breathing slows. Her cheeks, so round and pink from the sun or wind, look nearly edible in softness. Long black lashes rest upon those cheeks, and her tiny mouth twitches slightly as sleep takes hold. It's an image worthy of canvas and paint—these two weary travelers at a moment of perfect peace.

My eyes catch a framed photograph on the mantel beyond my brother. He might be around eight in the picture, smiling as he stands beside a stream with a trout held up in one hand. He always smiled most when out in the woods or with a fish in his hand.

I make Conner a peanut-butter-and-peach-jam sandwich on Mom's bread (not from my squatty loaf), spreading the home-made jam extra thick.

His footsteps creak on the floor, and the light of the kitchen magnifies the tired lines in his face. "I laid her down in the guest room," he says. I know he's thinking that the room was once his own, and now his child sleeps there.

Putting the sandwich on the table, I get a cup and pour him a glass of milk. "No coffee for you. You need to sleep."

"But Mom and Dad . . . ," he begins, then sits at the table. "I've hardly slept in the last week."

"You're home now, big brother." I come behind his defeated shoulders, stunned to feel the tightness of his muscles beneath my hands.

"Alisia might have nightmares. If I don't wake up—"

"My room's right across from her," I assure him but then won-der how to comfort a frightened child. "We can talk tomorrow. Why don't you go—?"

"It's okay. I'm sure you're wondering."

"Just a little," I say, and we both chuckle. I continue massaging his shoulders, feeling the knots slowly begin to give way.

"Several years ago, I was working a ranch in southern Texas when I met Rosa."

"I vaguely remember you living in Texas."

"I was only there six months or maybe less, and you were in college or something. Anyway, do you want to hear the story?" he says with his old brotherly humor.

"Yes, of course, go on." I sit across from him at the table. Surely I would've remembered that, but then my brother's loca-tions changed with the seasons.

"So I was driving cattle for this large outfit down there—"

"Driving cattle as on a horse?"

"No, on a buffalo." He takes a bite of the sandwich, smiling as he realizes what's in it.

"Don't tease. I feel like I'm talking to a stranger."

"That's what happens when you run off to the big city."

"You didn't stick around either. But back to horses, Texas, and becoming a father—I'm a little behind on your life."

I'd believed Mom and Dad kept me updated on my brother's life, but not nearly as much as I thought, I was discovering.

"Rosa worked at the local bank. By the third week of depositing checks at her window, I wanted to marry her. We'd end up talking for so long her supervisor came over and told me to just ask her for a date. You know how antilove I always was as a kid. Then it was off to the wilderness where you don't find many available girls with morals and ethics and a Christian faith, let alone a full set of teeth."

I laugh but sense a sadness in my brother. "Until Rosa?"

"Until Rosa. There's too much to the story for tonight. But I found her again five months ago. I knew God brought us back together for a reason." He stares at the last bites of sandwich on his plate, his thoughts miles away. "We were spending a lot of time together, but then, one night when I went to pick her up at this women's Bible study, she wasn't there. By the time I found her, it was too late."

"Conner, what happened?"

He paused, staring at the table. "She's dead, Claire."

My hand grasps his, but no words come. A wave of nausea washes over me as I process what he's just said and realize what my brother has been through. I want answers that pile upon one another, and I feel grief for someone my brother loved but I will never meet. There's a sleeping child in the other room who will barely remember her mother.

"Conner, I'm sorry," I say, lame words at a moment like this, but what else is there to say? "And Dad and Mom don't know about any of this?"

He shakes his head, the tiredness so profound there's no emotion in his stare.

"Are you staying for a while?"

"I don't know what I'm doing; this is all quite a mess."

"I guess it is."

"No, it really is, more than you know. But I'm tired, sis. Wake me when Mom and Dad come home, will you? I'll stay on the couch till they get here."

I hesitate. "Can I do anything?"

"You being here has meant everything," he says, bringing instant tears to my eyes. "I can't believe you're here."

"Me neither." I marvel for a moment at how it all worked out. "I love you, Conner."

In the living room, he's asleep within minutes, his boots dangling over the arm of the couch. Outside, my car is still packed with my little world brought home. The girl is asleep in his upstairs bedroom; Conner's world has come home too.

As I gently untie and pull off each of his boots, I'm struck by the wear on the thick leather. Where have these boots taken him? And what has he endured without us? Looking at Conner, his eyes closed in sleep, tears stream down my face for my brother and the journey he's taken.

---

Some remnant of a dream encases me. My eyes are still closed, yet my conscious side becomes aware of morning, early morning, and that someone is staring at me. It's a strain to open my eyes. As I do, I discover another set of eyes mirrored back. For a moment, I can't identify this child or my location—the dream I've forgotten lingers in this foggy, predawn world.

Alisia. My niece. She stands unmoving at my door, dark hair matted and tangled after a day of travel and a night of sleep. I sit up, surprised anew at what a night can bring, what profound changes in the way you view life. Yesterday I was not an aunt, and now I am—this child's entrance changes everything in our family. My brother is a father. My parents are grandparents. When is her birthday? What gifts will we buy with Christmas a month away? In an instant my mind captures a future of ideas so implicitly different than it was yesterday's dawn.

Enthralled by her somber gaze and dark eyes, I wish to pull back the covers and invite her into the cocoon of the down comforter. We could giggle and tell stories and make plans for pancakes with hot cocoa. But I don't know her yet. And so we look at one another, studying and memorizing. She must be confused, yet there is no fear on her face.

Then she bursts into tears, and the suddenness of it confuses me. Her cry rises to a howl.

"Alisia, it's okay," I say, hopping from the warmth of bed into the cool room. I race forward, then wonder what to do with her. Pick her up? Hug her? Get Conner? I've never been an aunt before.

"Mom, Mom," I call as I run down the hall.

It's my brother who comes up the stairs, wiping the few hours of sleep from his face and squinting until his features are puckered. "Where is she?"

"She came into my room. I was just looking at her, and then she started crying. I'm sorry."

Alisia's cry turns to a whimper when she sees Conner, her arms reaching out to him.

"I'll take over," he says, slinging her up from the floor, which takes the whimper away. Alisia gazes at me over Conner's shoulder, her chubby hands clinging to his arms. "How about some bubbles in your bath?" Then comes a string of words in Spanish, and I marvel at my brother, turned instantly into a father.

Breakfast together—Mom's thick pancakes, Dad making a mug of hot cocoa for Alisia. They've quickly fallen into grandparenting, even if there are unusual silences in the spaces between our conversations. We're together, and this beautiful child amazes us, and yet much is unsaid. Last night my parents must have heard the story. My weekend in the city and drive home took me into a sleep I didn't awaken from. I barely recall getting from the living-room chair to my bedroom. Now that I work at *The Tidal Post* and have Mondays off, my week feels off balance. I keep thinking someone should mention getting ready for church.

Alisia quietly eats the pancakes Conner cuts up and pours syrup over. Her long dark hair, still wet from the bath, is brushed away from her face, and she wears a little summer dress that's faded but clean. Dad found an old booster seat in the attic and cleaned it up, which sits her high against the table.

"Or did you have plans, Claire?" Mom has been talking to fill the silence, and I've missed that she's been talking to me.

"What?"

"Shopping. I thought you and I could pick up some things for Alisia and your brother."

"Sure, yeah, of course." There seems to be an unspoken rule that we won't discuss the details of my brother's arrival with Alisia in the room.

An hour later, we're at Wal-Mart in the little-girl section, buying items I wouldn't have thought of immediately: several winter outfits, socks, undershirts, rubber bands that won't tangle her hair, a soft pink blanket. Our conversation turns to the decision of whether to get the Little Mermaid underwear or the set with hearts and stars.

When Mom puts a new booster seat in the cart and begins looking at toddler beds, I finally ask, "So, are they staying for a while? And what do you think of all this?"

"They'll be staying awhile," Mom says, and I catch more worry than excitement in her tone. "I'd like to get a few toys too. Conner doesn't want her overwhelmed with stuff, but a few little toys will be fine."

"Mom, what's going on? There's something you aren't saying." I've witnessed the nervous chatter in her since breakfast. For a moment, she stares into the cart, then at a rack of kids' stuff and finally at me. "I can't answer what your brother should tell you. Honey, I'm sorry. I don't know what's going to happen, but we need to be praying for Conner, and I really mean that. He could be in a lot of trouble. He's going to need us."

Holding a packet of Little Mermaid underwear, I watch my mother push the cart down the aisle and away from me. The last time I heard such a tone in her voice, perceived her worry in such a way, was when Conner went fishing and was lost overnight during a freak summer storm.

My brother in trouble? What exactly did that mean?

# Sophia

*It amazes me to consider the journey that brought us here.*

We share sections of the paper over steaming tea and warm scones. For a treat, I put a record on the old phonograph, an LP of light folk music I bought in Europe back in the fifties. The sound through the horn has a scratchy quality from the needle that echoes just right with the crackle of fire and turning of pages.

Tuesdays are *Tidal Post* days. Sometimes there are grammar mistakes or a caption in the wrong place, or the ink might bleed through and underline odd sentences on the next page. My grandparents read the same paper; it's been around that long, though under different owners, of course. It's as local as local can get with even a section that digs into the archives and reports what events were important ten years ago, twenty-five years ago, and then fifty years ago. That's one of my favorite sections.

*The Tidal Post* gets distributed every Tuesday morning, but Ben usually gets an early copy on Monday afternoon when the bound bundles arrive at the doorstep of the paper's office. When Ben swings by, the publisher and office staff wave as he pulls out one copy and shuffles back toward the docks. Tuesday morning, as the paper is delivered to the good citizens of Harper's Bay, Ben arrives with our copy. We then sit at the table—or by the fire if it's an especially cool morning—and discuss the local news. The weather is always a main topic, along with the fishing news and tidal charts for the week ahead. We also speculate whether the editor went too far in reporting explicit details, or we debate whether a big chain store should build in Harper's Bay.

Sometimes it's a scandal of one kind or another. Once a council member embezzled city funds; another time a citizen dressed as a Pilgrim was arrested for public drunkenness. And then, of course, there was the infamous robbery of the Seaport Bank, where robbers tunneled through the underground sewer and popped up in the center of the lobby instead of beside the main safe.

I like Tuesdays.

My fingers get inky as I turn the pages and peruse headlines and photographs. Those reporters get some of the best pictures of kids at school or at local events. I often think of the reporters with their cameras, clicking away and capturing a piece of the world.

A name catches my eye beneath one of the articles. "Is this new writer the same Claire you met?" I ask.

"Yes, the Claire I rescued."

"You mean the one who came here?"

"Yes, the one I rescued," Ben says, waiting for my sarcastic reply, which I decide I better give.

"She did her own rescuing, as I recall."

He chuckles. "But I did rescue *you* from an invader from civilization."

"Interesting," I say, returning to the paper while avoiding Ben's little comment. "So she's working at the paper now. Wonder how that happened."

Ben folds his section and looks at me. "Sure are curious about that girl, aren't you?"

"I suppose so, though I don't quite know why. Nice little story she wrote."

"What? No critique. No condescending laughter at the dangling modifiers or backwoods vocabulary?"

"Disappointing, I know. What will I do for entertainment if this girl stays in town?" I read over the text of Claire's visit to the wreck site of the *Josephine*. "This must have been the article she was working on when I saw her on that boat."

"That's interesting that you saw her out there. And along with your curiosity over Josephine Vanderook—you're just filled with intrigue lately."

"It's disrupting my routine, I must admit."

"Mercy sakes, we wouldn't want that now."

"Looks like Wilson Bridge continues to be debated." And our discussion moves on and around the subjects of the paper as Ben refills our tea, and then I heat up another kettle of water for a third cup.

The paper finally folded and set aside, Ben makes his final stretch, indicating it's nearly time to leave. "I've got to work up my flirtatious spirit for my trip to the historical society."

"Mrs. Crow would do anything for you," I say. And suddenly, the feeling bubbles up quite unexpectedly. "You know, Ben, I'm ready to go to town." This brings the usual surprised smile from him. I think he still nearly believes—or hopes—that one such statement and its subsequent outing will officially end my life of seclusion, and one day I'll be ready for trips to the cinema, going to restaurants regularly, having visitors, and buying a cell phone. Seems by now that train of thought would have long died in him, but it hasn't.

"And what brings the lady from her cave?" he asks, knowing my supplies are stocked. "A new Christmas dress or some holiday shopping perhaps?"

"Not a bad idea since we'll be there. But I want to see that memoir myself, unless you think Mrs. Crow will lock the door when she sees me coming."

"She might think about it, but you are the local celebrity."

"You promised to never say those words about me again."

"Oops. I think I can still get a copy of the memoir from Mrs. Crow. Perhaps you'd like to bring along your little artifact for the museum while we're at it. I believe there may be fines and jail time for unlawfully commandeering salvage from an archaeological site."

"Finders keepers, losers weepers."

"Tell that to the judge."

"It was on my property, so how do I know it came from the wreckage? Maybe it washed ashore from some other boat."

"Hmmmm," he says, drawing it out between disapproving lips, but smiling with the raise of his eyebrows.

Holiday waits at the front door with tail wagging.

"Now why exactly do you want to see the memoir?"

"I don't know, just have that feeling today. Maybe for research and curiosity. And I want to see you work your magic with Mrs. Crow."

"You might make things tough."

"I think you can handle it."

"True, very true," he says, straightening his collar in exaggerated form.

I whack him with my section of the newspaper, making him double over in laughter and mock pain.

After nearly a year I'm going back to town.

# The Memoir of Josephine Vanderook

Days passed before I could open the trunks. My thoughts could find no answer for their presence, though my trepidation over the contents outweighed curiosity for a time. Surmises included the idea that perhaps Eduard had sent ahead some purchases he had made during those hours he had disappeared in San Francisco. At closer inspection, however, I recognized a number of the trunks as ones with personal belongings we had loaded in Boston.

The household help rarely spoke to me. Mr. Alden had been hired as head butler, and his authority dictated perfection from the others. At last I enlisted the accompaniment of Mr. Alden to open the trunks.

"There are more crates in the carriage house also, ma'am," Mr. Alden announced when I sought him that morning.

The crates and trunks all contained our personal belongings, household goods, clothing, effects that we had brought on the ship's passage. Glad that I was for their survival from the shipwreck, I wondered why so many had been shipped overland. What thought propelled Eduard to pull them from the hold and send them overland? I recalled the unexpected cargo he spoke of in San Francisco. A cargo he did not elaborate on, and that had been a surprise to me. Added space might have been needed in the overstocked hold, and the addition of dozens of passengers would have further aggravated the space. Had he pulled our personal belongings for additional room? They were questions whose answers had sunk to the bottom of the sea with my husband.

What bittersweet pleasure to open gifts from him. One trunk contained paper-wrapped yards of fabric and a hatbox containing two nearly ostentatious hats. Certainly he envisioned our opening such treasures with glees of exclamation—as if Boston society had waltzed into Seattle. My dismay over his long absences and moodiness in San Francisco were displaced for a time, now envisioning him leaving the ship to shop and think of our future together. A future we no longer had.

Later I would find the documents. Eduard had included a copy of his will and papers for the shipyard and our home. Why had he put his trust for these important papers into overland carriage and not in the ship he had built in his family shipyard?

My beloved Eduard. Somehow that kind and generous man turned a corner and was involved in a wrong. I knew it when I found the documents, even though I denied it at first. His behavior those final days confirmed it. As the stairway of truth began, a tremendous fear erupted in me. Had extra cargo contributed to the terrible accident and the loss of all those lives?

# Sophia

*Ours is a love that is known, though not often spoken of.*

The path from Ben's lighthouse to the dock is worn. Ben escorts me gently and carefully from the wooden dock into his little fishing boat. I sit low in the seat that Ben put in just for me, although he never admitted as much. It's a comfortable seat that doesn't jostle me against the side. Ben hands over a thick wool blanket to wrap around my shoulders, but I am already nestled within my down jacket, gloves, and a hat that will make my hair barely presentable once we arrive in town. Ben won't take me unless I follow his instructions to dress accordingly.

"You picked a chilly one. If the road wasn't closed, I'd take us in the Chevy."

"But it is closed, and I haven't been on the water in what . . . a year? Today is the right day."

"Last year was a warm day. Stay bundled or you'll catch your death." Ben's concern over the weather makes me smile. My bout with bronchitis several years ago is no doubt in his thoughts.

Ben makes some adjustments on the motor, and it roars to life. The water is fairly smooth in Ben's narrow harbor, thanks to a natural break of towering black rock. Gazing back, I take in the sight of the tall white lighthouse and flash of light from the bulbs at the top. We move through a maze of rock, encrusted at water level with starfish, sea anemones, and waving seaweed.

Then we hit the open sea with the first jolt of waves and wind. It surprises me how good it feels to be upon the water with Ben behind the rudder. We bounce upon the waves, the cold salty air invigorating against my face.

Always the memories of youth return as the wind whips our hair. Days of summer warmth and winter chill, of us jutting over waves along this very jetty. It's as if I can see the movement of time—children growing through adolescence and into adults—while the memories play before my eyes.

Ben and I would take this route as teens, escaping the boredom of the Point, for at that age, town brought the excitement. He would rise before dawn to complete his chores and escape his father. We'd meet in late afternoon with backpacks to stay at the Turluccio house for the weekend. Ben would attempt a "wild ruckus ride" as he called it, to sprinkle my clothes and hair (much to my angry cries) before arriving at the harbor docks, where Phillip and Helen would be waiting.

I catch Ben looking at me now, either trying to read my thoughts or checking to see if I'm getting chilled. "Remember Operation Breakout?" I shout.

He nods and a smile seems to take his worry away. He yells over the motor, "Once Phillip read *The Swiss Family Robinson,* we were destined."

We both laugh at that truth. Phillip initiated the idea, but we were all part of the planning. Helen insisted we take a vow of silence about the expedition—our reputations would be destroyed, and good girls didn't do what we were doing. She was often the voice of propriety.

Helen also knew the tricks to planning our escape. She and Phillip would say they were going to the Point for the week—Phillip to work at the lighthouse and she to stay with me. I would do the opposite and say I was staying a week in town with Helen. Ben always had the hardest time with his father's tyrannical law;

he even volunteered to run away for good. Helen steered him back on the path of logic and came up with a brilliant scheme. Even more than putting his son to work, Ben's father believed in the importance of vocational skills. Ben would tell of the opportunity in town to learn some building skills for a week (a stretch of truth, Helen reasoned, always hating to lie). It was almost strange that it worked so easily. Our only concern was if a parent spoke to another in town during the week, but it was such a rarity that we decided to risk it.

We left on a Sunday, right after church, the second week of summer vacation. Church was a twist of guilt over the lies it'd taken to implement the plan. But as Ben reminded us as we hopped into the boat, it was our last summer to be truly free. We were all fourteen years old. It was the summer between youth and high school. Phillip's school break would be cut short with football practice starting in August.

Within a half hour, civilization behind us, we stood on the rocky shore with miles of coast and forest before us. We secured the boat, unloaded supplies, and then stared for a moment. Both fear and exhilaration hit us—we were free for an entire week. Ben let out a war whoop, and the rest of us joined in.

Shelters were built in the shade of cedars, with two rooms for sleeping—girls and boys. We dug a fire pit, speared fish, picked berries, wove grasses, and hung them like Indian necklaces and war trophies around our necks. For hours we swam, and the water felt like the most freeing space on earth. The waves frolicked with us. We could feel the power, how they played with wild abandon.

Helen's and my braided hair became frayed by the second day. Phillip had studied local plants and knew what was edible, but no one was brave enough to try the mushrooms. We decided to never return home; it was the wild life for us. Skin turned brown, dirt packed beneath our fingernails, and bruises and cuts were adventure wounds. We made pacts, blood brothers and sisters, and talked about the things we'd do someday. Laughter, sun, salt, and water—days of youthful exuberance.

A week later we said good-bye to the woods and shoreline that had been our home. Hunger came upon us, along with the fear of worrying our families, and of course, we could have been found out and not yet know it. Civilization felt strange—being apart, sleeping in a bed, eating at a table. In the end, Helen and Phillip confessed all to their parents once the guilt became too much. Their parents told mine, though the adults decided against telling Ben's father. High school began with three of us grounded for months. But one week in the wilds changed us, formed a bond that would remain our entire lives.

The boat jars hard upon a wave, and Ben glances at me with that concern creasing his brow again. The two of us have lived a lot of years without the Turluccio siblings. We're too old for the wild-ruckus ride, bones too brittle and easily bruised. We're too old to swim within the untamed waters. At our age, we should no longer be in a small fishing boat upon the bay. Yet Ben and his boat and the sea are old companions. For him, the route from lighthouse to harbor is as familiar as my sea walk, perhaps more so. There is little thought involved, just face to the wind and an unconscious gauging of waves and rock.

I wonder if he could live without it. I wonder if he could say farewell. But we are old. One day he could disappear out here—the sea rising up to swallow all trace of him. Would he not be safer inland? Such concerns have been simmering within me.

The waves smooth as the boat maneuvers around concrete barriers and marked buoys into Brothers Harbor. A certain nervous flutter arises as I see people and the outside world around me and recognize my need of existing in it.

We arrive at the docks to the usual salute of curious and startled stares. Fishermen who heartily greet Ben stop short upon seeing the oddity of me. A few tip their caps. Some I recognize from childhood; we nod and are cordial, even smile on occasion. Change comes slowly here. A new boat may be at dock or one of the pubs along harbor row recently painted, but mostly it's the unchanging environment of sailors and boats, nets, coffee brewing, bilge pumps spewing water from the holds, the scent of sea and fish and men at work.

"Hiya, Ben," a fisherman calls from a large boat. He holds a crab trap in his hands, then seeing me, tips his head. "Hello, ma'am," he says and returns to work.

Ben tosses me a grin and gestures to the mass of equipment, vehicles, and portable buildings set up on the south docks and parking lot for those television people. "That's the big to-do in town."

Groups of people and a line of children wait at a gate. "They give tours?"

"Inviting the local community to tour the History Network observatory is a good PR move," Ben says as he cuts the motor and the boat coasts forward, tapping the side of the wooden dock gently. He leaps out with the agility of a young man. The floating dock dips and sways beneath him while he ties the bowline. Then he extends his hand. "You've returned to the land of the civilized at an exciting time. Would you like to add a tour to your itinerary?"

"Perhaps on the way back." Interesting to think of that team doing as I'm doing, seeking the stories of people now gone from this earth. I wonder why we are so intrigued by others. Are we subconsciously seeking answers to our own questions by investigating the past?

"Your wish is my command, but I want to get home before it cools off too much this afternoon."

"Then off to the museum," I say, trying to subside this nervousness.

Ben keeps his old Chevy pickup parked at the docks to get around town. The truck groans when he starts the engine, then warms to purr contently beneath us.

Along the route from the harbor to downtown Harper's Bay, Ben points out various changes within the town: the new Taco Bell that went in the summer before, the closing of several small businesses, a housing development in place of a lettuce field, the remodeling of the movie complex. I've never eaten at a Taco Bell or most of the other fast-food restaurants in town, nor have I seen a movie at the theater that's now being remodeled. Strange what the monastic life does for a person considered a citizen of this area.

We pass street signs that never fail to make me smile. It took until I saw a bit of the world and then returned to realize that a sign announcing a Tidal Wave Evacuation Route is something of an anomaly. The great waves of 1925 that crushed the downtown districts of Crescent City and Harper's Bay and the less severe but damaging 1966 tsunami have led to the implementation of evacuation routes and sirens around the harbor and downtown areas. I still find it comical to imagine people fleeing down the street, screaming out the direction of the signs as a gigantic wave bears down—I imagine some Japanese godzilla type. Oh, the things that amuse a hermit.

The Harper's Bay Historical Museum resides in an antiquated white house with clapboard siding that was once the residence of good Doc Harper, who also owned much of the downtown. The women who volunteer within the society take their responsibilities seriously. There are community service projects, fund-raisers, socials and teas, historical discussions about the importance of preserving the aging buildings.

The museum parking lot is usually empty for the most part, but Ben tells me that in the summer it has two or three more cars.

Hilda Crow has been museum curator for thirty years. As the

granddaughter of Doc Harper and the widow of the former town mayor, Mrs. Crow feels the weighty responsibility to preserve the town's history and to record the happenings and gossip in as accurate and profound a manner as possible.

Though Doc Harper helped prosper the town, his history alludes to a shadier side than Mrs. Crow will admit in her museum. Receiving an unexpected inheritance of gold as a young man elevated him from a dockworker to the most important man in town. Although he wasn't really a doctor, somehow he took the name, along with renaming the town after himself. In those days a man of wealth and power could do almost anything.

Mrs. Crow's outside hobbies are nonexistent; her veins pump the blood of Harper's Bay and nothing else. Except, I believe, she's spent many nights imagining herself as Mrs. Ben Wilson—something I perceived decades ago, much to Ben's insistence otherwise.

Hilda Crow doesn't like me. I'm a rue in her life—for one because I keep her from Ben. The other is the rue of *my* life—my somewhat celebrity, which has, of course, dwindled considerably over the years. Yet somehow it diminishes the Doc Harper legacy within our town and forced her, she believes, to include my life and success in the society's museum. The last time we spoke she said, "It's my responsibility to record all history. Whether you like it or not, Sophia, your books sold enough, and then your mysterious disappearance made you famous. If you'd set that novel in some fictitious town or decided to disappear somewhere else, then we wouldn't have this problem." It would seem that after fifty years, she'd get the idea that my seclusion was not an attempt to gather more fame.

The Chevy makes a few sputters as Ben turns off the engine in the museum's parking lot. Several vehicles are in the lot; one truck says Bay Construction on the side. Ben shuffles ahead of me to open the door. "Be nice," he says under his breath.

"What does that mean?" I say as a bell jingles. My heart is suddenly racing, and I fear the walls of the museum, the people all around. *Stay calm. You can do this.*

"Welcome to—," comes a hearty greeting that abruptly halts as the image of me must have come into view. My eyes take a moment to adjust after I walk inside. Hilda Crow appears older than I remember, or perhaps it's the kinky curls and blue tint of her hair when for years she'd kept it in a brassy blonde beehive.

"Well, Sophia Fleming, welcome," she says formally. "And, Ben, good to see you." Even Ben gets more formality than he's used to, punishment perhaps for being with me.

"Good day, Hilda," Ben says in his cheerful manner, ignoring her crisp demeanor. "What's all the excitement about?" He motions to several workers through an archway in the original parlor that is used for special exhibits—my display was in there for a while. The abrupt sound of a Skilsaw cuts through the usually silent museum, making Mrs. Crow and me jump nervously.

"They were supposed to be finished mounting the displays yesterday. That's why you don't hire family. My grandson can be incompetent. The new exhibit opens in the morning, so they'll have to work through the night if that's what it takes to be ready." Frustration creases Mrs. Crow's forehead, and she speaks in an amplified tone. "We're already having a few media visits today and it's not quite ready, for goodness' sake. Sorry I can't show you around, but be my guest and take a peek at what's happening. Just watch out for the workers. I'll catch up with you in a bit."

And with that Mrs. Crow scurries past the stairway that leads to rooms displaying the more modern years of Harper's Bay, including the tsunami, the shipwreck, and most likely my display, among others. Ben and I turn to one another and chuckle as we hear Mrs. Crow chastising someone in the other room.

"Do you think Josephine's memoir is in there?" I ask.

"I doubt we'll be getting the copy of it today."

"I think you're right; it'd put Mrs. Crow over the edge, I fear. But let's look around. I haven't been here in years."

"Wonder why?" he says, referring to my last visit when Mrs. Crow and I argued over my display and I walked out angry after spouting, "If I wasn't a Christian, you'd be on the floor."

"She intentionally chose the worst pictures of me."

"She said it was because you wouldn't contribute any photos or information, so that's all she had," Ben says as I follow him through the living room and kitchen that appear as replicas to life in Harper's Bay in the late 1800s. We follow the carpeting that separates visitors from the roped-off antique-furniture settings. The old parlor holds the temporary exhibits that have displayed local artists' works, traveling exhibitions, schoolchildren's projects, and the historical society's original focus. The upcoming one hundredth anniversary of the shipwreck has brought down the upstairs display and created the opportunity for a whole exhibition on the *Josephine* and its night of terror. Some of the ship's items have been at the museum since being salvaged in the days following the wreck. Surely Mrs. Crow hopes the expedition team with its high-tech equipment will add more discoveries to the display cases.

We greet two men who are attaching a section of the ship's railing to the wall, then move toward the long display case containing remnants of the wreck: broken eyeglasses, navigational tools, pieces of rigging, a child's shoe.

Ben nudges me as we peruse the items. "You know what else should be in here," he says with a touch of humor.

I nudge him back, fighting the guilt as I think of the broken china pieces and the book sitting on my kitchen counter—a display of its own.

It feels strange to see these things within the confines of a museum, these belongings of people, parts of a lost ship, the broken limbs of dreams. Ben moves on, while I remain at the display case reading the map of the ship's journey before the wreck. The memoir of Josephine Vanderook doesn't appear anywhere.

Ben turns a corner, and a voice greets him. "Hey, thanks again for saving me the other day."

"My pleasure. Did you get your car towed?"

"Yes, it went straight to Kenny's and is running great, but he isn't quite sure what happened."

I feel like I'm eavesdropping and don't know whether to run for the next room or to stay put, but their voices are getting closer.

"Some cars are just fickle beasts. Sophia," Ben calls.

My feet are frozen for a moment; then they wind around the corner, and I meet the surprised expression of that girl.

"There you are," he says, taking my elbow and guiding me forward. "You haven't met Claire O'Rourke yet." His cheerful tone irritates me.

"Nice to meet you. I heard about your car trouble."

She's unnerved by my presence, appearing tense in her stance. Her voice loses its casual tone. "I apologize for showing up at your house, but I didn't know what else to do. Sure glad Ben arrived."

Claire O'Rourke has a sweet, youthful face with dark eyes; her hair is pulled back in a ponytail. Instantly I feel an odd connection with her—perhaps it's the two encounters, now a third, in such a short time. I'm not sure why, but I wish to know this girl, though of course I never will. She's wearing slacks and a white blouse, holding a notepad and pencil. Yes, she's the new reporter—another writer.

"It's just good you were safe," I hear myself say.

"Claire's working at *The Tidal Post* now. Oh . . . but you know that; I forgot." Ben's playing a game that only he is enjoying.

"Yes, I enjoyed your article about the shipwreck. Nicely done."

"Thank you," Claire says, seeming genuinely pleased at my words. "I'm here doing another story today."

"Really?" Ben says, smiling at her. "About what the divers are finding?"

"Yes, a follow-up of the first one. I'm meeting the head scientist in a bit, but I thought I'd look around the new exhibit first."

"That's why we're here too. We're intrigued by things that have come from the shipwreck all right." Ben gives me a look that pushes me beyond irritation to downright anger. What is he up to? I'm torn between fearing he'll start telling Claire about what I've found along my shore and wondering about this girl whose smile lights up her whole face. There's an energy within her that attracts me, even boosts the blood in my own veins. Oh, to be so youthful, filled with a vision, with a future to tackle.

When the conversation lags, Claire reaches out her hand toward mine. "It's a real honor to meet you, Ms. Fleming."

"I feel the same. You should come out to tea sometime." The invitation flies from my lips like some old etiquette returned after decades of hibernation—surely my mother's upbringing. We all are surprised by my words. Ben's smile is gone, and he stares at me in shock.

"Uh . . . that would be nice." Claire only slightly stutters.

"Well, yes, wouldn't that be wonderful? I could bring you out in the boat," Ben says rapidly before I change my mind. What's strange, I don't want to change my mind. I actually would like to have tea with Claire O'Rourke. What is happening to me?

"Maybe next week?" I say, again surprising myself. "Wednesday?"

Claire glances at Ben and back at me. "That would be nice, really nice."

CELEBRATE IN HARPER'S BAY
  Holiday celebrations abound in the community in the coming month, beginning with the Big Turkey Parade. . . .

# Claire

---

Thoughts, or rather worries, of my brother and Alisia were inter-
rupted by seeing Ben Wilson at the museum. Now my footsteps
sound like echoing taps on the tile floor as I walk away from
meeting Sophia Fleming. I'm having tea with her next week. I am
having tea with novelist S. T. Fleming.

Perhaps this isn't as amazing as I find it to be. From what I
believed, Ms. Fleming is still the recluse she's always been, coming to town only rarely and having no one out to her cottage on
the Point. Has something changed while I was gone? My earlier
conversations with Mom and Dad have confirmed what I
believed. And yet suddenly I'm going out there. Me.

Gazing down at the notebook in my hand, I see I've scribbled
next Wednesday on the paper, further proof that the conversation truly occurred. The museum clock chimes softly, reminding
me of my appointment with Roger Carlisle of the History Network. My notebook is shaky in my hands, and I try to calm
myself before Roger arrives.

"Did you see everything you needed to see?" a voice says from
behind the empty counter. Suddenly a head pops up, and Mrs.

Crow appears, holding a pile of papers against her chest. Perhaps it's the activity all around, but the woman hasn't looked me in the eye since I told her my name upon arriving.

"Yes, thank you."

"Good, very good. Channel 8 News will be here in an hour. If you have additional questions, give me a call."

"Sounds great, thanks."

"Did you happen to see that we have a local celebrity here?" Mrs. Crow says with emphasis on *celebrity,* making me wonder if she's being sarcastic or enthusiastic.

"Yes. I saw Ms. Fleming."

"You could add that to your article, you know. Would probably help attendance to the exhibit if people knew she's been in. They might think she'll come back."

"Well, my article is more on the shipwreck and items being recovered. But thank you for the suggestion."

Obviously Mrs. Crow doesn't like my answer and quickly makes her departure after saying tartly, "Well, if I can help you with anything else . . ."

I decide to wait for Mr. Carlisle on a bench outside the entrance. A breeze carries the scent of sea when I open the door, and the distant foghorn sounds at regular intervals. Thoughts of Sophia Fleming are a blessed respite from worrying about my brother. What would it be like to be a town enigma?

Much of childhood playtime revolved around re-creating events and people around us. The neighbor kids, Conner, and I might act out church or play Indiana Jones in the tangled woods behind our house—my brother was always Dr. Jones. After the neighborhood kids went home to chores or TV shows, and once Conner escaped into the solitude we both required at times, I would take my backpack of books, a Jell-O pudding pack and plastic spoon, and seek my own quiet place, where I most often played the role of S. T. Fleming. Winding down darkened pathways where the pines and ferns grew into a canopy surrounding me, I walked as a novelist tortured by words that wouldn't find their place upon the page. For hours, I could debate with the words, build my reclusive hideout, and imagine that television journalists were hiding somewhere for a glimpse of me. I'd write poetry—awful poetry I'd later discover—and work on stories of every genre, depending upon my mood.

Once I saw her. My mother and I were buying new sandals for summer when Ms. Fleming came into the department store and bought a straw hat. As my mother was paying for my shoes, I spied on her from behind a rack of clothing. She turned and winked before leaving.

I've been invited to have tea with S. T. Fleming. Even if it never happens, the invitation is meaningful.

Alisia walks with solemn steps for one so young. The backyard holds great interest for her. She stares as a black beetle meanders along the rock pathway, then moves on to investigate a shadowed hollow among the bushes and trees of the garden. Strands of hair rise and catch the afternoon light, and I find myself intrigued.

From the bottom porch step, the afternoon sun warms my face—the shade too chilly and the contrast between the two surprising. The yard takes on a grander perspective from this view—a child's view, Alisia's view. Massive sequoia pines surround the lawn, crowding in from the wood beyond. They look like a giant army from the beanstalk world. Smaller, fruitless mulberry trees drip with vines, and a large fern appears treelike; a rivet between bushes is a hidden passage into secret hideouts. I wonder if this green and shadowed place frightens a child or provides intrigue.

My unsuccessful attempts at church-nursery duty have kept

me away from children. Those outstretched arms toward mothers who rushed off to church, confident the cries would end, the miniature demands that so quickly turned to fits of anger over things like crackers and toys. I don't know what to do with arched backs, high-pitched shrills, or kicking feet. All my logical talks with the two-and-under group never get through. Finally a nursery worker told me that my ministry surely rested in other areas, and I was released from the schedule, much to my relief.

Children fascinate but intimidate me. Watching Alisia, I find the usual apprehension fade. She needs us. All the unspokens about her mother and the circumstances of her arrival bring the knowledge that this child has been through difficulties, some I'll probably never know or even comprehend. This child has survived more than my own sheltered life has encountered.

I want my life to be meaningful, but the *how* and *why* have always been in question. Yet sitting on the back-porch steps and watching this child as she touches the petals of a flower, this reminder comes from what has been a fog of busyness and five-year goals. What is it that I've felt destined toward? Somehow I got lost in San Francisco, though all the while believing I was on that path toward my dreams. Does Sophia Fleming find meaning in her seclusion? Did the outside world shake her so deeply that she fled to her childhood home to recover and yet never did? Something in this child and in that woman brings such thoughts, but the answers seem right beyond my grasp.

The doorbell rings. No footsteps echo through the house. My brother must be sleeping, an attempt to recover some of the hours lost, and my parents have gone to town. I glance at Alisia and wonder if I can leave her. How long can a child this age be alone? She hasn't put anything in her mouth or acted like the toddlers who must be toted on your hip if not playing within constant sight. Yet she doesn't seem old enough to play alone, though probably kids her age play for hours in backyards in every neighborhood. And I can see her from the front door, I surmise.

"I'll be right back," I say, wanting to include a directive like "Stay right there." Yet I've not moved into the role of instructor or disciplinarian, so it feels uncomfortable to me. Hurrying toward the front door, I make continual backward glances at Alisia while she watches a bug on the daisy bush.

The UPS man stands at the door with a clipboard. "Can you sign?" he says, tapping it with an electronic pen. The engine of the brown truck rumbles as it sits in the driveway.

"Sure," I say, looking over my shoulder through the house to the open sliding door. I no longer see Alisia, so I quickly sign the clipboard and grab the package. "Thanks." I close the door, rushing back outside.

"Alisia?" I miss the steps and race to the lawn, my eyes taking in the flower beds, the lawn, the fountain on the compact brick patio, the pathway to the bungalow, the gate leading to a long trail that goes to the sea still closed.

"Alisia!" All those missing-children posters, the TV shows, the milk cartons, the frantic thoughts all slap me as I turn back toward the house. Something makes me do a double take, and I spot her new red shoes barely sticking out from the shadows of the porch. Relief with a tinge of anger replaces the fear. "Alisia, what are you doing under there?"

She doesn't speak so I repeat the question, bending down to her level to see her dark eyes.

"I hiding."

"Hiding? From what?"

"Papa." She speaks calmly, but I perceive fear. Cobwebs have caught in her hair, and there's a smudge on her new shirt.

"Why would you hide from Papa? Is it a game? Fun?"

"Mama hide me." Suddenly I know that she's hidden this way from "Papa" and not just once before. As I reach for her hand, she hesitates a moment and then comes from beneath the porch. Her soft pudgy fingers weave through mine. And though I bring her back into the sunlight, she doesn't let go. She doesn't let go for quite a while.

"She's not yours, is she?" It's an accusation I immediately regret.

Conner is clean shaven, and his hair is still wet from the shower. He said he hoped it wouldn't scare Alisia to see him without his "hairy face," because she's been through so many changes lately. As he sits on the back porch swing, watching Alisia at play, I drop the words I could barely contain when he walked outside. Already Alisia seems to have forgotten that she was hiding from her "Papa." And I know without a doubt that the father she was talking about is not my brother.

In one instant his half smile fades, and it takes a few moments for him to look my way. "Not by blood, but in every other way possible."

"Where are her parents?"

"Everything I told you about her mother is the truth. Rosa's ex-husband had deserted them before I even met her."

"He was violent?" I say, thinking of Alisia with cobwebs in her hair, wondering how she didn't flinch as I pulled them out.

"He would have killed her too."

"What do you mean *too?*"

My brother pauses long and hard. "I found Alisia hiding under the bed."

"Conner," I whisper, suddenly more afraid than I've ever been.

"Rosa was dead; her ex was passed out and didn't even know what he'd done. I found Alisia and called the cops." Conner leans forward, elbows resting on knees, hands folded, his eyes watching Alisia as she runs toward a ball and kicks it. "*Bueno,* Alisia, very good!" She smiles and runs after the yellow ball. "The paper said her father escaped to Canada."

"He didn't want Alisia?"

"He told Rosa on the phone that he'd never allow another man to be Alisia's father. That's why I had to wait until they arrested him to come here; they arrested him last week."

"He threatened you? Conner, are the police helping you? Is there some kind of restraining order to protect you and Alisia?"

From the corner of my eye, I see Alisia kick toward the ball and fall backward. She lets out a small cry that pulls my brother from the swing to hurry toward her. As he passes me, he says, "We've been on the run for three months. The police don't know I have her."

# Sophia

*I need you to believe in me.*

<hr/>

It seems the night itself awakens me. The stillness in the room. The blue dusky light filtering through the windows. The only sound is Holiday's gentle breathing on his rug beside the bed. He hears every creak and rustle outside; no raccoon or deer is sly enough to outsmart those ears. Yet he hasn't raised his head or been disturbed from slumber. I pull the down comforter over my shoulders and tell myself to sleep. Certainly it's late, though I have no bedroom clock—I never replaced the one that broke in the early sixties. Time is fairly irrelevant to a life in seclusion.

After I've turned this way and that, adjusted pillows, and sighed for effect, finally I sit up, which awakens Holiday. "It's okay, boy," I say, sliding my feet from under the covers and searching the floor beside him for my slippers. "There, there."

The wood floor groans much louder in the deep of night, I notice while walking to the kitchen. The moonlight makes me wonder if I'm still asleep, the haze of a dream surrounding me. The hem of my white cotton gown sways at my ankles, and tonight I can almost believe that I am young again, young and untouched by the pain of living. I kick off my slippers to feel the cool wood beneath my feet. I am a girl, in this very house, dressed in a sleeping gown, standing in the kitchen and gazing through the window toward the sea. I'm drawn there, out there into the cold. It's foolishness; I'll catch my death, as Ben would say. Decade upon decade separates that girl from this old woman. But the longer I stand at the window, the more I want to go.

Finally, I'm slipping without socks into my untied boots and wrapping the thick couch blanket around my shoulders. The back door opens as if of its own accord.

And I let myself forget for a moment. With each step I allow myself to journey back to a night so long ago when I walked this path, drawn to this place by the surf against the rocks. The yearning of eternity beat then as now with the same clarity and depth as the waves. A longing came then so clear it ached, bringing visions of what might come upon the dawns of tomorrow. What hopes I had so long ago. So easily I tossed wishes to the stars. So easily I opened myself to welcome what God would give.

Now I seek that girl who was me. And with that, the years between her and this return. In a moment I remember it all.

Years ago I walked from this place on such a night, determination moving my steps. I would write and shape beautiful words upon the page. The years would pass while I went through school and wrote and wrote, but when doubts or months of procrastination came, I would remember that night by the sea and the belief that I could do anything. And so the words would rise again. Words and the worlds they created. I found sweet solitude within them. Later came New York, parties, accolades, and people who seemed to bring the vision to life. But they turned in sharp succession to disillusionment and restlessness. The writing angst that had created paragraphs beneath my fingertips soured when intruded by expectation.

Then a night of flames, nearly beautiful but for their evil. A fire and screams that have haunted my days and nights. A loss that took the remains of that girl who once stood in this place, the girl I've nearly forgotten.

The waves are a heartbeat against the rocks. The cold slides from the sea and wraps around me. I realize I'm shivering and marvel at the foolishness that's brought me into the night and down the path to the sea. I will catch my death of cold—words all older people find themselves saying once we shed our carefree dresses of youth for the sensible attire of age. Though I shiver, I pause a bit longer to gaze out to the shimmer and dance of light on waves. Like the past calling me, reminding and stirring those old longings of something untouchable, I allow myself to listen and feel. I wish to swim within those waters again, to swim in the reflected moonlight as if adorned in a diamond dress.

At last I turn back. I'll need some tea and a bath to rid the chill before I crawl into bed once again. I may catch a cold, but it doesn't matter.

For a moment, I was young again. Such is a gift and wonder at my age. And the reminder stirs a longing to dream again, to believe that I do have a future and a hope.

On such a night, I can believe in tomorrow again.

HARPER'S BAY POLICE LOG
  Harper's Bay Police responded to 231 calls the week of
November 17-23.
  Conner O'Rourke, 26, was booked into county jail Novem-
ber 21 on kidnapping charges.

# Claire

*An* infinite sadness.

This emanates from my brother's being, and yet there is a peace in this sadness that I attempt to understand. We are separated by glass, our hands touching without touching, phones against our ears connecting voices. Conner appears younger and smaller in the oversized orange jail suit beneath harsh fluorescent light.

"It was the right thing to do," I say, trying on the supportive tone but wondering if it was. He turned himself in, the decision made and done before I knew about it. But could there have been another way? Did he have to do it so quickly? The social-services people most likely will take Alisia away from us, especially once Conner makes bail and returns to the house.

"I know it was. I know for certain. I shouldn't have stayed hidden so long, but I didn't know what to do. All I wanted was to get Alisia to Mom and Dad without it being dangerous to any of them."

His certainties are something we do not share.

"Are you okay in here?" I ask, every prison film and story filling my thoughts. He has no bruises, at least none visible.

"I'm good. I have a cell to myself right now. Guess God knew it'd be a good time for me to be in here; seems the county's a little low on crime this week." His chuckle echoes strangely through the phone line. "Listen to me, little sis. Don't worry. I mean it. Whatever happens, I'm okay. I'm better than okay, really. This is hard to explain, but you see, I've been wandering around for so long. Wish I'd stayed with Rosa when we met. But I didn't know if I could be a father to someone else's child then, didn't know what I thought of marrying someone who'd already said those vows. It took some years to figure out, wasted years we could've been together. And finally I guess I'm right where I should be. Funny, huh?"

"I wouldn't go all the way to funny."

"Ironic then. But it's so simple right now. I have nothing but God. Today I was reading the Beatitudes in Matthew. 'Blessed are the poor in spirit' and all those strange paradoxes. And for the first time, I kind of understand them. Here I am, poor in spirit. Another version says, 'Blessed are those who realize their need for him.' And then I found in THE MESSAGE: 'You're blessed when you're at the end of your rope.' Sounds like an accurate description of me right now."

Conner pauses, resting his elbows on the table with the phone against one ear. "When there's no one to help but God himself, that's when we're blessed. It's strange, but I feel blessed, even in here with my future and Alisia's unknown. I've never seen God in such ways before; that's pretty amazing. Wouldn't recommend it for everyone, but for me, right now, I can actually say I'm thankful for it."

I stare at him, wanting to burst into tears, desperate to wrap my arms around him beyond the dividing glass wall. He seems weak and strong at the same time, lost and found, poor and blessed.

"What can I do?" I whisper and put my hand against the glass once again.

He smiles and puts his against mine, his fingers inches longer. "Take care of her for me. She's seen too much for such an age. Give her a childhood back. You know, I'm so glad you're here."

"God's intricate planning," I say with little energy. Conner's more settled in his faith than I've witnessed in years, even while wearing an orange jumpsuit and sitting in the county jail.

Later, as I walk across the prison's parking lot, it hits me: My inmate brother amazes me. He sees his need for God.

# The Memoir of Josephine Vanderook

———— ❦ ————

*A windswept world.*

That was the place upon my memory with every dawn. Seattle held nothing for me. No amount of coaxing could get me to its streets or into the new society erupting in the town. The arrival of my father-in-law dipped me deeper into the yawning abyss. His words were sympathetic, but I understood in immediate terms that my survival felt like a betrayal to him. My life echoed his son's death. Within a week it was decided that I would return to Boston. After my return, I would keep secret what I had discovered about that night.

John and Karen awaited my arrival at the train station. There appeared for a moment a glimpse of compassion within Karen's expression, this woman who had despised me from the beginning, resenting that I was her sister by marriage. Karen Vanderook wore the newest fashion, a hat matching her fitted traveling suit. Her eyes roamed over me in surprise. Assuredly I appeared in such dishevel from my travels and from the sorrow that plagued my days and nights.

I found my dear Boston to also be empty of life and hope. Facing each day became the task. There is a deep coldness to loss. I would never have known it or believed in the strength of grief—how easily it can drown you, how you wish it to sweep you away.

These many years later, I do not know when that storm began or how far back it brewed within Eduard. The years would pass, and other storms have come and gone. Nothing is left untouched once the sun returns.

I am no longer innocent. Too many cries fill my ears in the night. My husband's face in death appears more easily than the features of that boy I once loved. My questions have accumulated without answers. The wisdom of age is the knowledge of what we do not know. The dreams and visions of my youth are beyond my grasp. They are cast away, unrequited. And yet my poor spirit is blessed—oh, how it is blessed. Almighty God has found me. Only when all is stripped away, our souls desperate for him, will we see the vision of God himself.

# Sophia

*What is between us cannot be explained.*

———— ❧ ————

I've chastised myself all day. Why would I not once but twice invite someone to break into the solitude of my house? Already I struggle with the restlessness that accompanies my rare visits to town. Seeing the outside world disrupts my peace here. And now Ben's son is coming for tea. I've paced and dusted and arranged couch pillows. Holiday's eyes follow me, but his head rests on his outstretched paws with as mystified a look as a dog can carry off.

Bradley Wilson's life has come to me through the filter of Ben's fatherly pride and worried concern. I still think of him as a young man even though he's in his fifties. He couldn't guess the things I know about him. In the sixties, Bradley traded college graduation for communal living in San Francisco. Later he borrowed money from Ben to start a small business, outdoor muffin stands around the city, which eventually failed just like his first marriage. Bradley's forties brought a change into his life. He remarried and opened a successful sandwich shop in a small town in northern California—Ben says they're the best sandwiches around. A few years ago Bradley repaid every cent of the money he's borrowed from Ben over the years.

I've seen photos of Bradley and the changes through eras, hairstyles, and age, the slow metamorphosis into a balding, slightly overweight man whose blue eyes are a mirror image of Ben's.

Ben as a father. Even with the stories and photos and times he disappears for visits, it doesn't quite sink in. Of the thousands of Ben memories, none include him in the role of father or grandfather. Bradley was in college when our friend Helen died, and Ben returned to the Point several years after her death. I'd been here for nearly twenty years by then, having lost my parents during that time. What kind of parent was Ben? The times we talked about those years, Ben admits his shortcomings. The shadow of his own father was something he fought to overcome, resulting in Ben's heightened leniency. He once commented that the cause of Bradley's struggles was due to his parenting—"giving a lot of meaningless stuff but I couldn't show him my love." Perhaps Ben's consideration of moving inland has much to do with making up for past mistakes.

At the sound of a knock on the door, Holiday barks and hops from his spot beside the hearth. I glance around once more; there are three places set at the table and the kettle simmers on the stove. Varieties of tea litter the tablecloth, enough for an entire tour group.

After a deep breath at the door, I open it to Ben and his son. The look on Ben's face surprises me—such pure pride that I've never seen. Suddenly I realize that his two worlds are finally fusing, his loved ones meeting for the first time.

"Hello, Bradley," I say, reaching for his hand.

"Nice to finally meet you, Ms. Fleming." He smiles, and I'm surprised at what warmth is found within his face. The photos have not captured his kindness.

Bradley follows his father's lead in removing his boots, though I try to persuade him against it. Ben has his own set of house slippers here; Bradley appears smaller in his bright white socks sticking out of the bottom of his slacks.

We find seats, Bradley sitting unknowingly in Ben's usual place, which feels awkward to me, as if something is sorely out of place. *Just relax*, I tell myself.

"Did you get seasick at all?" I ask.

"No, that patch really worked." Bradley thumbs through the tea varieties. "Dad tells me you're a writer."

Ben and I look at one another and smile. It's oddly refreshing, humbling even, to have someone know nothing about me, not look at me as an oddity or even care that once I was a literary somebody.

"Yes, though I don't do as much as I used to."

"I'd like to write a book someday." Bradley speaks the words every writer hears from others.

"You should," I say and mean it. It's great to see someone with dreams still vivid within them. Perhaps that was my attraction to that Claire girl—as if the future hung on the horizon of her sight. My future often feels like a ball and chain dragging my every step.

Bradley brought photo albums, which take nearly an hour to get through. By the end, I've seen his family, their vacation to the Grand Tetons, his sandwich shop, their house in the small town of Cottonwood. *No, I've never been there before. Maybe a visit would be nice. It gets how hot in the summer?* A wave of tiredness rolls over me as I realize how a social visit can drain my energy.

Ever watchful, Ben notices the change within me, although I fight to cover it with another cup of tea and a slice of banana-nut bread. He rises from his chair. "I noticed you've used up most of the wood on the porch. I'll move some up for you; there's possibly a storm coming in. Then we need to head back."

"Let me help," Bradley says, closing the final album.

"Oh no, it'll just take a few minutes. You finish that last tea. It'll warm you before we're on the water again." And then Ben is out the door, already changed into his boots.

An awkward silence rests between Bradley and me for a moment; then we speak at the same time.

"I enjoyed your—"

"What kind of tea?"

We chuckle at the bumble.

"I'd hoped we could talk alone," Bradley says.

I already know where this conversation is going. "Is there something you can't say with Ben around?"

"In a way, yes. You see, my father is quite fond of you."

"Really?" I take a slow sip from my teacup with yellow roses on it—a gift from Ben some birthdays ago.

Bradley shuffles in his seat. "You're mostly what he talks about on his visits."

"Well, there's little else for him to talk about. We don't have many exciting things outside of one another here on the Point."

"Yes. Exactly. That's what I've thought. There just isn't much out here for Dad anymore." *He surely didn't mean that the way it sounded,* I tell myself as my stomach makes a sickening tumble. "Dad mentioned it to you, right? That I think it'd be best for him to come live with us."

"Your dad is capable of making his own decisions."

"He won't leave because he'll feel like he's deserting you." Bradley pours four spoonfuls of sugar into his tea as he talks. "I'd help in any way to get some assistance for you too."

"Why do you want him?" I ask, suddenly tossing politeness and wanting the truth.

"What . . . what do you mean?"

"Why do you want him to leave this place?"

"We love him. I love him. I want to spend time with my father in these later years. He could get involved in our church. It's a good church, and he sure has liked it when he's come for a visit."

Bradley goes through a list that I think perhaps he actually wrote down at one time. He's probably one of those people who writes all the pluses of a subject on one side and the minuses on the other. The side with the longest list wins. What could be on the minus list? Having his father as a constant in his life? Future decisions about Ben's health? Who will entertain him? Who will bathe him when he can't any longer? And what rest home is affordable and offers the best care? I want to ask him about the list and his motives for plotting out Ben's future.

"And I want to know that he's safe."

The last straw falls. I speak slowly but with distinction, fighting to not raise my voice. "You want. You want to know he's safe, and you think he likes that church, which by the way, he doesn't really care for. You want to keep him in a controlled environment so you don't have to worry about him or feel guilty that he's living in the lighthouse alone. You want these things. But what about Ben? What does *he* want?"

My social graces are certainly gone.

Bradley stares at me for a moment, but not with anger as I expect. He nods and then says softly, "What you say is all true. I do want these things. But I also have tried to consider his feelings. But are you certain my father doesn't want to move? Do you really know, Ms. Fleming? Or do you want to keep my father here because it's what *you* need and what *you* want?"

The front door opens, and Ben walks in with a gust of wind behind him. "If we're going to get you back to the hotel tonight, we'll need to get going."

When we say our good-byes, Ben apparently senses an uncomfortable air between us. His expression questions me, but I look away.

"I'll be by tomorrow then," he says to me.

"It was very nice meeting you, Ms. Fleming," Bradley says, and I'm surprised by the sincerity in his tone. "When it comes down to it, I want what's best for all of us."

"Okay," I whisper. And then the house is empty again. It hasn't felt this empty in a very long time.

Afternoon light has faded into dark shadows. I sit in my chair, growing cold as night approaches. The wind clatters against the shutters outside, and Holiday occasionally raises his head to wonder at my stationary condition.

My stable life is crumbling around me. The faster I try to uphold the walls, patch the mortar, fix the structural damage, the faster it falls and disintegrates within my grasp. *God help me.*

Over time, much of my faith has been stripped down to its bare bones. I love God so deeply and fully, so amazingly. I know I need him, completely and desperately. I know that only by the grace found through Christ do I have freedom from this world. And yet, nothing else is secure. Is it enough? I'm supposed to say that it is.

Too many years are upon me. Shouldn't age and years of prayer develop a depth of wisdom that will light my path? And yet I feel as if I know less every year. The ignorant security of understanding what life is about has faded, my need for God and his grace increased.

Sometimes we're taken and stripped down to nothing, and then even more is taken away. All my stories are about it—about the need and search for grace—amazing grace, mysterious grace, confusing and desired and aching grace.

Tightening the blanket around my shoulders, with my journal and Bible open on my lap, I consider this life of solitude. When I came here, it was a temporary escape from the world. My mother, never knowing how to show affection or comfort, gave me blessed time alone. And somehow I just stayed.

But have I wasted this life, buried the talent, allowed a blinding so as to achieve my own desire to be alone? Were we all destined for greatness? Or are some of us designed to be the worker ants? Can we all rise from the sleep of complacency and change the world? I still wish to believe in such ideas and am surprised that they were asleep so long.

All the greatest men and women have met with great mistakes. Will I see the journey of my own lined up to contend against the few eternal successes—something like what I imagined of Bradley's plus and minus list? Or is it our humanness and our mistakes that bring us closer and deeper and more desiring of that untainted thing we all yearn for . . . grace. Grace. To truly be granted grace.

Today I was faced with myself. Bradley held up a mirror and I saw me—how I've wished to escape myself at times.

Bradley was right. More than half of my desire for Ben to remain is selfish. I want him to stay. I want him to need me. But it is I who have needed him all this time. I do not know how to live without him.

And yet I know so clearly now. I have to let Ben go.

Vine Creek Community Church will begin holding prayer meetings prior to Sunday services each week. Topics for prayer will vary weekly but will include community needs and world events.

All are welcome.

# Claire

The past days provide ample excuses for not attending church this morning—jail visits to Conner; meeting with lawyers, a social worker, and police officers; my assignments at *The Tidal Post*; and toughest of all, time with Alisia. Alisia has lost another person in her life; she's not allowed to see my brother since he's accused of kidnapping her. She blames me. I seem to represent the loss, or perhaps she believes I made him leave.

By a miracle, for it can be called nothing else, my parents were granted temporary custody, approved due to their former foster-care license and the fact that Conner gave up his chance for bail to ensure it. My brother will remain in jail. He may be extradited for trial in the state of Washington.

What if I was still in the city? My parents and brother have needed me through all the paperwork and meetings, and I've needed them. While exhaustion coats me like tar poured over my entire body, my parents seem revitalized by this little girl who's entered our lives. She doesn't blame them for Conner's disappearance.

Mom enters my room at 7:30 to see if I'm up, waking me in the process and asking if I'm going to church. She's cheerful, too cheerful for the early hour and for the circumstances. In that gentle voice, she reminds me that Uncle Artie had called with hopes of our attendance at the special prayer service for Conner. Uncle Artie is the pastor of Vine Creek Community Church.

Church. I'm not sure I can face it.

Head tucked beneath my pillow, I attempt a return to sleep's lair. But soon enough I give up. My overactive mind busily contemplates—*worry* might be the more truthful word—the day's events. How will it feel to return to my home church after living in the city so long? This is not the usual visit, returning for a holiday amidst handshakes and hugs and saying good-bye. This is returning to the fold, perhaps for good. They will know about Conner's arrest. Alisia will be stared at, despite the best of intentions. Should Alisia go to children's church? Thinking of the list of rules my parents signed for temporary guardianship, I wonder if she can be out of their sight, even at church. Avoiding it this week seems the best plan.

I watch them from the arched entryway to the kitchen. Dad at the stove, his back toward me. Alisia, encased in ruffles, squirms at the kitchen table. My mom found the dress in a specialty shop downtown and bought the matching set of bloomers, tights, shoes, and hair "pretties."

"Here you go," Mom says and gently wraps a large dish towel over Alisia's dress, tying the ends like a bib. It reminds me of the many times I ate Sunday breakfast in my slip or embalmed in an oversized dish towel. Dad has made the pancakes this morning; they sit in a wobbling tower on a cookie sheet in the center of the table. Mom's pancakes are always in a neat smaller stack on her white platter, sprinkled with powdered sugar just for looks. Mom's look better, but Dad's outdo hers in taste.

I notice the Spanish dictionary open and turned facedown on the table beside my father's coffee cup. Dad arranges a smiley face on Alisia's plate from the varying sizes of pancakes.

"Papa funny," Alisia says along with some Spanish I cannot decipher. French was the language I took in school, although everyone said that Spanish would one day be more useful.

"Good morning," I say, walking in. Alisia's smile fades, and she looks down at the plate as Mom pours syrup over her pancakes. This has become her typical response to my attempts at friendliness toward her. I lean toward her. *"Buenos días,* Alisia."

"Good morning," she says with a defiant frown as if to say, *Duh, I may be only four, but I know some English.*

"So we'll all go to church, it looks like." My father grins.

"Except for Conner," I say and instantly regret it for the effect my sarcasm has on my parents, the cheerful facades falling from their faces. "Sorry. I think I'll just go take my shower."

"Take a cup," my father says, handing me his forgiveness in a coffee mug.

Coffee, shower, usual routine of hair, makeup, and trying on several outfits before finding the right one (leaving piles of discarded shirts and blouses like forgotten limp dolls all over my bedroom floor), and I'm ready for church. In the backseat of my parents' car, Alisia stares at me from her car seat.

"She doesn't like me," I say when she frowns at my smile. It's amazing how scrunched-up eyebrows make her even cuter and yet can irritate me so. I made promises to my brother about this child, and I'm at a loss as to how to fulfill them.

"Don't be silly." Mom turns in her seat. "She just knows you're a little nervous around kids. I should have made you baby-sit more often."

"I didn't like baby-sitting."

"You might have learned to like it."

"But would the children have survived in the process?"

"You have a point." Mom is surely recalling little Tony and the emergency room incident, my final tryst with the world of baby-sitting. Evil Jr. became his name after he painted his little sister's head with fingernail polish while I was cleaning up crayon artwork from his bedroom wall. One emergency-room visit, two frantic parents, and a long night later, I was finished in this town, whether I wanted to watch children again or not. Which I didn't. Evil Jr. is in high school now and was recently arrested for selling stolen property. Some things can only be proven with time.

"Where Daddy Conner?" Alisia asks, as she's asked every few hours for the last several days.

Mom usually takes up the answering of this, but while talking to my father, she didn't hear the backseat request. And Alisia's looking at me.

"He had to go bye-bye," I say. "He'll be back."

"No!" she cries in anguish, a lost look in her dark eyes. "Want Daddy!" Words in Spanish follow.

"It's okay. Want your dolly?" I ask, picking up the rag doll from the seat and handing it to her. She launches it forward between the seats and continues crying. Mom and Dad try soothing her to no avail. I too wish to cry and demand my brother back. He's been out of my life for so long, yet suddenly I need him—for Alisia and for myself.

Perched just outside of downtown along a row of balding hills near the bay, Vine Creek Community Church welcomes visitors or hails travelers with its sign by the highway. There's always some cute saying on the board, and today's reads: Let Some Sonshine Brighten Your Day. I've often wondered where my uncle gets those clever sayings. Is there a Web site, book, or could it be that he thinks them up himself? I'll have to remember to ask.

My father drives slowly down the long gravel road, through a grove of trees until the windswept hill reveals Vine Creek Community. The original, white-steepled building is surrounded by a flock of additions, which house the classrooms, kitchen, and fellowship room. A small courtyard and playground connect the old church to the new.

As we walk toward the entrance of the church, I want to pull Alisia close. She frowns when I put my hand on her back. The refreshment area is set up under the breezeway that connects the sanctuary with the outbuildings. We receive a few hearty greet-ings, people coming toward us with smiles and concern.

"Claire, it's so good to see you," my uncle says. Uncle Artie, my mother's brother, has been the pastor here for twenty-five years. His thick arms encase me in a hug that leaves me breathless. We both pull away with tears on the rims of our eyes, knowing with-out words what the days have recently been like for our family. He bends down to meet Alisia, who hides in the folds of Mom's dress.

"Oh, my goodness!" comes a voice and a tap on my shoulder. "Claire!" The voice is that of Jill Watley. She's several years older than me, and we became friends through church plays, outings, and youth group that led into singles group. I know Jill works at the church now as a secretary and ministry director, filling the various roles when a volunteer is lacking, which is often, I'm sure. She's gained several pounds through the progression of years and dresses to such perfection that with her flawless makeup and hair she could be a model in a catalog.

"I heard you were in town. It's so good to see you."

"Thanks. You look great as always," I say, eyeing my parents, who are engaged in conversation with some church members and Uncle Artie and are proudly introducing Alisia as if she were their blood granddaughter.

"Thank you. You look great too. I heard that you might be back for good."

"I'm not sure yet."

"If you need a place to stay permanently, let me know. I hear things like that all the time. Would you stay in Harper's Bay or go up to Crescent City?"

"I don't really know."

"Would you want a roommate?"

"I haven't thought of it."

"I heard about your brother." Jill lowers her voice at this.

"And what did you hear?" A defensive tone leaks in.

"Oh . . . well—" she suddenly sounds regretful—"just that he took that little girl, trying to save her life, of course, and he was arrested. And there is the prayer service today. I helped to plan it."

"He turned himself in."

"Really? Well, you know how things like that get changed." She attempts a laugh. "If you stay in town, I could sure use help with the Christmas program—it's only five weeks away. Our singles group is still on Wednesday nights, and in a few weeks we're having a karaoke night. You're still single, right?"

"Yes."

"Great. We always lose the good ones."

*Does that mean I'm not a good one?* I want to ask.

"Claire, remember, we're on your side," Jill says, and I soften beneath her kind smile.

"I'm sorry. It's been a bit overwhelming, that's all."

"That's what we're here for, times like this. It's easy to forget, but in times of need, hopefully the church family will be there." Jill rushes off toward the refreshment table—the Styrofoam cups are getting low.

I stand there not wanting to join my parents in what has grown into a small clutter of friendly banter around Alisia; I move instead toward the refreshments. The church bell rings, indicating prayer time, and the groups head toward the entrance.

"Do you want me to hold you?" I ask Alisia, expecting a quick no. She shakes her head but takes my hand, seemingly feeling as sensitive to all the eyes as I do.

"See, it just takes time," Mom says.

I'm unconvinced that it'll be this easy.

The prayer service blends straight into church. I've stayed at the edge to avoid people during the break, finding my energy drained with every small-talk encounter, though I appreciate the words prayed aloud for my family. Especially here, in this place of sanctuary—a room with pews that can hold over two hundred people, stained-glass windows along the sides and a front stained-glass cross, a stage with pulpit and arrangements of plastic trees and plants, and microphones and a piano.

I'm here again, but this time no longer a visitor. My brother is in jail, and a little girl sits on my father's lap. How was I so lost in my own world that I didn't know anything of Conner's life? I'd never heard of Rosa, a woman who would change his life—all of our lives. Conner speaks of her often, how they had planned to marry. But their plans for Conner to adopt Alisia once they married had brought Rosa's ex-husband storming back into their lives—something they wouldn't know until too late.

The pew feels harder than I remember, the room warmer. I notice my uncle's repeated words. He says "and the Lord's peace" six times.

I need to ask forgiveness. My ears attempt to listen, and my eyes cease their analysis. Gazing around at the people in the pews, I ask God to soften my heart, to take away the criticism that wants to erupt within me. I want to love these people. And I'm surprised, in one of those guilty realizations, that my uncle's message is about grace. If only grace came without the need for it.

---

The usual nervousness that I feel when arriving at the county jail is quieted today. I chat with a guard as I go through the visitor processing. I pull up a plastic chair in the glass-and-steel cubicle and see my brother enter on the other side of thick Plexiglas.

Conner smiles, and that deep sadness seems replaced with something I can't quite pinpoint. "A prayer service for me and Alisia? That's amazing." He appears genuinely surprised that people would make such an effort.

I notice his face already looks gaunt, though I've asked him every day if he's eating enough at meals. He promises he is, but I wonder how the confines of a boxed world are affecting Conner's spirited nature. The walls of a classroom and our own house have always closed in around him. Will this not destroy him?

"The entire half hour was all for you, and probably forty to fifty people attended."

"Pretty humbling to think of them doing that for me," he says, and then weariness shadows his features. "Rosa would love to know that. It was her faith that helped bring me back. She prayed every day for Alisia and for me, even when we weren't together. I wish you could've met her. You would've really liked her. She always was smiling and optimistic. It's hard not letting the bitterness get me."

"She'd be happy that you have Alisia."

"I know. Alisia keeps me going." His demeanor lightens as he changes the subject. "Aren't you meeting with the famous S. T. Fleming this week?"

"Yes. Isn't that something?"

"I want all the details. I've never read her book."

"Books. She wrote two. She's just remembered more for the first one."

"And I'm guessing that you've read them both."

"And not just once." I smile.

"What are they about? People talk about how strange she is, but few talk about the books."

"They do in literary circles. I actually liked the second more than the first. Seemed like she was reaching for something else, while the first book was more of a story she'd experienced—at least that's my guess."

"Will you ask her things like that?"

"I don't know. What if she doesn't like people asking about her writing? Could be why she's all alone."

"I'd guess any writer would love talking about her works. By the way, what do you dream about?" Conner leans his head against the partition, holding the phone to his ear. I expect to have some joke attached to this question, but he seems serious.

"What do I dream about? It's been a long time since someone asked me," I say, wondering if anyone has ever truly asked.

"Same with me. Griffin Anderson asked me that today."

"What was Griffin doing here?"

"He and Ben Wilson came. Guess they visit jailbirds like me on a regular basis."

"That's nice, I guess." I'm not sure what I think of them coming to visit my brother as if he's a wayward in need of ministry.

"They're great guys; we had a good time talking. Good to be reminded to still dream while I'm in here." And by his weary yet hopeful expression, I'm suddenly glad for these visitors to my brother. "You were always a dreamer."

I smile, recalling how easily my mind could drift into the clouds. "It can make you lose touch with the moment though."

"So tell me."

"What? My dreams? Well, until a few weeks ago, I planned to work my way into being a reporter in the city, spend several years doing that, try for some Pulitzer Prize-winning stuff, and write novels in my spare time. Just a few things like that." I laugh at it now, at how far away it seems, how unimportant when stacked alongside jail cells, orange uniforms, and saving a child's life.

"But what do you dream about? Not your goals. What is it that beats within you?"

I'm unsure what he means. "Aren't my goals also my dreams?"

"They're the means to reaching toward what's inside of you. But what is your thing?"

"Is this what Griffin asked you?"

"Actually, yes."

"Figures. I guess I want to feel like my life has meaning, what everyone probably wants. But mine seems to include words; words seem to find me often. Once I had a dream about words."

"Tell me about it," he says.

"It's kind of corny, but all these words were whizzing around my head like butterflies in a wild dance. I kept trying to catch them and wished for a net to capture big heaps of them."

"You're kind of odd; know it, little sis?"

I smile at his smile. "Yeah, I know. And what do you dream about, my even odder brother?"

"Swimming."

"That's not what I expected."

"For some reason, that's what I think of nearly all night. I want to just swim. There's something about it I can't explain."

"Wait a minute. Is this a goal or the thing?"

A buzzer sounds and I fear that our time is up. Instead, the guard at the door moves aside, and another visitor enters on my side. The older man moves slowly toward the booth past me as a young man in an orange jumpsuit walks into the visitor area on Conner's side of the wall. We both watch for a moment before looking through the glass at one another. The phone is warm against my face, and I wonder how many people use it in a day.

"Sis, what are you afraid of?" Conner asks, and for a moment I see fear in his eyes.

"I'm afraid of you not coming home." Sudden tears fill my eyes.

"No, I mean, what in this life are you afraid of?"

He doesn't want to talk about himself or the district attorney's case piling against him or what it's like beyond that visitor doorway. These are the things I want to hear about, to discuss, to say it'll be okay, even though I can't be sure. Instead I have to think and search inside for the fear that comes to me most.

"I guess I'm afraid of having no significance."

He nods slowly. "Yes, I can understand that. I think that's why I've wandered so, searching for meaning."

We are silent for a moment. The old man in the partitioned booth beside me is agitated, cursing into a phone.

"So do you know what scares me?" my brother asks, a slight grin on his face.

"That they'll have mystery meat for dinner tonight?"

"Good one, sis," he says, crossing his eyes. "No, I'm afraid of Pilgrims."

"Excuse me, did you just say pilgrims?"

"That's right. And you know, there are pilgrims, and then there are Pilgrims with a capital *P.*"

"The ones on the *Mayflower* and what others?"

"There are also pilgrims who are people in search of something. Those are good pilgrims. It's the Plymouth Rock Pilgrims who scare me."

"And why do they scare you, or do I want to know?"

"I have a reccurring dream about them. I really have nothing against them in the real world. But in the dream, they were riding horses and chasing a friend of mine. I was in the sky, for some reason, trying to warn my friend, but he wouldn't listen. He had stopped talking to me, and nothing I did would make him hear me. The more he pulled away from me, the closer the Pilgrims came."

"This could be a horror flick."

"It gets worse."

"Worse than Pilgrims on horses? I don't think Pilgrims had horses, by the way."

"The Pilgrims were trying to reach my friend, to turn him into a Pilgrim too. I didn't know why they wanted him, but they sure did."

"So you're afraid of them now."

"Wouldn't you be?"

"Sure, though there aren't that many running around, except it is almost Thanksgiving. What's today, the twenty-third?"

"Yeah, you better watch out. I mean, I want to be a pilgrim, one who goes in search of something. But I don't want to be the other kind, the one in the little suit who chases after people."

"You're a little odd, brother."

Conner opens his mouth to respond when the inmate beside him starts yelling. I can hear him through the glass. The man beside me kicks his chair over and shouts, "Then you can just rot in there!"

Guards rush toward the inmate, and another on my side takes the arm of the man. One guard motions to my brother; Conner falls to the floor with his arms and legs spread. In a short scuffle, the guards drag out the inmate who continues to shout, but he doesn't struggle. Another guard approaches Conner. I expect Conner to be taken away, but after a few moments and conversation between the two, my brother rises from the floor. Slowly he picks up the phone, visibly shaken.

My phone has been pressed into my ear, and my arm is shaking. "Are you okay?"

"Fine, just fine," he tries to assure me.

"Conner, I'm scared for you."

"I'm afraid too. But, hey, blessed are the fearful," he says with a wry smile I find impossible to match.

# Sophia

*What more can I say?*

ʼBen arrives for *Tidal Post* Tuesday. First thing he asks is whether or not I am okay; translated, do I want to talk about what had happened during Bradley's visit? I instead ask whether the article had been run about him and Griffin.

He hands me section one with a sigh. "It didn't turn out the way I hoped."

## THE TIDAL POST

LOCAL PROFILE
CHRISTIANS QUESTION CHRISTIANITY

Local residents Ben Wilson and Griffin Anderson meet every Monday morning at Blondie's, not just for the biscuits and gravy and coffee, but to discuss the Bible and their Christian beliefs.

"We've been meeting for two years now," says 77-year-old Ben Wilson. "We've talked about everything from end-times prophecy to whether Jesus turned that water into wine or into grape juice."

"Our age difference hasn't mattered at all," responds 24-year-old Griffin Anderson (local artist of Rooftop Rd.). "We both feel a need to explore the depths of our faith, not just accept what is culturally Christian. We want to really know what God and Christ are all about."

Interesting words for two of the best-known Christians in our area. Griffin's award-winning sculptures all include some spiritual element, though not often identifiable at first look. His best-known work is Superman, which appears to be a superhero holding up a red-and-black globe. Spiritual themes are in

abundance, Anderson explains, but he likens his work
to something like the parables of the Bible.
   "I'm not sure how I'm affecting the world. Right now
I'm just drinking coffee with Ben on Monday mornings
and asking God to guide both of our paths."

Ben says, folding the paper, "We did say more about the Lord
than they included."

I chuckle at his disconcerted frown. "And if you had a five-
point message, would they have printed it? Would it have
changed any life? I doubt it. Readers will be intrigued by the
truth of your words. You're a Christian who doesn't have everything figured out, as if any of us do. So you're seeking to really
know who God is—what else could be better expressed?"

"You're just trying to make me feel better."

"And it's working."

"Maybe a little."

"But be prepared for intruders arriving with Bibles in hand
on Monday mornings."

"You think? I really enjoy being with only Griffin for now."

"Could happen. Maybe you should change mornings."

"Maybe."

As we sip tea and read the paper, a thought strikes me: *How
many more Tuesdays will I have with him?*

"Are you still having her come out?" he asks, reminding me
that Claire O'Rourke's visit is scheduled for tomorrow. "Do you
want to change it to another day or cancel altogether? I've felt
bad about my part in that."

"As you should," and I attempt a frown. I take a slow sip of tea,
savoring the slight aroma of Earl Grey. "Might as well go for a
record in visitors, as long as it doesn't become the top story in
next week's paper."

"I'm sure it won't." Ben grimaces. "Guess that's something to
talk with the little lady about on the way, just to be sure."

"Do you have section two?" I ask, looking through the pages.

"As a matter of fact, I do," he says with suspicious enthusiasm. "Here you are." He hands the folded section to me awkwardly, holding the edges closed.

When I open it, a thick manila envelope slips out. "What is this?" I ask, opening the clasp. Then suddenly I know. "Did you go see Mrs. Crow this weekend?"

"Sure did."

The papers slide out, pages and pages of copied handwritten print. And I have it. The date indicates it's one of the final things Josephine wrote.

"Don't think I've forgotten that you have those artifacts from the shipwreck." He uses that fatherly disapproving tone.

"What artifacts?" I say in feigned innocence.

"Are you going to tell me what kind of book it is? I've noticed it missing on my recent visits."

"We've had company, and it's just been so busy," I say with a smile. "And it's taking forever to dry. But it seems to be some kind of ledger, maybe of the cargo or something."

"I won't ask about turning it over again," he says but is really asking.

"As soon as it's dry enough to read—it's gruelingly slow."

"Yeah, when you stare at it half the day. But I won't stick around," Ben says, finishing the last drop from his cup. "You have plenty of reading to do."

Carrying the pages to my comfy chair after Ben leaves, I anxiously begin to read.

*The Memoir of Josephine Vanderook*

*I would have followed him to the end of the world. . . .*

**ADVERSARY STRIKES AGAIN**

At the site of Wilson Bridge, a graffiti message and damaged heavy equipment are the most recent evidence that the self-named Adversary of Change has struck again.

The graffiti message said, "Save Wilson Bridge. Join fight with Adversary."

For three years, Old Wilson Bridge has been the topic of local debate. The decision whether or not to destroy the old bridge will be decided at an upcoming city council meeting.

Police continue to investigate the sabotage at the bridge-construction site.

# Claire

Worry. I'm letting it shadow the hours of my days.

Alisia is having nightmares. We all awaken to her cries, my mom rushes to her room, and I stand at the doorway, helpless. Despite momentary breakthroughs, I am still the symbol of my brother's disappearance.

"Where's Daddy Conner?" she asks, almost exclusively to me now.

"He had to go somewhere," is one of my lame excuses.

Tuesday, back at work, I was handed my inaugural newspaper with my first byline. Bittersweet. Within that paper is also the record of Conner's arrest.

Even with a couple of assignments Rob has given me, my

schedule is slower at the beginning of the week. As I work on an outline for the two stories, my phone rings.

"Griffin's bringing the sculpture over at lunch," Mom says. "You'll be here, right?"

"Of course," I say with a smile.

Several hours later Mom, Alisia, and I watch Griffin back into the driveway.

Alisia describes it best. "Wowie!"

Griffin laughs as he drops the tailgate on his truck. He hops in the back and begins removing straps and bungee cords that have secured the metal sculpture in place.

"It's perfect," my mother says. "Better than I could've imagined." And I have to agree.

"Griffin made Garden Man," Alisia says, then tries to climb into the truck bed.

Coming up behind her, I consider pulling her away. Instead, I lift her up. She seems surprised that I help her. The sculpture is twice her size. The gardener holds a packet of seeds in one oversized hand and five flowers in the other.

"I added this one since you arrived," Griffin says, bending down to show Alisia the smallest flower in the gardener's hand. "That one is Alisia."

"That's me," she says proudly.

The sculpture is an eclectic blend of quaint, contemporary, and creative. Upon closer inspection, I recognize some of the elements of his creation: alarm clocks for eyes, stove dials for buttons, and copper vines and leaves weave around the gardener's legs made from coffee cans. It's astounding how things thrown away have been combined into something this amazing. And yet, even as I recognize this fact, I'm awed by what truths it carries.

After Garden Man, as he's now called, is put in place for my dad's arrival this afternoon, Griffin sits in the porch swing and

I on a cushioned wicker chair, the sculpture now part of the front yard décor. Mom is making hot cocoa, and Alisia colors a picture on the table between us. Her eyebrows scrunch together in concentration.

"You like your church in Crescent City?" I ask, wondering why he no longer attends Vine Creek.

"Yeah, it's a great group, and I like the drive—driving gives me ideas for sculptures. I still go to the singles group at your uncle's church. Before my dad died, he was invited to the church in Crescent City. He hadn't gone to church since my mom left us when I was in junior high. So I went with him and stayed after his death." The porch swing creaks as Griffin leans back. "I bet your uncle is glad to have you back."

"I actually haven't talked to him much yet. Once I get used to the whole feel of being home again, it'll be better." He smiles, not taking my words as criticism, which I don't intend. "I read the interview about you and Ben."

Griffin nods, seems a little embarrassed. "Of course you would since you work there. A few people didn't quite get it. But it's brought a lot of discussion."

"About what?"

"A few friends don't understand why I hang out with Ben. But he's such an incredible person. And we're in the same place, trying to discover things that are easy to take for granted as a Christian. Guess what Ben and I seek is like the difference between looking at the sea from the beach and diving into the water, searching all around.

"I want to swim and know as much as I can. You can stare at the ocean for years and think it's the same scenery, but when you start swimming in it, you realize how vast and beyond our discovery it really is. I hope I'm always discovering new things about God, even if it hurts and I make mistakes, even if I feel like it might drown me."

Something in his words, in the passion stirring his eyes, moves me in a most disconcerting way. I can picture myself on the beach, toes digging into the sand as the waves pull beneath them while Griffin swims ever farther, diving deeper, and shouting at discoveries beyond our sight.

"Your brother and I were talking about this."

"Ah, now I get the swimming thing," I say with a smile. "And pilgrims versus Pilgrims with a capital *P?*"

Griffin laughs. "Exactly."

"You and Conner must have talked for some time."

"I went there again this morning. When he gets out, I think he's going to join Ben and me for our Monday discussion group."

"To discuss pilgrims and swimming?"

"Among other things. Mostly, we've been searching for who Jesus is."

*Who is this person?* I ask myself. "Everybody has times of doubt."

"It's not doubt. I really want to know. Not know just who Jesus is in my eyes or in someone else's. It's like how people view . . . maybe the president or a celebrity. They gather ideas from the news, tabloids, interviews, and then create an image of their own making that's often nothing like who the person really is. But they don't really know that person. I want to know who Jesus *is.*"

His words jumble me up. If anything in my life is a sure foundation, it's that I know who Jesus is. Jesus is the Son of God, who came to walk in man's shoes and to redeem the world. Jesus is the Beatitudes and that baby in a manger. He is the risen King I sing about on Sunday mornings and while listening to Christian music in my car.

Of course I knew who Jesus was—and is—right?

"And I want to set the record straight on that prom-night disaster."

"What prom-night disaster?" I say, fully knowing what he's talking about.

"I would've explained years ago, but you wouldn't listen. Then that made me angry at you. Over time, I figured—what was the point?"

"What is the point?"

"The point is you had the wrong idea that night."

"Really? How was I wrong when you dumped me for another girl on prom night?"

"I guess you do remember."

"Vaguely." I frown and he smiles.

"I apologized seven years ago."

"Well, a little sorry was a sorry excuse."

"If you would've let me explain. Now you've held it against me ever since."

"No, I haven't . . . well, maybe a little."

"You want to know what happened that night?"

"It's a million years ago."

"Yeah, I can tell. As you might recall, it was clear you weren't interested in me other than as a date for the night. You barely talked to me. Then at the dance I ran into Nicki Carpenter, who'd been dumped that night by Randy Blake. Nicki and I had been friends for years, so I tried to cheer her up a bit. You were in your own little bubble and didn't notice me either until, of course . . ."

"The final dance." Strange how quickly that night comes back to me. I hadn't wanted Griffin to be my date; the guy I was interested in brought a girl from another school. In fact, I'd nearly forgotten about Griffin until they called for the final dance. Some friends pointed out that my date was already taken and that Nicki Carpenter was draped over his shoulder.

"Nicki kept crying even when I tried to cheer her up with a dance."

"She looked cheered up."

Alisia rises from the table, knocking several crayons off. "This Griffin," she says with a shy smile, handing him a paper.

He pulls her onto his lap and talks to her about her depiction of him beside Garden Man.

Moments later, Alisia slides from Griffin's lap and picks up a paper from the table. Holding it behind her back, she comes to me. Her dark eyes stare into mine, and she seems to hesitate, though expectation fills her features as she hands me the paper. "For Auntie Claire."

The picture brings tears to my eyes, but I fight them, not wanting to frighten Alisia. Flowers of various colors and sizes cover the white paper, and in the center a little girl holds the hand of a bigger girl. Alisia has drawn a picture of us.

As I look at the picture, I think of my old goals for life and the future. Everything I thought I wanted. Suddenly, there's nothing so amazing as a picture from a child and the discussion of who Jesus really is.

---

My assignment is to check the progress on the new bridge and get photographs. This time, I notice the orange signs stating the road closure as I drive out to Wilson Bridge.

Nearly completed, the new, sprawling Wilson Bridge will change the sharp descent of Highway 7 to a smooth glide over the wide gorge cut by Wilson River. Below, though not fully beneath, stretches the strip of the old bridge and the subject of community debate. The county wants to blow it up; otherwise people will use it for easier access to the river instead of going across into Edgewood State Park. Locals say it's all about money for the county and the state. An entrance fee is required to enter the park, while old Wilson Bridge is free. And, of course, the fact that the old bridge is considered a local historic site is argued.

Weeks ago, I crossed this bridge in early morning weariness, the fog hiding its height (one hundred and thirty-five feet, I discover) above the rocky waters below. Pulling to the side of the road, I realize I've parked in the same place my car broke down, the black boulder still beside the road. The earth rumbles with heavy equipment. Those usually sleeping yellow dinosaurs are awake now, grumbling at their work of pushing, scooping, dumping.

A worker, seeing my press badge, hands me a bright hard hat that's much too large and slips immediately over my eyes.

"Thanks," I say. He nods, not catching my cynicism. I mean, really, there's nothing above us to warrant a hard hat, but state rules, I know.

A burly man with an orange shirt tucked into jeans that hold in a bulging belly pulls out earplugs as he walks toward me. He stuffs the earplugs in his jeans pocket and shakes my hand. "Ms. O'Rourke, I'm Reagan Montgomery, the site supervisor. Nice to meet a member of the local press," he says wryly as I wipe my hand discreetly against my legs after it's released from his firm grip. "Are you writing this story?"

"Yes, taking over for the usual reporter who covers these things—she's out for a while."

"Lemme guess. Margie Stinton told you to torment us in black-and-white once again? It's been nearly a month, so I guess it's overdue."

"I don't get your meaning."

"You new around here?"

"New to *The Tidal Post*."

"Ah. Well, Ms. Stinton has her mind made up about our project. She writes articles without even interviewing us. Think her very first headline when we started the project was something like 'Saying Good-bye to Small-Town Life.' That riled citizens from their peaceful mornings to march around the site and promise us a fight all the way. I'm just trying to do my job. Don't care if I build a bridge here or up in Oregon—they tell me where and I build it. But anyway, what are your questions? I gotta get back and check the rebars along the western railing."

"Sure. First, an update on the bridge completion. It says here that you were hoping for a December 17 ribbon-cutting ceremony."

"Yeah, about a month ago we were. Looking more like after Christmas now. We got pulled off for a week to help another crew down in Eureka, then returned to some equipment trouble—sabotage actually—which I don't think made it into your paper."

"We did one story about the sabotage. Is this the second case?"

"Third. We even have the police patrolling a few times a day. The latest one happened last night. The police just left a while ago."

"Can you show me the damage?" I say, pulling out my notebook from my shoulder bag.

Mr. Montgomery pushes his hard hat back with a grin. "Sure thing. I've still got one dozer down. Want some photos?"

After finishing a roll of film on the bridge development and a bulldozer with flattened tires and wires cut in half, I gaze across the bridge toward the forested roadway leading to Edgewater State Park and at the end, Orion Point. Sophia Fleming is there at this moment, only a long walk away. I'm having tea with her tomorrow. I'll once again be on Orion Point.

Back at the office, the phone is ringing when I come out of the darkroom with the negatives ready to print.

"Claire, someone for you on line two; wouldn't give a name," Loretta says, leaning over Katt's receptionist's desk.

"Okay," I say. "Maybe it's that secret admirer I've been trying to get."

"That's what I was thinking, or maybe a cute stalker," she says as if thrilled at the thought. "I wish I could pick out someone to stalk me, someone good-looking and nice, not creepy."

"Aren't all stalkers creepy?" I ask, sitting in my cubicle.

"Not the one I have in mind," she says with a wicked smile.

I have to stop my laugh as I pick up the phone. "This is Claire O'Rourke."

"Thanks for taking my call," a male voice says.

"Who is this?"

"I'd like to remain anonymous."

"Anonymous?" I say, turning toward Loretta, who hurries over.

"I have a story for you."

"Uh . . . and what is the story about?"

"You were at the bridge-construction site recently when those people came and did damage to the equipment, right?"

"Um . . . yes," I say.

"I know who keeps orchestrating these things."

"And you want to tell me?"

"I know there was more damage done last night. I know a lot of what's happening. Is there a reward? We could meet and talk about it."

"Sorry, but I can't meet with a stranger for a story I know nothing about."

"Maybe that construction crew will pay a reward for the information."

"I don't know, but you should go to the police with this."

The phone goes dead.

"That's strange," Loretta says. "We get weird calls from time to time. We'll have to call Deputy Avery about this one though."

I hang up the receiver.

"Will you include the anonymous stranger in your article about the bridge?" Loretta asks. "That might be what he wants—a lonely guy who wants attention."

"There was another incident at the bridge last night; someone damaged a piece of equipment. The foreman didn't want to talk to me at first. He thought I might be like Margie. The guy on the phone seemed to know something."

"Wonder what the bridge people thought when they met her," Loretta says offhandedly as she sits on the edge of the table across from me.

"Who?"

"Margie."

"They've never met her. The foreman said she never talked to them before writing articles about the bridge construction. What do you think of her?"

"I've never met her either. I've been curious since she started writing for us several years ago. But I've never so much as seen the woman. She works all freelance. It's weird, 'cause for a while I was really trying to meet her. I e-mailed about us going to lunch, but then she'd cancel or the plans wouldn't work out. Finally, I just gave up."

"She has e-mail?"

The front door opens and Leonard walks inside.

"Hey, Leonard, you've met Margie Stinton, right?"

"Nope. I never could figure out how she got such perks. All she does is e-mail in her articles and we do the rest."

"That's called being a freelance writer," Loretta says.

"Yeah, but she's the only one here who gets to do it."

"Then why does she have a desk and everything?" I ask.

"The only thing there is her nameplate. She's never used the desk as far as I know."

I turn in my chair and open the drawers and cabinet on her side of the cubicle. Except for a dead spider in the file drawer, they're empty.

"Has anyone here met Margie?" I ask.

Loretta and Leonard shrug and appear as dismayed as I am.

When Rob comes into the office later, we're all waiting. "Who is Margie Stinton?" comes the assault on him.

"Whoa, hold on. What's going on?" he says, holding up his briefcase.

"We were talking," Katt says from her desk. "Not one of us has met Margie Stinton."

Loretta sits on the edge of Katt's desk, crossing her cowboy boots. "And when Claire was at the bridge-construction site today, the foreman said he hasn't met her either, even though she's written several articles about the project."

"Never let freelancers into a local paper," Leonard adds.

"So who is she?" Loretta asks.

"She's a local freelance writer who turns in her articles on time. I don't know anything else about her. I've never met her in person."

Another round of questions:

"What?"

"No one has met her?"

"How do you hire someone you've never met?"

Rob sets his briefcase down. "Okay, several years ago I was asked by a community member to hire her. They offered extra advertising for the paper, it was on a temporary basis, and I could reject any article I didn't like. A sweet deal. Never needed to meet her. I thought she might eventually come on staff, even set a desk area up for her and such, but it's worked just fine this way."

"But don't you think it's strange that no one knows who she is?" Katt says, coming to sit beside Loretta. "We tried to look her up in the phone book and on the Internet. Nothing except for a Margie Stinton in Florida."

I lean against a file cabinet and try not to chuckle at the perplexed expression on Rob's face.

"I'll check out a few things and let you know."

So now we're all wondering. Who is Margie Stinton?

Designs

# Sophia

*Remember...*

<hr />

I've been glancing around the house again, looking for something to dust. Any visitors at all, let alone two in the same month—what was I thinking? This Wednesday morning brought another round of house inspection. And I'm tired after reading into the life of Josephine Vanderook well into the night. I cut some wiry geraniums and put them in a vase on the table. The book and broken china are safely tucked on a shelf in my book room.

Claire O'Rourke will be coming here. It feels different than when preparing for Bradley's visit. I try to distinguish the two, understand what I feel about this.

Bradley came to Orion Point to show his father he was willing to see where he lived. But Bradley had really come to garner more support in winning his father. I remind myself that it isn't a competition, but one of us will win and the other will lose. And I already know the outcome.

My eyes go to the kitchen window every time I pass it, wondering if I'll catch a glimpse of Ben's boat with that girl Claire bundled up in the wool blanket. I get a unique flutter of nervousness at every outside noise. She surely finds me a curiosity. Has she told many people of our meeting and this visit? Will it cause some ripple effect with me getting invitations and greetings from the community? I decide if she stares too closely or takes any notes, Ben will have to make her leave.

My life has long been filled with a routine of practicalities mixed with thoughts and prayers. Contemplation has been a companion. Yet I will mostly be remembered for a book I once wrote. A book about two boys and two girls during the summer of their fourteenth year. Important people in publishing and the media grasped on to my writing; some continue to quote it as a favorite, to refer to the characters as friends, which continues its presence on the bookshelves. Every year it sells fewer and fewer.

And it seems so long ago, the actual writing of it. I wonder about the words I chose so carefully, about the characters I left upon those pages. Never have I returned to them—surely they are abandoned orphans in the fictive world. But they didn't want to leave. They didn't want to leave that summer and the place I invented for the real world in which they lived.

And so I will be remembered for a book. Few know of this life here, the time upon my knees in prayer, the weeding and pruning of my garden, my footprints along the sea walk. My epitaph may speak of words I wrote, for it is all people have of me. They do not know that I've prayed for them, for hours and for days. For the families I read about in the newspaper who've lost a loved one from their midst or experienced some tragedy or scandal. For the townspeople of Harper's Bay as I've recited their names one by one. Then the names I'll never know but I pray for anyway— for our nation and the nations of the globe. For soldiers, migrant workers, professors, convicts, the lonely and oppressed, the lonely and prosperous . . . I pray for you out there who have never heard my name and for the ones who have. My seclusion began in heartbreak but changed through a life of prayer, the monastic life perhaps one of the greatest in eternal terms.

What is life like for Claire O'Rourke? I think about her routine, her dreams, her favorite ice cream. What will it be like to hear her voice in my house? What would it be like to be her friend?

First Bradley and now Claire—their coming seems to carry the outside world with them. That old life is not dead to me. As I sit in my chair, I recall that intricate outside world. At first I felt such intimidation as a small-town girl thrust straight from college into strange and wondrous New York City, launched into society— a place that allowed for oddities, scandals, diversity, but not religious devotion. Parties above me in topics and style. There was hurt when invitations were extended all around except to me, though I told myself not to be hurt. After all, I was young and from a different landscape (oh, why can't the heart ever obey the mind?). Still there were banquets and sometimes my own name was honored, bringing kisses on both cheeks, hugs, and handshakes for the words I had written while alone in deepest solitude.

I began to adapt to it, or rather I was transforming into the image of who I needed to be—no longer hesitating over clothing choices and sometimes turning down invitations just because I could. Travel became less intimidating, especially after traveling in Europe, meeting book people, and thinking of Phillip being in some of those same cities during wartime. When the second book was released, critics were harsh but it didn't matter; others (the ones who would offer more contracts) loved the novel.

And then that short trip home, the class reunion, and the day that changed my path forever. The weekend began with the four of us together again. It ended with Phillip dead. Phillip, who had endured a war, miraculously survived battles, and returned a hero—one simple decision took him away.

The wind chimes on the front porch clink, drawing me back, reminding me that someone will once again invade my space. Suddenly I don't want it. Maybe I'll go on a walk at the scheduled time, leave a note.

"No, I can't run away; right, Holiday?"

He lifts his head and grunts before lowering it back to his fuzzy rug.

I've run away before.

After Phillip's death, New York lost its luster when I returned. It appeared cruel and unkind upon my return. It didn't care about my time away, the extra days needed to attend a memorial service. Schedules and parties and events had been shifted, and now its patience wore thin. A book tour was set to begin, despite the harsh reviews of my newest novel; the public still reached for it from the shelves. I was on the roster of my publishing house's plans for the future.

Outside my New York brownstone, the city moved and breathed. People walked from here to there; yellow cabs breezed around Buicks and Cadillacs; cashiers in stores punched keys and put clothing and food into bags and baskets; a street musician sat at the corner singing; and I was one speck within that metropolis.

My business suit pressed and hat pinned firmly in place, I appeared an outward model of the professional female writer. My book tour began at a store in Manhattan. Inside were wood paneling, pipe and cigarette smoke, rows of books.

Some time after my reading from the new novel and answering the usual questions—including how to become a writer like me—and partway down the line of autograph seekers, I began to cry. Just one tear at first. One long, slow, surprising tear that stopped me with pen upon book until it splashed into a pool upon the page.

The rep from the publishing house was the suave-salesman type, the kind who could mediate an international crisis but crumples under the weight of a crying woman. I excused myself and found the bathroom—more wood paneling and a smoke-stained ceiling. After knocking lightly, a bookstore clerk squeezed inside and handed me her cloth kerchief without question. Later she escorted me out a back door, where the cab she rang was waiting.

Without phone calls or explanations, I took a plane home to Orion Point. It seemed I slept a week with the sea outside my window, my mother bringing food and silent comfort and taking care of the concerned queries that followed me back.

Weeks later I quietly returned to the city—grateful for its anonymity when I needed it—to pack my belongings and instruct the movers on their cross-country journey. My agent, accustomed to his writers checking into sanitariums or falling into drinking binges, chastised me for not calling him, then encouraged me back toward what could be, what I was jeopardizing, and what he'd diverted—the impact of a canceled book tour and an angry publishing house. He thought the critics had harmed another fragile writer's psyche or that a new idea sent me into the coastal wilderness I'd written about in my earlier novels.

Weeks and months would pass into years. From time to time, someone would make the trek out to check my progress—agent or publishing rep—to whom I gave no update. Later, travel expenses were traded for certified mail. When I failed to reply, eventually that too faded away.

The past is like a coat I put on every morning, defining me in many ways. The future will soon come knocking. This tea, as simple as I try to make it, is not simple at all. Claire will mean something to my life—I know that somehow. Will her arrival attempt to pull away this coat of the past?

## Claire

Ben was waiting at the docks, smiling at my thermos and lifting his own to show he'd had the same thought. The morning is unseasonably mild with a cheerful sun upon the docking area.

Ben's small fishing boat passes the larger vessels, and he waves to a fisherman, who is taking advantage of the warmth to air out cushions and mattresses around the deck of his boat.

Once we begin to bounce upon the water, extending beyond the first bouys, the breeze nips my nose and cheeks. The forested, rocky curve of Orion Point appears against the morning gleam of silver sea. Our destination.

*Be yourself, be yourself.* These are the words I keep repeating in my head and have been saying all morning. Before I left the house, Alisia climbed in my lap while Mom gave me instructions as if I were a child again: *"Call her Ms. Fleming. I want a lot of details. Take this plate of cookies. Oh, you have truffles. That's nice, but remember to use your manners."*

I'm meeting S. T. Fleming. In fifty years, perhaps only a handful of people have taken this journey from the harbor to the lighthouse and then to the Fleming cottage.

Such is the impact of this meeting, something I could write about, something to tell children or a niece in future years.

## Sophia

*I will always be with you.*

---

Footsteps on my front porch, Holiday's cautious bark, door opening. Ben knows by my expression that he has to stay. What if there's nothing to talk about? What if the conversation lags? What if she asks something I don't know how to answer or don't want to answer?

Yet Claire is the nervous one, more nervous than me. She hands me a gift-wrapped box from the Harper's Bay candy shop, while she apologizes for her casual attire of jeans and cream sweater. Says that if they were driving and not coming by boat she would have dressed better. I think she looks pretty, her cheeks rosy from the sea. I'm wearing my usual polyester-blend pants, but I did iron a blouse for the occasion and took extra time putting my hair in a neat twist. I ask about the ride across the bay. Too cold? Did she get wet? She laughs softly—strange to think how long it's been since I heard another woman laugh in this house.

"He called it the wild-ruckus ride," she says, explaining how Ben tried to scare her on the way out. I laugh at that. And suddenly her presence here reminds me of the first warm day of spring when I open the windows and let in light and fresh air.

"You could show her around," Ben says, and I'm reminded that yes, this is something people do with visitors. I didn't dust the other rooms, and the book room is where the memoir and shipwreck artifacts currently reside.

After avoiding the book room altogether, we return to where Ben watches us expectantly.

Claire seems drawn to the line of photographs along the top of the china cabinet. "Is that . . . ?" she asks, staring at a picture, then turning to me. "Do you mind?"

"No, not at all."

Seeing her pick up the frame with the group photo brings a smile to my lips. It has sat there so long, losing its luster, yet I perceive the photo from Claire's viewpoint and chuckle a bit.

"That isn't . . . ?" She hesitates, obviously doubting what her eyes are telling her.

"Yes, that's Hemingway and that's Evelyn Waugh. The others aren't as well-known, but they were great writers too."

"And this is you?" she asks, pointing to the girl I used to be. A girl whose thoughts and dreams have grown and changed from the seeds that began them.

"Yes, that's me."

"It must have been amazing being among such a group of writers."

"It was a pretty staggering time for me. A girl from the Point hobnobbing with the likes of these—not that we were very close. But there I was, wearing the wrong outfits to the right parties. Sometimes wandering around like a bull in a china shop; other times feeling invisible, though not enough for my comfort, mind you. Then other times I'd be the center of too many eyes. It took time to fit in." My honest words to Claire surprise me, though I find it easy talking with her.

A lovely naïveté shines in Claire's eyes. Such ideas appeal to her, draw her—she's dreamed such dreams. How I remember those lofty thoughts of someday being successful, someday having my words in print and seeing my name on a book in the bookstore. They can bubble up into desire to see it again. I could pull out some of my writings, more than enough for several collections of stories, and perhaps more than one novel is there among the ramblings. A publisher would pick it up just because of the buzz and preeminent sales the buzz would create, whether the words were coherent or not. Once again I could find myself in the midst of the New York literary scene with social circles as numerous as corner shops.

I tell Claire about the parties, conversing and thinking in separate spheres, seeing the images as I speak. Ben stirs the fire, adding another log, probably stunned to hear me share stories, some I've never told to him.

"What was he like?" she asks, touching Hemingway's face.

"A flirt," I say, and Ben rises from the fireplace, looking our way. "This picture was taken in 1954. We were at a party put on by the publisher. Mr. Hemingway's short story had just won the Pulitzer." I recall how the critics in the previous years had said his best work was done; then came *The Old Man and the Sea*. "I was so intimidated by the thought of meeting him. But he called me over, knew my name. Said, 'Well, S. T. Fleming, how do you like these parties?'"

I can't help but smile at the memory I've allowed to gather dust. Mr. Hemingway sat with arms stretched over the back of a couch. His white beard trimmed perfectly, eyes holding a hint of both sadness and flirtation. A big man, some said, with a bigger ego; others said his deepest fears haunted him day and night. I was intrigued and terrified at the same time. His wife was talking to an editor in a cluster of people, glancing up and discussing a painting on the wall. And Ernest Hemingway, sitting there between two beautiful women and recently the winner of the great literary award, soon to win the Nobel Prize, began flirting with me.

*"I'll have to buy you a drink sometime, Miss Fleming. Think of the future you have ahead of you—just beware of those words now. Don't let them torment you like they do most of us."* As the memory washes over me, I'm silent a moment. "Less than ten years later, when I'd been living here for several years, the headlines told that Hemingway was gone."

Hemingway, the great adventurer who had made his home in exotic locales, hunted, and lived life to its wildest form, was dead by his own hand.

"It wasn't all glitz and glamour," I say, remembering how it could be quite impairing. "I would've probably followed the same path as many—turned into a snob, an alcoholic, or expecting the world to move over for the artist. Success and a little fame can do strange things to a person."

"Is that why you left it behind?"

I hesitate and suddenly feel I'm trusting too quickly. "You might say that had something to do with it."

"Fascinating though," Claire says softly. And then she's looking into the framed photo of my Phillip. There's a physical leap within my chest as she asks, "Who is this handsome guy?"

Ben and I have made inept attempts at discussing Phillip over the years. We mainly find solace in the memories and humor of our youthful exploits. But when we've tiptoed into the visions of his time at war or that last night together, we get mired in the loss and the guilt of surviving. Except to the Lord and Ben, I have never spoken of Phillip to another soul in fifty years.

She watches me with interest, reading me, it seems.

"He was a very special person to me . . . to us," I say, though Ben seems busy again with the fire. "We grew up together, but he died young."

"Oh, I'm sorry," she says, staring into Phillip's black-and-white image. How little you can see of him from the photograph. Just a handsome face, eyes that peer from yesterday, a proud American GI. His mannerisms and laughter, his smile so shy, his hands strong yet gentle while holding mine, the way he could embrace me as if everything had disappeared around us.

"Tell me about your return to Harper's Bay." I say this to change the subject. We sit at the table for tea, and it seems my question opens the floodgates. As she explains everything from the night alone in her car to her taking the job at *The Tidal Post,* I find myself enjoying every minute, asking questions, greedy for details. For a time, I get to live in her world, something so foreign and new to me. We talk about her brother, and I'm surprised she would share these details with me.

"Why is life so confusing?" she asks with a sigh.

"Wish I could give you some advice, but I've been asking myself that same question, especially lately. Plus, I'm a little out of civilization."

"Getting out of the loop for a while sounds good to me. Maybe not for the next fifty years though," she says with a laugh, then looks worried that I've been offended.

I laugh with her. "I don't recommend it."

When Ben joins us for tea, we talk about Claire's family and then Ben's lighthouse. It's surprisingly easy the way we talk and drink our tea as if we've done this for years. And quite unexpectedly, I want this to be habit, not one solitary visit. Then I realize that this old coat won't leave me. The past is who I am. And yet maybe the future holds more than my fears have allowed me to see.

## Claire

A sponge oversaturated. Taking in the cottage of S. T. Fleming, the conversation, attempting to visualize her life so many years secluded in this place, I feel near frantic to gather it all in, and yet there's just too much.

As I sit by the fire on a worn and comfortable sofa, I realize that many of the belongings in this house are probably older than I am. Time is hard to comprehend at twenty-four; I know this. Five years for me holds much promise and changeability, but for Sophia five years has been the passage of a short time. At least that's what I'm guessing.

Sophia shows me around the cottage casually, as if she can't really see what it looks like from the outside anymore. I feel nervous and intimidated—like visiting a grand museum after hours with full access to all the treasures. Imagine touching the paint of a van Gogh. That's how I feel picking up that framed photo of Hemingway and Waugh and this woman in her youth. Everything seems of value to me, and the author is my tour guide.

The kitchen overlooks the back deck and gardened pathways. I stop there a moment to see what she sees. A small space looks out to the bay, and white furls churn atop the waves like little sails. Lining the windowsill is a row of varied vases, holding differing stages of plant life: a seedling popping from soil, a miniature rosebush with yellow buds, and a geranium cutting taking root in water. Her dish drainer holds one clean teacup, a clear glass plate, a silver fork and spoon.

A bedroom turns off from the hall and toward the front of the house. Sophia's bedroom goes toward the back. She offhandedly refers to the front bedroom as her junk collection, and we pass it without opening the door. Of course, that is the room I most long to see. My imagination takes flight as I picture everything from dozens of secret manuscripts to the petrified corpse of some past intruder. Oh, how imagination can fly far and wide.

Her compact bedroom is neat and tidy—brass bed covered with a hand-stitched quilt and down comforter. The scent of age and dust is heavier here, as if the years had leaked into the edges and fermented there; perhaps the pressed-in walls and closed door have locked it all inside. A dresser, French doors that open to the deck speckled with potted plants. Books, including a Bible, *Shipwrecks of Northern California, Pop Culture, What's So Amazing about Grace?* and *Contemplative Prayer* are stacked on the bedside table. A pile of novels rests beside these. I notice Sherwood Anderson's *Winesburg, Ohio,* a Kafka, and *Peter Pan.*

Sophia Fleming, in her solitude, seems more prone toward gardening and books than toward decorating. Apparently the old paintings on her walls have been there for years, because she appears surprised when I point them out. Her great-uncle painted them—a ship on Harper's Bay, a seagull in flight, and a flower growing from rocks by the sea.

Nothing really matches, and nothing appears planned or thought through in terms of interior design. But everything finds a tidy spot where it's probably been for years, in the place of its use or disuse. Photographs to gaze at when one remembers they are there, an immediate journey down memory lane. The most recent-looking photo is of Ben and Sophia, in her garden perhaps. By their clothing and ages, it appears to have been taken in the sixties. Her home is a usable, somewhat sentimental environment, where time stands frozen or at least is resting.

For a moment, the ascetic appeals to me.

Time issues resolved, days stretched before me, books I could read, plenty of time with God. Rest, oh rest, and silence inside and out. For a short time as a child I pretended to be a nun. My parents were vaguely troubled that I'd convert to Catholicism. It probably had more to do with Julie Andrews and *The Sound of Music* and hopes that I'd be led from there to the love of my life. There were days of thought and interest in such a small and peaceful life. I just didn't like the rules and commitments and duties attached. *If only I could be an independent nun,* I'd think. My woods became my own convent where I'd walk and pray in calm solemnity, until my brother would dive from the bushes like Rambo and send me screaming back to the house. Perhaps this crazy recluse of Orion Point has found the existence we all somehow sought.

I haven't seen a television here, unless there's a home theater hiding in the secret room, but she has a radio and stacks of newspapers and magazines—*The Tidal Post, USA Today, Coastal Life, The New Yorker,* and *Better Homes & Gardens*—in the living room.

Sophia's golden Lab watches me, not with suspicion but with curiosity, I believe. He stays close to his master, following us from room to room and now resting as if asleep at her feet, though on occasion an eyelid raises toward me, then closes again.

"How do you get supplies?" I ask as Sophia places a log on the fire and pokes it daintily with the iron poker until the flames leap up its sides.

"Ben is my lifeline to civilization," she says, turning to smile. I wonder what her salt-and-pepper gray hair would look like hanging down her back. Suddenly I hope to be as beautiful and graceful at seventy-something. I wonder if Ben notices and what the two of them must share.

The morning gives way toward noontime, and I sense a weariness in Sophia, though her smile and conversation have yet to dissipate. She seems to enjoy our time as much as I do, but my mother's manner warnings are alerting me that it's time to go.

I do so unwillingly. This woman has a drawing effect on me. I'll probably kick myself for all the things I've forgotten to ask. Perhaps I can come again or we'll write one another or . . . somehow I hope to know her better.

# Sophia

*If we do not have tomorrow, I hope you know I love you.*

---

*A*re you all right?" Ben stands with his hat in his hands, late evening casting itself over him like a drizzling rain. He so rarely comes to the house after sunset, especially after he's already been with me today.

"Of course. Come inside. I've cooked chicken noodle soup."

"Campbell's?" he asks with a smirk and a raised eyebrow.

"I made it myself, except for the canned broth."

Over steaming bowls of soup and oyster crackers, I notice Ben studying me. "Ask if there's something."

"I just want you to tell me. You've had a lot of things happen in a very short time. You aren't the best about admitting some things to me."

"As if you are." I know what he's referring to. It's been over a decade now, maybe it's approaching two, when my life went dark for a while. "Ben, don't worry. I can't explain it, but I know God is taking care of things."

After two bowls of soup, Ben leaves, though I wish him to stay. I would've let him smoke his pipe in the house for once, beat him at cards, but his evening chores awaited.

After he's gone, I think again to that time of my deepest depression. It was sparked by memories I hadn't visited until that time, memories I can now hold and remember, though not without pain. Memories like Phillip's funeral, with the usual solemnity, but also with a feeling of honor within the grief. He was a war hero and hometown boy. He'd saved lives and exhibited bravery in the midst of battle. Then his life was cut short in another act of heroism. The entire town was in mourning. And I felt guilty to be alive.

Phillip's parents held me close, his mother's embrace unresolved to the loss. Phillip's sister, Helen, could not be consoled, so Ben escorted her from the service.

"I always thought the two of you . . . ," Mrs. Turluccio said in my ear, touching my hair and face as if I embodied the future she'd never have with Phillip.

Everyone had pictured us together, Phillip and I included. There had been others in our lives, people we'd tried on in attempts to get one another out of our systems or as an experiment to see if someone would not only suffice but amplify. We might think so for a while. I believed I'd found love in New York, but it was really admiration and the need to be admired. Phillip had an attachment in Austria, though I suspected it was more a mission of mercy, the hero in need, and I had never really needed a hero—or so I assumed.

Then suddenly there was no hope for us at all. He was dead. There was no getting a moment back. I'd never envisioned life without him. Even if our love didn't lead to marriage and happily ever after, Phillip would always be essential to my existence—I believed it so and could not fathom a world without him.

Day by day, I faced that world. My seclusion on Orion Point would pass the years and soften the grief. Until the restoration of the clock tower, decades after the fire that took the original. Its completion touched something within me. It became a physical reminder of how life moved on, how the past was gone, how Phillip was forgotten. Even a town hero gets left behind.

All those decades of missed moments, a clock tower reconstruction, a forgotten hometown boy. Then Phillip's birthday, the knowledge that he would be an old man. And yet he would always be young in my memory. I couldn't conceive of him at sixty-five. I wished to have him here, let myself imagine us together all those years, what his belongings would look like in my house—our house—and how easily we'd live our lives. There would be the annoying habits and bickerings, but then we'd have our walks, tea before the fire, sharing books and movies, going on travels, maybe even in a motor home, attending church and community events.

I had none of these.

I didn't get a life with him.

All the things I'd never have came to me again. For weeks, I barely ate or slept. Reading Phillip's old letters became an obsession, and I knew nearly each word by heart. I held one-sided conversations, the ones I wished to have with him. My imagination almost took over reality. For days and days, I didn't stray from the house. Life's darkness no longer felt like an enemy; its embrace was my comfort.

Then late one morning Ben came to the door. He said he no longer believed that I was "fighting a flu" as I'd said. He insisted upon coming inside. The few dishes I'd used were dirty in the sink, the fireplace's coldness revealed its disuse, and my appearance surely frightened him—I'd bathed but done nothing with my hair. He cleaned, built a fire, made tea, tried to talk to me. I sat beside him in a chair with a down comforter wrapped around me, a chill awakened in my bones.

"You can't let it take you," he said in one of the few confrontational acts of his life.

"What do you mean?" I asked, trying to gather the energy to perform. Instead I began to cry and cry. Ben held me for what seemed like days or weeks, months perhaps, the way time warped.

Ben had brought mail with him. A packet of letters. The fourth-grade teacher at Harper's Bay Elementary annually instructed her students on letter writing. That year I became the recipient and meticulously answered them all, even when the questions were humorously blunt, "Are you crazy like my dad says?" Usually the teacher edited such questions.

On that night, Ben read each one aloud. Somehow Ben's tender ministrations and the letters of children became the hands of healing.

Tonight, something in the memory tugs at me. Going to my bedroom, I rummage through the many stacks of papers I've saved. And finally I find the bundle from that very year, wrapped in a rubber band. And yes, the tugging serves me correctly. Inside the bundle I find a letter from Claire O'Rourke.

*Dear Mrs. Fleming:*

*Hello. My name is Claire O'Rourke, and I am in fourth grade. My teacher's name is Miss Murdoch. I have two cats and a dog, but my hamster ran away from home one night, and we can't find him. I live in Harper's Bay. We learn about the history of our town. We learn that you live on Orion Point that is by our town.*

*I like to read and play hide-and-go-seek and make forts in the woods. I like to read books the very best. Do you like making forts? Do you have a pet? My cat had kittens, and you can have one. Someday I want to be a writer like you. And maybe I can come live with you. Then I won't be so far from my mom and dad, but I can think a lot and write and come visit them.*

*That is all. My teacher says I should be a writer because I write a lot more than most kids my age. This letter is long. My teacher is showing us how to write a letter and how to write in cursive.*

*Sincerely,*

*Claire O'Rourke*

Holding the pages of Claire's letter to my chest, the tears gather in my eyes. Ah, the Lord has already used this girl in my life. And here, years later, he brings her again.

I think of how sometimes God puts people together, maybe more often than we realize. We can disregard it, lie to ourselves, find the reasons why it's impractical. But something within the creation of them connects. I've been afraid of it. There is something fearful in revealing our true selves, allowing others to peer intimately inside. It takes such trust, and none of us is completely trustworthy. It's a risk, and there will be disappointment, opposing views, disenchantment, but the fusing of two imperfect lives is something of the divine.

Do I dare? The idea of it sounds romantic and ethereal. But such fusing can be ripped apart. I nearly did not survive it once. In truth, I'm not sure I completely did.

Yet Claire is in my life, and I'm drawn to her, to her spirit and the unspoken that speaks to me, the connection I cannot explain. She is something found, and I hope to know her.

# Claire

* * *

The afternoon is full of assignments: photos at the library, copy-editing, working on an article.

I feel strangely protective over my time with Sophia. That afternoon Mom and I discuss it, and she agrees that even though Sophia didn't ask, I need to be careful to guard her privacy. It hadn't occurred to me how this day, with such an amazing time with Sophia and Ben, would need protection. I'm now part of shielding her as Ben has done for so many years.

While I color with Alisia, I see my father struggle with a mattress on his way toward the bungalow. He seems unsure why he continues to remodel, whether it's for me or my brother or someone else.

"Sometimes God tells you to build an ark, plant a garden, or remodel an inventor's studio. You don't ask; you just do," he says as I help carry the full-size bed into the studio that smells of fresh paint. "You had a phone call about that unmarried group that meets tonight."

"Unmarried group—what kind of a name is that?"

"Oh, maybe it's called the singles group. All the groups get me confused: young marrieds, married, singles . . . anyway, it got me thinking you should do things with kids your age."

"Dad, did you just say, *kids* my age?"

"Sorry, you'll always be my girl."

I'm on my way to the "unmarried group" as Dad called it. I've been in similar groups before, and in a way they're all the same. A group of single people varying from college age through middle age. Discussions revolve around finding a mate, saving yourself or resaving yourself for marriage, how to live the single life, how to prepare for being a good spouse, and on and on. Some come in search of the love of their life. Others are bored and it's either this or the club scene, which they've tried and given up on. Some are divorced or attempting to survive heartbreak of one kind or another, or seeking solace, friendship, or a promise of something more than the loneliness and failure of the moment. I'm not sure where I fit.

"You came," Jill Watley says with a sincere smile. I'm introduced to Beatrice and Maryanne, two others in the group. We meet in the church parking lot and wait until Charles arrives, a guy in his forties whom I've seen at the bank. We load into Beatrice's minivan to carpool to tonight's big event. No one told me what the event was until I got in the car.

THINGSTODO

On my computer, this is the title of a document file of things I want to do. This file, along with others like PLACESTOGO and BEFOREIDIE, are together in the hard-drive folder called LIFEGOALS. But nowhere in any of those files and especially inside THINGSTODO and BEFOREIDIE have I included what we're doing tonight.

Karaoke.

And not only karaoke, which in and of itself might possibly be fun in a place like New York or say, Hollywood. But not karaoke in Harper's Bay. Not karaoke in Harper's Bay with this odd eclectic singles group on a Wednesday evening at the Shamrock Grill that the group rented for the evening. Harper's Bay has one place for karaoke, and we're here.

The story behind this, I discover, began at their New Year's party. Each person chose one thing they wanted to do before the year's end. Maryanne wanted karaoke. Unfortunately, they delayed that activity and now I'm part of the group.

"Does Pastor Artie know about this?" Charles asks me as Beatrice pulls into an empty parking space.

"I knew nothing about this," I say with my hands up.

"It was the only place around with karaoke," Beatrice says, defending her position as activity planner. "We're doing this for Maryanne, remember."

"I'm so excited!" Maryanne wiggles in her seat like an eager child.

From the depths of Beatrice's minivan I emerge, wiping off crackers from my faded jeans and the back of my black sweater—guess I was sitting where her two-year-old's car seat usually rests. Thus arrives the Vine Creek Community Church Singles Group to the doorway of the Shamrock. We carry trays of cut veggies and mini quiches along with bags of other goodies.

Low lights cast a haze over the large rectangular room decorated like an Irish restaurant—lots of dark wood, a framed map of Ireland, shamrocks mixed with fishing nets, and some of the local prizewinning fish immortalized on plaques over a trophy case.

"Well, there they are," Griffin calls, looking up from where he's leaning over the pool table. I recognize his opponent, Andy, who moved back to Harper's Bay a few years ago after going to school back east.

"Top o' the evening to you, lass," Andy says while he twists the blue chalk over the end of his cue. "Welcome to the Shamrock."

"Nice accent. Maryanne thought you were meeting us at the church," I say, setting down my coat and purse at the counter. I greet the waiter, who looks like he could be a member of the Hell's Angels; he has a nice smile despite his missing bottom teeth.

"Why carpool a few blocks? I told Raul and Andy to just meet here," Griffin says and hits a striped ball into the corner pocket. Raul is checking out the photos of local sports teams along the wall. "We couldn't get lost."

"Beatrice probably wanted us to come as a group." Andy sticks up for diplomacy's sake. He better understands group dictum, or perhaps he, unlike Griffin, is conformed to it.

Seeing Andy and Griffin together, I'm struck by the contrasts and the likenesses. Both profess faith in Christ, have been friends for years, are good at pool it appears, yet Andy's more the preppy type, the stereotypical guy you'd want to bring home to your parents. Griffin is more of an enigma. Messy-styled hair, artist, a guy with few answers but many questions. From the way he orders a Coke from the waiter, I get the feeling they're friends too.

"Let's get started!" Maryanne rushes toward the stage, looking it over as if it's a natural wonder. "I can't believe we're really here doing this!"

"Me neither." Singing in public is about as desirable to me as doing stand-up comedy. Not my strong suit. Give me some paper and time to write something clever or beautiful, and I might have a shot. Give me a month or two to practice one song—in the shower, car, my living room—then maybe. My voice isn't terrible; it's unreliable. Sometimes in the middle of a hymn or worship song just as I rise on the crescendo, I'll squeak or croak shockingly.

"Everyone, this is Smokey," Griffin announces to us, pointing to the waiter. Yes, Smokey the Waiter. "He'll get you set up there, Maryanne."

From beneath a multicolored lamp, Griffin looks at me, our eyes meeting longer than reasonably expected. For the life of me, I can't understand why his eyes grab mine so easily and why I get these flutters whenever he's near. I'm forced to admit that I would've been disappointed if he hadn't been here. My mind concludes that if I was trapped forever in Harper's Bay and forced to choose from the single males in town, Andy, not Griffin, would be the logical choice, though my emotions don't quite agree.

Griffin smiles and I wonder if he can possibly read my inner struggle.

Maryanne, Raul, Charles, and Jill surround Smokey onstage, watching him explain the karaoke equipment.

I join Beatrice at the long wooden counter, where she's organizing the snack trays.

"Have you tried the hot pizza sauce?" she asks, pulling the cellophane from the top of a casserole dish.

"No, but it smells good." My enthusiasm sounds forced to me.

Beatrice doesn't pick up on my tone; instead she dips a piece of bread into the cheesy concoction. "Oh, you're gonna love it," she says, handing the bread over.

"Mmmm. It is good."

"I'll give you the recipe. It's always a hit at potlucks. Charles always asks if I'm bringing my special goo to get-togethers." She smiles and glances in Charles's direction.

During our small talk about the ingredients, suddenly the reverb of the sound system screams through the room. I catch Smokey's grin as the others onstage grab their ears and jump at the noise.

"Let's get started," Raul says, taking over as announcer. "Get some goodies and prepare for a night of entertainment."

Griffin and Andy set down their sticks, both claiming to be the winner. We carry plates of snacks to the round tables, turning chairs to face the stage.

"Introducing Maryanne Tyler singing Natalie Cole," Raul announces.

Hair permed tightly around her face, overweight, and wearing a business suit for tonight's events, Maryanne is transformed when the music begins. She puts her heart into it. The spotlight blinds her view and envelopes her in a cocoon, where she becomes the singer she wishes to be. Perhaps it could be funny, seeing Maryanne up there, swaying and punctuating, *"L is for the way you look at me."* But it isn't. Actually I'm amazed by her.

Beatrice told me Maryanne found out she is in the early stages of cancer. Though her doctors expect a recovery once she goes through chemo and radiation, fear must surround her. And yet there is a beauty in her that reminds me of my brother. In the face of such obstacles, they seem to see God without a haze or fog. Their need is evident, and God is there for them.

For the most part, my faith has been easy for me. It's never been challenged or tried. Now, worries over my brother and Alisia can take over. My doubts over the future plague the present. Even meeting Ms. Fleming has brought another disconcerted challenge in that it must be kept secret for the most part. And what does that mean? During my latest visit to Conner, he asked whether I'd be there for Alisia long-term. He knows Mom and Dad will be there, but what about me? Will I be a constant in her life if he gets convicted and sent to prison? But what can I offer her? What will she gain from me?

Questions pile upon one another.

"You okay?" Griffin pulls up a chair beside me.

I nod, unable to speak for a moment. "I'm just unraveling a bit." And then I'm surprised and a little embarrassed for saying such a thing.

He doesn't look at me; we're both watching Maryanne. But his presence feels strong beside me, comforting. I didn't realize my fingers were clinging to the chair until I feel Griffin's hand over mine, gently pulling each finger from the wooden edge, then grasping my curled fingers within his own for a second. I could fall right over and lean my head upon his shoulder. I'd close my eyes and disappear for a few minutes or hours. I could sleep a thousand years.

Raul announces himself as the next singer. His eyes are closed, and he's swaying as he sings with his Indian accent "Do You Really Want to Hurt Me?" by Culture Club. Raul, our import from the Middle East, grew up on American music. His cousin mailed him old cassettes so he was listening to eighties music in the nineties, and it seems he never stopped.

And quite suddenly, I care for these people. The feeling comes over me like a cloud drifting across a searing sun. The criticism I emit so easily is softened. Beatrice, back at the bar rearranging her hors d'oeuvres, her gifts of affection for us. Charles and Andy join Raul, swaying behind him—three men of different backgrounds and ages, each unique and unassuming. Maryanne, lover of karaoke, facing her first round of chemo. Ministry-minded Jill with her graphs and plans and desire to make a difference in lives, who seems to finally relax as she smiles my way. Even Smokey wiping down the tables with a grin on his face. I see the fragmented beauty of grace in their lives despite continued struggles. Beautiful mosaics formed by broken pieces.

"Quit analyzing the meaning of everything and lighten up a bit," Griffin says, nudging me in the ribs.

"I'm not analyzing," I say. "At least not everything."

Griffin rises and returns to hand me a pool cue. "Seems I recall you used to be pretty good."

"Still am," I joke, knowing that within moments, I'll reveal the years since I've played. As a dedicated journalist-to-be, what time have I had for playing pool? "I'll let you break, though."

"Generous of you." We move to opposite ends of the table. In a quick fluid motion, his cue cracks the triangle arrangement of balls, sending them flying in all directions.

"I think you're actually enjoying this," he says.

"What, the karaoke?"

"All of it."

"Maybe I am."

"It's about time." He sets his stick on the table. "You know what? Come on; let's give Maryanne a laugh."

Before I can say, "How?" we're on our way to the stage to sing a song for Maryanne.

# The Memoir of Josephine Vanderook

A time of weariness can upend a future.

I married Walter after meeting him twice and at the encouragement of my father-in-law. I married Walter because I was too weary to fight.

He was an influential man in Boston, established, of society, and would care for me the rest of my life. These were the assurances of my father-in-law. After the discoveries of the documents and my telling of the events before the shipwreck, my father-in-law believed that Eduard had been aware of something that may have contributed to the shipwreck. He would not discuss it with me, despite my attempts to do so. And soon after our return to Boston, he brought Walter to the house.

Never in my childhood musings would I have thought to marry a man like Walter. His age alone, that of my father-in-law's, had kept me from believing his interest was anything more than gentlemanly concern. How foolish in retrospect, for except in such vulnerability I would have seen the advances of the man for what they were.

Walter tried to love me, and perhaps his love was of a magnitude that he could not choose the right paths of expression. I endured the first years of his awkward affection until at last we settled into a comfortable existence. Truly, and God knows the hours of my prayers, I tried to find something with Walter of what I had experienced with Eduard. Respect was gained and contentment grew with the years. My children were gifts of my marriage to Walter. Without them, I would have died long ago.

But love and passion I no longer had. I have never outgrown my desire for what I had with Eduard, brief though it was, compared with the span of years.

Only now, after years of longing and attempting to reclaim him, do I find that what I truly desire has been waiting all along. A greater love, pure and unblemished, unfailing—and how Eduard's love failed me—has been found.

This life journey makes little sense to me. There are many things I have relinquished. Yet, in the lying down, there is always the gathering up.

# Sophia

*My dearest...*

---

*I* return the book, china pieces, and Josephine's writings to the kitchen table. I need to give them up. I know this as surely as I know I must give up Ben.

Carefully I open the cover of the book to check its progress. The pages might possibly take weeks to dry, perhaps longer without opening them up. Yet I fear damaging the binding or that, if I attempt to dry them, they'll simply disintegrate. Portions of pages are decipherable. Numbers written in ink, maybe details of supplies. Lists of names—the passengers—and their cargo?

My patience should be as fit as a long-distance runner after living my hermit existence, but my patience is ever wanting. *Hurry and dry little pages. Dry.*

As I regard the passenger list on the *Josephine* before its last fateful journey, my mind drifts. I sometimes think about all the alternate lives each person faces. I wish to live a dozen, not that I want to trade this one in. Sometimes those people out sailing the world are who I wish to be. Or, if I could retrace time and change many things, I'd hang out in Oxford with my writing buddies, discussing myth and theology over a cup of strong coffee. The newspaper depicts stories of intriguing professions like photographer, war correspondent, or jazz musician. I consider what it'd be like to simply drive a car again—without destination—just to drive and see towns and states and countries. How I wish to live in other shoes for a while.

It's all those unlived lives.

Two lives have suddenly found their way into mine. One passed from this world when I was just a child. The other is this girl who touches my space and thoughts. It's as if the three of us are the past, present, and future.

Leaving the book on the table, I decide to take my thoughts to prayer. I wonder (as I wonder so often of many things) what it all means. In my mental cinema, I picture each person I pray for. Begrudgingly, I add Mrs. Crow to the images and feel my heart soften for her as I do. The last face is Ben's. I've captured him behind the motor in his boat. He's turned his head my way and is smiling at me. My Ben. And so I pray the names, reciting from the *The Book of Common Prayer*.

"Almighty God, I entrust all who are dear to me to your never-failing care and love, for this life and the life to come, knowing that you are doing for them better than I can desire or pray for, through Jesus Christ our Lord. Amen."

It never ceases to amaze me how hard kneeling is—the joints complaining and my rational mind telling me that I'm too old and that God can hear my prayers from the comfort of my chair. Someday my knees may not let me up. Or I'll catch my death from the draft along the floor. The excuses are valid.

Yet there is something amazing about kneeling, the humility and greatness of need that well up within me as I find my place there. It is my way to pray.

I repeat the last prayer again and again, knowing that God needs to hear it but once, if that much. But I need it. Perhaps that is one key to prayer—speaking what God already knows. Sometimes we simply need to admit it aloud or to rest before his feet.

I will remain a student of prayer, drawn to the mystery. Something spiritual happens beyond our sight. It's a laying down of our lives for one another and for ourselves and for God.

Tomorrow I will send an invitation for Claire to visit again.

And soon I must tell Ben that he must follow the path the Lord is opening before him. Even though that means we must say good-bye.

THE TIDAL POST

```
WEATHER NEWS
STORMS GATHER FORCE
  Meteorologists predict an onslaught of storms sweeping
down from Alaska. . . .
```

# Claire

Our first Thanksgiving with Alisia. The idea of a painful sit-down meal with Conner absent brought Mom and I to discussing options. Dad had the best idea. We all volunteered for the church's annual Thanksgiving feast for the community. I peeled and mashed potatoes, Mom helped in the pie department, and Dad took part in transporting people who couldn't drive. Even Alisia enjoyed handing out napkins and silverware.

Conner asks the usual question, "You did videotape it, right?"

"Of course," I say. "Just call me Spielberg."

I've quit asking how he is. He doesn't tell me anyway, but I've learned to gauge him by the circles under his eyes or the slouch of his shoulders. He's always better on days that Griffin or Ben or both have come to visit. Now when he sees me, he wants every detail of Alisia's progress with her counselor and with life in general. Today he seems more defeated than usual.

"You'll have days of tape to watch when you get out."

"Did you hear the latest?" He leans into the phone, his elbow on the metal table. "No, of course not; I just met with my lawyer

253}

this morning. We have the hearing next week to see if I'm going to trial in Washington."

"No."

"Not the best news?" He rubs his face. "I made a mistake, never should have brought her all the way here. But it was all I could think about, just getting her to Mom and Dad. Didn't know I'd have you here too. But still, I should've gone about it differently."

"You saved her life. No matter what, you saved her life."

He looks at me, tears in his eyes, nodding. "If you could have seen her, so afraid, so very small. I want her to have the life she deserves, a childhood like we had. It's kind of heartbreaking that her blood relatives don't want her, not that I'd like a fight."

"We want her," I say, and then we both have tears in our eyes. "We want you too. We're all together, a family. I'm finally understanding how much we need each other. And what it means to truly depend on God. You've shown me that, Conner."

Desperately I want to embrace my brother and grow angry at the glass that separates us.

"Tell me something from bizarro world, Claire. Tell me a story so I'll feel good. That's how people get through things, moment to moment."

I try smiling, remembering our love for bizarre tales. "Bizarro world!" we would shout when something strange happened. It takes me a moment to think of something I want to tell, something worthy of bizarro world.

I wish for complete confidence that by Christmas we'll all be together. I actually envision an *It's a Wonderful Life*–type ending, the doorbell ringing, and Conner standing there all smiles and joyful. But it hasn't worked that way for Thanksgiving. And that reality has destroyed my secret hopes in the instant miracle.

As I tell him a bizzaro-world story that includes Leonard's breath and Loretta's plan to get a perfect stalker, I see his expression change. Moment to moment. If only it could last.

# Sophia

*I have made many mistakes in this life.*

⊰ ❖ ⊱

I've tried to say it. We've ignored it through the holiday. Ben didn't even tell me if Bradley invited him to Thanksgiving, but I know he must have, because he does every year. Certainly Ben, too, knows this was our last Thanksgiving together.

We're on our second day of turkey sandwiches, and a few slices of apple pie remain.

"Thanksgiving is my favorite holiday," Ben says in between bites.

"And why?"

"It's unpretentious. There isn't all the hoopla over it like so many other holidays. It's simply a day to eat food, be together, be thankful. It's just a great day. By the way, how has the reading been?"

"I've read the memoir. It has some surprises in it."

"Like what?"

"Well, Josephine figured out to a certain degree that her husband was involved in something illegal." I tell about the extra cargo and their belongings sent overland. "And then the things she doesn't say. One thing is clear: She never got over losing her husband."

"Interesting. I attended that little exhibit opening at the museum. Mrs. Crow is worried that those scientists will discover something different from the information she put into her display cases."

"Did you have a good time?" I ask, suddenly feeling that old sense of being left out. It comes and goes. Some years have passed without my missing the outside world at all. Sometimes I've yearned for community events. Mostly it's church I miss; on Sundays I think of going to church. I've even dressed and walked the path toward Ben's house, only to rush back before he could see me.

"It's something I'll never forget," he says with a chuckle.

"What's so funny?"

"Mrs. Crow said that phrase. I've always thought that's the strangest phrase."

"Do you know how often I say *huh* when I'm around you?"

"Think about it. During some important event in their life, why do people always say, 'It's something I'll never forget'? Of course they won't forget it. It's only the minor things we forget anyway."

"Unless you have Alzheimer's."

"Even then, the forgetting is out of your own control."

"They say it because there aren't words to describe what they really feel. Our language just can't quite capture it. You're just one of the few who actually hears it."

"It makes me chuckle." He sets slices of apple pie on our near-empty plates. Ben is the pie cook. He stole the recipes from my collection, but he makes pie better than I do—something about his light and flaky crust that I've never been able to beat. "There goes the last of the pie."

"And it's something I'll never forget," I say as seriously as I can.

He points his fork at me, laughing.

We talk awhile as we eat our pie. That thing stirs within me. That subject I've avoided for days. It must be said. "Ben, I need to talk to you about something."

"Sounds serious." But there's humor in his tone.

"It's about you moving inland. Have you been thinking about it?"

He plays with a few crumbs on the china plate. "Of course. Every day."

"And?"

"And . . . I don't know."

"Ben, this is very hard for me to say, so here goes. You need to go. You know it, and I know it."

"Speak for yourself. Tell me how you know."

"If I wasn't here on the Point, would you be staying?"

His gray eyebrows furrow as he considers this. "But you are here."

"I can't be the reason for you to stay. You've been the one to tell me I can't stop change. You've said that for years."

"I'm not trying to stop change. But I can't leave you out here alone."

"See? You know inside that you want to go."

"I didn't say that."

"You didn't have to."

"What if you married me instead?"

"Funny. You're just full of good cheer today." I let myself laugh this away, though I'm inwardly shocked to hear such words.

"And what if I'm not kidding?"

"But you are. After all these years, of course you are." I can't read his expression. Is it hurt, humor, or what? "Why would we do something that silly?"

"Just an old man's desperate thought, I guess."

"Maybe it's time for both of us to change."

"So you'll be moving off the Point too?"

"Yeah, right."

He ignores my sarcasm. "There's a guy in town who asks me every year if I'm ready to sell the lighthouse. He and his wife have always dreamed of living in one."

"It's a seller's market."

"Yes, it is. I'm going to Bradley's house next week. I'll be giving him my answer. He wants me to move there soon, before winter hits too hard."

A wave of panic washes over me. So soon? "I can understand that; the pass gets snowed in sometimes. And then I'll come visit in the spring."

"Sure you will."

"Well, you can come visit in the spring."

"You could come with me." And suddenly I see in his eyes just how torn he is. On one side is his life here with me. On the other is his son and the chance to try something new. But to leave the Point?

"Ben, I can't. This is where I belong."

He nods slowly. "I know."

"Tell you what though. Next week I'll turn in the things from the shipwreck." It's all I can think of, an attempt to change the subject as if to make it go away.

"Okay, next week. You sure?"

"Definitely." With that we shake hands as if making a solemn oath, which brings a grin to us both. I think how in letting go, there should at least be the satisfaction that I did the right thing.

But there's no satisfaction, none at all.

Storms

# Sophia

*May what God grants us be used to amplify the lives of others.*

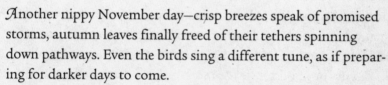

Another nippy November day—crisp breezes speak of promised storms, autumn leaves finally freed of their tethers spinning down pathways. Even the birds sing a different tune, as if preparing for darker days to come.

Ben and Claire arrive as I sweep my front walkway. Ben takes the broom and shoos us into the house. For a treat, I have apple cider with cinnamon sticks, orange slices, and cloves simmering on the stove, filling the house with fragrances.

"It smells wonderful," Claire says, unraveling her scarf and smoothing her hair as we walk inside. From a backpack, she takes out several books she's brought me—some new fiction titles I've wanted to read.

Sometimes you don't realize how much you miss something until you have it again. I knew I wanted her to come for another visit. Now that she's here, making me laugh, the days between seem somewhat duller. Ben seemed pleased to leave us, happy that I have a girlfriend, which is amazing after decades and decades without one.

We talk as easily as before, yet again it surprises me since our differences are more of a canyon than a gap in age and worlds.

I find myself telling her about my childhood exploits with Ben, Phillip, and Helen. We laugh and sip the piping hot cider.

"If this is too personal," she says, which sends a nervous shiver through me, "please say so. But your first book, it was about you and your friends on the Point, right?"

"Yes, though it was certainly fictionalized," I say with a smile, thinking of those days of writing it, of creating something new from one week of childhood. I've wondered what Phillip thought of the books, as we never discussed them much. The writing was too close to me then; I was too afraid to ask, too fearful that he hadn't understood what I was trying to say.

"I hope this is all right to say," Claire says, and I inwardly smile at her nervousness. Yes, she knows what writing means to an author, the pouring of heart upon the page. I hope that we have many days of talking ahead of us, of becoming so comfortable that she'll not broach a subject gingerly. She'll know if it's okay to discuss or not discuss. "As much as I loved the first book, your second one always intrigued me a little more."

"Really?" This does surprise me. Only Ben and a few others have ever said this. "I'd be interested in the reason."

"My theory has been—I can't believe I actually get to ask you this—" and there's an excitement that lightens her features—"that the first was sort of a recapturing of the past, but the second was more of an abstract collection of discovering life as an adult. Did you intentionally put in symbols like the sea being kind of the eternal in the story, the Point as in pointing a way, things like that?"

"Some intentional, some just happen on their own. Do you use symbolism in your writing?"

"Some are intentional; some just happen," Claire says with a grin. We talk about her writing, the computer files of the fiction she's been working on. "I get petrified that I'm terrible, and I'm an awful procrastinator."

"Sounds like a writer," I say, telling how even the greats get crippled with fear. I want to volunteer to look at her short stories, but then what if they're terrible? Before my mind can hold back my tongue, I say, "Why don't you bring some of your work next time, and we'll make it a writers' day."

Ben comes inside, and the conversation turns to Claire's brother and little Alisia. I feel like I know them now. Then she relates the intriguing story of the mysterious reporter.

"I assumed she was on staff like all the rest of you," I say, recalling that Margie Stinton's byline has appeared in the paper for several years. "It would be interesting to read her back articles and maybe get an idea about her. She must have a lot of influence in the community or with a community member."

"That's true. I'll have to ask Rob about that."

"Are you doing any more articles on the shipwreck?"

"Yes. I've wanted to do one about Josephine Vanderook."

"You have an interest in Josephine?" Ben asks as he takes our cups, refilling them at the stove.

"She's such an intriguing person."

Ben glances long and hard at me as he brings the mugs back. "I've thought so too. What about you, Sophia?"

"Yes." I wish to kick him under the table. Should I tell her that I have items from the wreck and about the copy of Josephine's memoir? I wish to toss reserve to the wind but find myself holding back.

"Do you think it was more than just a storm that caused the shipwreck?" Claire asks, brushing a long strand of hair from her face.

"It always is," Ben says.

"What do you mean?"

"Well, in my experience, there are always many depths to events, a lot of history behind what actually happened before that night. A storm, for instance, is the gathering of wind and rain into a pressure system that then erupts against the land. There is a past, a present, and a future to it." I consider Ben's words, thinking of the storms of my life and no longer about the weather pattern that took a shipload of lives into the sea. "Sometimes it takes a great storm to finally reveal truths to our lives."

"Ben the Philosopher," I say. "Is this what you and that Griffin boy talk about on Monday mornings?"

"Sometimes. We talk about all kinds of crazy things."

"Ben brought me a copy of Josephine's memoir," I say, deciding to throw a bit of caution to the wind. "I've been reading about her."

"That must be fascinating. I've been meaning to check out the archives at *The Tidal Post* for articles about the wreck."

"Here's an idea. I'll keep reading the memoir and let you know if I find anything of interest, or maybe pass the copies on to you when I'm done." Am I committing too much with her?

"You two sound like sleuths," Ben says.

"Gumshoes," Claire says with a laugh. "We'll start our own private investigating business after we solve this case."

We laugh and I think how odd to even joke about it. I would have never done so without her.

Claire plans to return next Monday for morning tea, and it seems a long way off. All these years and I've never wished for a telephone to chat with a friend until now. I want to hear the next installment of who Margie Stinton is. I want updates on her brother. The outside world holds more interest now than ever.

But soon after Claire leaves, fear washes over me. The archives. *The Tidal Post* archives may hold more information than I want told if she looks into the year 1954.

For there, she will find the story behind Phillip's death.

# The Memoir of Josephine Vanderook

My Eduard died at age thirty-three.

I am an old woman now.

Did he lose his love for me? This has haunted me as much as the sound of that storm.

What words can I leave my children and grandchildren and generations to come? What wisdom can I impart? My life has been lived fully; I've felt the depths of sorrow and the heights of love. I have wasted years and only knew their precious value too late. But my faith in God has been my anchor, my strength, and my security; yet it is such a personal journey that I hardly know how to convey it.

Whether in youth or in age, we all depart this earth. If we live long, pain will find us, but such is only a shadow of love. And so to my children, grandchildren, the generations to come, and to my Eduard, I say, "I have loved. I have loved and lived with a passionate heart—perhaps not enough, but can there ever be enough? I only hope all will attempt the same."

THE TIDAL POST

July 28, 1954

OBITUARY

PHILLIP TURLUCCIO

A memorial service will be held for Mr. Phillip Turluccio on August 3, 1954. Mr. Turluccio died July 25, 1954. He was born October 17, 1926, in Harper's Bay, CA, and has been a longtime resident of the community. Mr. Turluccio enlisted in the United States Army, serving in WW II and returning as a decorated officer.

He was 27 years old.

Mr. Turluccio is survived by his parents, Stanley and Vera Turluccio, and his sister, Helen Wilson.

# Claire

---

*H*arper's Bay has dressed for the holiday season. Lights and decorations liven up the downtown area, and Christmas carols play in shops and over the radio. My weeks are marked by putting the paper to bed, visits to my brother, lawyer meetings, singles group, lunches with Griffin, teas with Sophia, Christmas shopping, and creating holiday cheer with Alisia.

Alisia welcomes me home from work, carrying two Advent calendars that mark the days until Christmas. My mother made one of them out of cloth; the other one Dad had bought for Alisia and holds a small chocolate for every day of the season. Usually she's tried to save part of the chocolate for me, but often only a nibble remains by the time I arrive home.

The days jump one upon the other.

One morning as I'm sitting at my desk, copyediting an article, Rob walks inside, arriving earlier than usual.

"Can I talk to you in my office?" Rob asks, winding around the receptionist station.

"Sure." I stop by the coffeepot and fill two mugs, knowing that he too has a better disposition with a cup of coffee in front of him. He thanks me, then indicates that I should close the door.

"I e-mailed Margie Stinton, and she finally got back to me," Rob says. "I asked if we could meet."

"And?"

"She wants to remain anonymous and questioned why I suddenly have an interest in her personal life, especially now that she's taken some time off."

"Why would a freelance writer want to remain anonymous? Loretta said there was no listing for her in the phone book either."

"My first thought: I wondered if it could be S. T. Fleming," Rob says, leaning toward me as if to read my reaction.

"The thought crossed my mind too, but she doesn't have a computer." And with that admission, I've also confessed to knowing her fairly well.

"Okay then, what about that night your car broke down at Wilson Bridge? You told the police that a male and a female arrived, and they were arguing."

"Yes. I couldn't tell their ages, though."

"This has me wondering. Margie has mentioned a grandson in past e-mails, one that she didn't seem to get along with. You had that anonymous phone call from a guy; perhaps it was one and the same. And remember that editorial we ran about the Adversary of Change?"

"Sure, the person said he'd done the bridge sabotage."

"Margie forwarded it to me, but she wouldn't include the e-mail address she received it from. I talked to Deputy Avery about it because he thought it'd lead the police to the person. I couldn't tell him, had to use the whole 'can't reveal my source' line to protect Margie's information. And Margie also likes to make up words that really mean nothing, which reminds me of the Adversary using the word *influctiveness*. Maybe . . ."

"This is really strange. Are you thinking that Margie is involved in the damage to the bridge?"

"My suspicion is swinging that way."

"What are you going to do?"

"A bit of investigative reporting." Rob rubs his hands together and smiles.

I grin, picturing Rob with a hidden camera in his lapel. "Let me know how it goes." I rise to leave.

"And I need to ask you about Sophia Fleming," he says.

"What about her?" I say, sitting down again as if I'm at the principal's office.

"I heard that you've established a friendship with her. You've even been to her cottage several times. Talk about a scoop."

"I've really enjoyed meeting her."

"It's quite remarkable." Rob leans onto his desk, a Post-it note sticking to his elbow.

"Yeah, maybe a little."

"No, it is. I've lived here my entire life, and Ben Wilson has been her only contact for as far back as I can remember."

"It's not something I'd want to write about. She's become a good friend, and I'd never want to break her trust."

"I understand. However, if you ever want to do some writing about it, of course, we'd like the scoop, but I have other contacts with bigger publishers. You might be surprised at some of the contacts this paper man has."

"Thanks, really. But I don't have plans for that," I say before leaving the office, a little shaken by Rob's interest and such prospects. Not that it hasn't crossed my mind—crossed and left quickly. It's easy to forget who Sophia really is when we're together laughing and talking about life. But some of our conversations would be of great interest to the publishing world. And the real reason behind her seclusion is still the question I'd like to ask.

For some time now, I've wanted to search the archives. But I've delayed, letting busyness be my excuse. This evening after everyone leaves for the day, I stay behind and enter the back room with its long metal shelves holding the copies of every paper since 1882. Each box contains fifty-two editions of *The Tidal Post* covering every week in that year. I've justified why I'm here, after telling Sophia I'd look for articles around the time of the shipwreck. My hands turn black with ink as I flip through the 1905 and 1906 boxes for any new information.

I stand before the archive shelves for a long time. I'm curious about Sophia's return to Harper's Bay and the fire Cap Charlie talked about on the weekend of the reunion. There will be articles chronicling her success as a writer. And it might give reason behind her seclusion.

But I don't want to know this way.

---

Later that night, rain falls in long moving sheets over the windows. Without wind, it's like a gentle waterfall flowing over the earth. The outside lights along the walkway cast warped light through the rain.

A restlessness pervades my sleep. My thoughts travel to Sophia Fleming's stone cottage, and I wonder if she too finds it hard to sleep tonight. I wonder how she's lived upon that point of isolation. What is the reason for her shutting out the world?

A trace of betrayal rises from time to time as I consider our many moments in the past few weeks. A connection was made, an identification of two souls that caught a glimpse of each other. Our discussions about what God means to us—two women of different generations with the same God. I think of the words of Josephine Vanderook she so willingly agreed to share. And then my question, which took guts to approach, the question whose answer had been riddled with speculation for decades. "Why?" She'd shrugged me away, yet how can I really blame her? A secret so long kept is hard to finally voice.

Should I confront the question or ignore it? Will the torment of not knowing force me to ask it? Would it harm or relieve Sophia to tell her own tale?

I know that within months of her class reunion, Sophia Fleming would dissolve from the public eye after missing several book signings on her national tour and then canceling it altogether. Perhaps it wasn't the blow to her writer's ego. Perhaps it wasn't writer's block or that she was a one-book wonder. Perhaps it wasn't any of what the media speculated when one of its future literary giants fell from grace and disappeared without an explanation.

Perhaps instead it was a broken heart.

Perhaps I will ask her.

# Sophia

*I have wanted to tell you . . .*

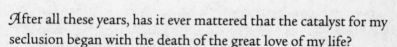

After all these years, has it ever mattered that the catalyst for my seclusion began with the death of the great love of my life?

Tonight as the sky cries in long sheets of tears, I find Phillip's letters, the ones he wrote during the war. I have stacks of them, but the ones toward the end contain the words I've read and memorized.

For months his war letters included jokes and funny stories, retelling the antics of the other guys: Piper snored like a billy goat; Herbie swore worse than a sailor but danced like nobody's business; Turk cooked a mean hobo stew; and Nick had infamous hair that was sleek and in place. *"I think it stayed put even during battle,"* Phillip had written.

But I knew there were truths Phillip wasn't revealing. What was he feeling? What was he facing? Finally he wrote the letter that spoke of truth. Oh, how it hurts to untie this bundle of letters tonight, even after all this time since his death. Phillip no longer feels the horrors of these stories. He's been dead so long, passed into peace. And yet that he ever felt such terror continues to haunt me. Why is it that the best of us often die first?

The letter, his words of old, must be read again tonight. And tomorrow I will pass them to Claire; they've too long remained in my care.

*December 30, 1944*

*Dearest Soph,*

*You want the truth? It becomes easy to fool Mother and Helen. I should have known it wouldn't work with you. My stories are accurate tales. But what mother and sister and friend want to hear of the dangers and horrors of war? How do I explain that the boy who left you all will not be returning? I lost him only months ago, yet it feels as if he died long ago. You have asked enough times for the truth, and today I want to tell someone.*

*Sgt. Harry Ross has a wife and little boy back home. He liked to pull pranks on us guys and tell jokes at the toughest moments, keep our spirits up and the tension down. He actually liked the C rations, would eat our extras when we let him. And Sgt. Harry Ross died today in filth and mud in some field near Bastogne, Belgium. I shouldn't be telling you this, but I can never fully explain it.*

*We all have final letters to our families tucked inside our pockets, with promises from our buddies that they'll send them home if we don't make it. I can't send his letter; it's ruined with his blood.*

*Oh, Soph, I try to picture you in college so far from home, and I want you safe and happy and going to dances, laughing that marvelous laugh of yours. I want to be there with you, wearing a college jacket, not this uniform covered in dirt and my friend's blood.*

*I can't say if I'll even send this letter to you. But I sure wish for a day to sit on the beach together and watch the waves. We wouldn't even have to talk, just sit close and watch the whitecaps off Orion Point. I'd hold your hand and know that someday everything would be okay. Sometimes simply imagining a day like that helps me through a night. Night is when I get to think. The days, we're on guard, wary of every noise and movement, sometimes lost in a battle that could take your life in one moment. But at night, I'm at the Point, feeling the crisp Alaskan breezes and holding handfuls of coarse granite sand. Don't worry that I'm lost completely, though on days like today it feels like I could let myself get swallowed into this muddy foreign earth. My faith is still with me, but I wish I'd never discovered the devastation that God sees.*

*You asked for the truth. Forgive me if it was more than you wanted.*

*All my love,*
*Phillip*

---

It is morning now. The storm has settled into a restless sleep for the day it seems. Claire sits in Ben's chair and holds Phillip's letter in her hands, a tear escaping down her cheek. She is the first person to share his words.

"This whole stack of letters chronicles the journey: he and Ben landing in France, then traveling north to Belgium, where they lost so many in Bastogne, fighting step-by-step into the Third Reich itself, what would later be called the Battle of the Bulge. The 11th Armored Division pushed along the southern border of Germany and into northern Austria. Phillip's letters were usually the truth, but sometimes he'd attempt another light version. Once the floodgate opened, I became the confidante of his heart."

"Incredible," Claire says, holding the letter tenderly in her hands. It's the way she holds the paper that makes me love her. She understands. She can perceive through his words and my silence of his life just how great a life I lost. The years have softened the guilt of surviving and calmed the anger of wondering why such a person had to die so young.

There's silence as she folds the letter along the worn fold. I see her eyes return from wandering the past. "May I ask what happened during the years after the war and when he died?"

It's the question I've asked myself again and again. Why didn't we get married and start a family? Why didn't I comfort him when the war haunted his nights? Why did we take time for granted? I know the series of events, but I still wish to change each and every one of them.

"Everyone was getting married when the war ended. Ben and Helen had married before he even enlisted. Phillip and I wanted to start a life *together,* not with him off in some foreign country. And yet, I feared if he died over there, I'd regret forever that I wasn't his wife. Then after the war, I was in college. He traveled the States for a while, worked various jobs, spent some time in South America; we wrote one another continually. Then my sudden success soon after college. . . we were young, thought we had all the time in the world."

Claire nods, but I know she can't fully understand even though she grasps for the truths. Some things can only be known with age. When you glimpse the inside of someone and then lose that person, it's hard to ever get over that. The glimpse is like discovering some secret realm through a crack in a stone wall. You want to go there, explore awhile. That's what I've struggled to relinquish.

"I would like to tell you about the night Phillip died. I've never told another person on earth."

"Sophia," she says softly, "only if it isn't too hard to talk about."

"Sometimes the story wants to be told. Guess it's long overdue." As I begin, it seems to rise from memory so suddenly that I'm swept back to that night most inexplicably.

"The four of us were together again on that warm summer night in 1954. Ben and Helen had a baby-sitter for their son, a rarity for them. Phillip had driven up from Texas, where he'd been living on his grandfather's ranch. My flight from New York was late so I barely made it in time for the reunion. Although the ten years since high school graduation had been packed with activity, it seemed impossible that the four of us hadn't been together since the day Ben and Phillip shipped out. Returning to Harper's Bay and our old high school was like revisiting something familiar you'd nearly forgotten about, yet it'd been with you all along.

"After several hours of reminiscing and attempting to catch up with countless people, the four of us plotted an escape while we could. Phillip and I deflected a dozen inquiries into when we were getting married. Ben quickly tired of dancing. Helen avoided the women who were also mothers; she grew tired of comparing baby weight and stages—this was a night out.

"In high school, we'd vowed to climb the clock tower. It was one of those ridiculous high school ideas that should never be attempted, but because it shouldn't be, the wanting was amplified. After leaving the school and cruising our old haunting grounds in Ben's 1948 Thunderbird, someone suggested stopping by the tower on Courthouse Street. We sat beneath the stars and contemplated how we'd reach the top. It actually appeared quite doable, though Helen and I wondered about our dresses and heels. If we could reach the side fire-escape ladder, it would be easy going to the top.

"'Why haven't we ever done it?' Phillip asked.

"'Maybe because it was a crazy idea among teenagers,' Helen said. 'We're too old to do stuff like this now. What if we got caught? I'm a mother, for goodness' sakes, involved with the women's church league, and Ben just started a new job.'

"I couldn't help but laugh as Helen attempted to convince herself more than the rest of us. She always had a wild streak to contend with, one that ran strong within her veins.

"'Okay, we should do it. If we don't do it, we'll never do it.' Those were words Helen would always regret."

Claire sits cross-legged in the recliner, elbows on her knees. How strange to return to that time and place, as if it's not my own story, as if it never happened. "There were some kids inside the tower, lighting little caps or something. We never reached the top, were just starting up the fire escape when the kids heard us and got scared. A fire started, and while the other kids ran out, one boy just froze up there, too afraid to come down. Phillip and Ben went on up and inside the tower to save him. They reached the boy, but Ben and Phillip were separated on the way out."

I think of that boy they saved. Ben told me he served in the Vietnam War, came home to open a business, and started a family after battling alcoholism. They talk from time to time. He's older than Phillip ever got to be.

Claire has tears in her eyes, and I'm surprised to find them falling down my own cheeks. Days slip away, lost love never loses its bitterness, and moments of regret visit us all. And yet, sitting here with Claire, somehow the sharing of it makes the burden all the lighter.

# THE TIDAL POST

STORM WARNING, SMALL-CRAFT ADVISORY
  The U.S. Weather Service has issued a small-craft advisory for the coming weekend. A fierce storm is expected to arrive by Saturday morning and last through the weekend.

# *Claire*

---

The cold seeps down to my bones as Ben takes me back to the docks. The waters are dark gray, and fear takes hold while we ride in his boat from the Point to Brothers Harbor. We don't speak the entire trip back. Ben must know of the revelations dispensed within the stone cottage.

Sophia gave me her trust and her vulnerability. She gave herself. I'm not sure what to do now, though I hope to be worthy of such a gift.

As Ben battles the waves that are rougher than usual, I think of him, not just of Sophia and Phillip and lost love and sorrow. I wonder how Ben has lived in his lighthouse, making sure the bulbs are blazing into the darkness—beacons of warning to the lives bobbing and traveling upon the great waves. Phillip was Ben's best friend and brother-in-law. And then he would lose his wife years later. But he's stayed the friend and confidant to Sophia all these years. He's loved her; I know this. He's loved her and allowed her to carry the torch for Phillip, both rejecting a life of love together in the process.

The salt air fills my lungs, stings my face, and makes my eyes water. The sea with its infinite movement and depths. The sea I am so small against. The sea with secrets it does not tell.

"Storm's coming in," Ben says.

"Claire, oh, you just missed a phone call," Loretta says after I race through the glass doors of *The Tidal Post* to escape the rain that's begun to fall. Christmas music plays over the radio, and Loretta's been decorating the offices. "It wasn't your stalker either unless he disguised his voice. He'll be out of the office unless you can catch him really quick."

"Who is it?" I say, setting down my satchel as if it's a hundred-pound weight. My desk chair welcomes my weary body with a creak of complaint. "Where is everyone?"

"Rob's meeting with Deputy Avery, and everyone else is here and there. But the guy who called you is from one of those big important New York magazines you always read. The one with really, really long articles."

My closed eyes suddenly open. "What guy? What magazine?"

"Here's the message."

I gaze at the name, at the title of the magazine, then back at the name Harold Jacobsen. "Why would he be calling me?"

"Call him back so we can find out. He was leaving for the weekend."

And then I'm dialing and asking for Harold Jacobsen. "This is Claire O'Rourke."

"Hello, Claire. I'm glad you caught me before I headed out for some much needed R&R. Supposed to be great weather at the Vineyard."

"Uh," is all I find to say.

"Now I'm sure my call has come as a surprise."

"Um . . . yeah."

"Well, I'll be brief. It's come to my attention that you might have an in with a certain novelist who has never granted an interview since her seclusion in the mid-fifties. Can you get us an exclusive interview or at least your story of meeting S. T. Fleming?"

"How did you know about that?"

"I could say I have my source, but I'll just tell you—it was your boss. Rob McGee is my cousin."

"Rob?"

"Yep. I once tried to get him to New York, but he's addicted to being a small-town newspaperman. But then I have high blood pressure and ulcers, and he goes golfing three days a week. Tell me who's the fool."

"Uh," I say again.

Harold Jacobsen chuckles. "I'll let you process this for a few days. We'd want a two-thousand-word story. Either the inter-view—no Q&A—or an essay on your experience. Rob says you know our magazine, which is why he thought you'd like this shot. It'd be due in two weeks, and we'd give you above-base rate plus the opportunity to write more for us if it all works well."

"Can I let you know?"

"Of course. I'll be back Tuesday morning."

Then the phone is dead, and I'm holding it limply against my face.

Loretta says, "Well? Well?"

"They want me to write for them."

"Oh, oh, that's amazing; that's incredible. That's probably even better than I can imagine since I don't read that sort of thing, but I bet it's like winning the Publishers Clearing House Sweepstakes or getting a call from Clint Eastwood or something like that."

I hang up the phone as the conversation processes through my head. "It would be something like that, except there's no way I can do it."

Loretta purses her lips and tilts her head to the side. "Huh?"

"I need to get home."

Outside, before I reach my car, Loretta hurries out after me, Christmas bells on her lace-up cowboy boots ringing as she approaches. "Did you hear?"

"Hear what?" I say, finding her combination of Western wear with Christmas pin and Santa hat amusing. I hadn't noticed her attire before.

"Of course you wouldn't have; you just left. Rob called. Deputy Avery is on his way to arrest the saboteur. It's a grandmother and her grandson."

"So it's not Margie Stinton?"

"It *is* Margie Stinton, but that's not her real name."

Loretta rides with me as we discuss the revelation, the windshield wipers slapping back and forth. "Rob put the pieces together. It'll run as the top story for sure. This is the biggest news in Harper's Bay since . . . since . . . I don't know when. This story goes all the way back to the shipwreck even. Rob researched some hunches, and I guess our founder Doc Harper didn't quite "inherit" that gold that made him a rich man. He recovered it from the *Josephine.*"

"Rob found evidence of this? The *Josephine* wasn't supposed to be carrying gold, at least not from what I've read. Maybe that's part of why it floundered in the storm."

"Could be." As we turn onto Front Street, we see the police cars. "Guess Margie not only wanted to stop the historic site from being destroyed, but she also wanted to protect her grandfather's secret. I'm surprised she thought any of it would work."

As we pull into the Harper's Bay Historical Society, Margie Stinton, aka Mrs. Crow, is being escorted to the police car.

# The Memoir of Josephine Vanderook

There is a piece of land far and away from where I now sit and write these words. It's a rocky edge that adjoins earth to water and offered me life one night long ago.

My body numb with cold, I clung to those rocks that would save me. Their edges cut my hands and knees as I held on so tightly. The waves tried to pull me away.

Where was my husband that night? Did he go to the wheelhouse after his meeting with Mr. Lendon? Perhaps he died first, or he may have survived a long while. In the end, I lost him regardless.

At moments throughout my days, I think of that little piece of rocky shore. I wonder how it appears on a calm, spring day. I wish to walk the forested paths and find that place, to stand there and thank God once again. I dream about this, my eyes drifting through windowpanes and Boston streets, imagining the journey across our vast land to reach that tiny town.

I ask the almighty God to bless that place. Bless all who cling to the rocks and find salvation there. Bless their lives and the lives they touch.

# Sophia

*My dearest Josephine . . .*

The storm has arrived.

Words from Josephine's memoir return to me now as early darkness beats with the storm's fists against my windows, pressing close and causing me to pull out candles, a lantern, and a flashlight. *I could never recall exactly when the storm arrived.*

Meteorologists with their maps and computers report the arrival of weather systems now with some accuracy. Even so, those storms surprise us, as if they had been listening to our well-laid plans; the chain of secrets passing from breeze to breeze until the storm hears with a chuckle, rumpling up his billowed tops like the crown feathers of a rooster before he moves in for a fight.

"I can beat the storm," Ben told me before leaving with Claire. "I've been doing it for years." I frown at this added example of Ben speaking words that hint of double meaning, yet he doesn't make them clear enough to fully decipher. Such are his ways of expressing frustration, even if he doesn't realize it. Instead he believes he's keeping the peace, but it aggravates me to no end. If he'd swallow his pride and spit it out, and I'd swallow mine and just ask, we might actually get somewhere.

But where?

Questions for another time. Again I open the back French door—pushing hard against the winds coming from the sea and the north—to catch the darkening view of the choppy waves and hope to glimpse Ben, his hand on the outboard, the bow of his fishing boat bursting up and down upon the sea. The last cling-ing leaves fling from branches and fill the sky with their circus-act flight. I hear papers behind me scatter from the kitchen table, so I hurry inside after a wrestling match with the door.

Josephine's words are scattered around the kitchen floor, and the propped pages on the book flap in discord. As I check the dry-ing process, I notice for the first time an edge of a page toward the back of the book. Opening the back flap, I see it's not a page from the book but several separate papers folded and stuck as if glued to the pages because of the moisture. I peel one paper from the book, noticing how my fingers shake with age. It tears slightly as I open the folds. Then I behold in stunned silence the opening line:

*My dearest Josephine . . .*

It is from him. I carefully pull each page apart. The ink has bled from one to the other, and many sections are too smeared to decipher, but other parts are fairly intact. From the fragmented sentences I copy down words from the past.

*My dearest Josephine . . .*
   *I find this to be my way to speak what must be told. In days we . . . Seattle to begin our life together in a new land. It has been my dream and you . . . loved me enough to . . .*
   *I have made many mistakes in this life. The gold, which would have guaranteed us wealth and happiness in a new land, has blinded me. We never should have . . . with such a heavy load. Tonight I will tell Mr. L. it cannot continue. I will not put lives at risk. We must make port immediately and . . . This is the admission of my deep regret.*
   *. . . found this quote . . .*
   *There are places within us we do not often share,*
   *And sometimes do not know so well ourselves.*

*Places of longing and love,
of near-forgotten dreams and secrets we cannot speak of.
These places are sometimes found by others, and once glimpsed,
there can be no turning back.*

Josephine, ours is a love that is known, though not often spoken of. What is between us cannot be explained.

I remember the first day we met, though you may not remember. It was . . . library . . .

It amazes me to consider the journey that brought us here. Will you share your dreams with me? I need you to believe in me. Do you think of me? Do you still want to know me? Would you do it all again?

Remember . . . I will always be with you. Forgive me, Josephine. What we've shared is not conventional; it is not well understood. We should keep it in the ways that we can, because it is rare. And it is ours. Ours alone.

If you can forgive me . . . God, who brought us together, can also show us the pathway for tomorrow. May what God grants us be used to amplify the lives of others.

If we do not have tomorrow, I hope you know I love you.

What more can I say?

Your beloved . . .

It takes an hour to decipher all that I can from the pages. Then I sit back and read it over. Eduard Vanderook wrote his wife before his death. And the letter went into the sea with him, never to be read by her.

# Claire

The storm promises to be fierce; gusts slap against the windows and crack through the trees. Mom gathers candles and lanterns for the night and days ahead. Dad bends against the wind as he carries garbage cans and Alisia's toys to the garage.

Mom sets down a camping lantern onto the hearth. "I can't believe Mrs. Crow is responsible for the trouble at the bridge. I knew her grandson had been in trouble with the law in the past, but Mrs. Crow?"

I'm folding laundry on the couch, refolding a few shirts Alisia was helping with before her interest moved to the window, where she watches the leaves flying around the yard. "Guess she thought she could influence the community by writing slanted articles and then resorting to sabotage. Anything to stop them from tearing down that old bridge."

"You can't stop change. Is she in jail?" Mom asks.

"They released her until the hearing."

"Speaking of which, it's looking good for Conner."

"What do you mean?"

"I can't believe I haven't told you yet. Of course, we can't know for sure." Mom lowers her voice, ever mindful that Alisia picks up more than we expect. "The lawyer said a certain someone's real father confessed to what happened and that they might drop the charges on your brother."

"And you haven't called me about this? When did you hear about it? You should've called on my cell phone."

Mom gives me the details of the late-afternoon phone call and then her excuses—the news of Mrs. Crow and the storm warnings. "Claire, I've wanted to say this. You're doing a really good job with Alisia. I'm proud of you. Conner will be proud when he gets out. I don't know how we'd have done it without you."

I start to respond when Alisia cries out, "Garden Man!" and points out the window toward Griffin's sculpture tipped to one side, flattening some bushes in the flower bed.

"Grandpa will take care of him," I say, taking her away from the window.

"Auntie Claire, hold you," she says with arms stretched upward. I love when she says this. Having heard us say, "Let me hold you," she believes it means for us to hold her.

"It's okay. I'll hold you. We're safe." And she snuggles in my arms, a hand reaching up to take a strand of my hair that she wraps around her finger, twirling this way and that.

Night is coming. And so is a storm.

## Sophia

My sudden desire to share this remarkable letter with Ben reminds me again of the late hour. Now annoyance turns to worry. I step over the pages of Josephine's memoir resting like downed kites on the floor as I look out the front window, hoping to see Ben's red cap and flannel jacket, his head bent down against the wind as he walks from his lighthouse to my cottage. Surely he made it back and I didn't see him; I can hardly see the water and he could pass by in a moment. This is only one of my rationalizations as to why he's not sitting in his chair beside my fire, sipping tea, and looking in awe at Eduard's letter.

Then I have the front door open, facing the cold that feels even colder—can the temperature really fall that fast?—as the first drops escape from the sinister gray world above.

I'm plain worried now.

If he isn't here in half an hour, I'll go to his place and see if he's there. If not, he has a CB radio. After all those practice runs in case of emergency (the only way I could stop him from paying for a phone to be brought to the Point), tonight I may be grateful.

Maybe his boat engine wouldn't start and he stayed in town. Of course, he wouldn't brave this weather to get back to the lighthouse. He knows I'll be fine.

But he'd worry enough to try to get out here. Ben Wilson wouldn't stay in town overnight and leave me here, not without a word, not during a storm. He would try to reach me. And that's what has me worried.

## Claire

The phone ringing so late at night is abrupt and disturbing.

I find it in a grappling movement, thinking I need to get it before the incessant noise wakes someone up. Everything feels foggy and disorientated around me.

"Claire, it's Griffin."

"What's wrong?" An instant wave of fear fully wakens me. Now I hear the storm outside, pounding with gusty fists.

"Ben Wilson is missing. Ms. Fleming called from his light-house. I'm going out there. Thought you'd want to know."

"Pick me up."

A pause. "Okay."

Dad waits by the door with me, wishing to go with us. Mom has a fear of storms and with Alisia in the house, I encourage him to stay.

"If it's serious, I'll call you," I tell him.

As soon as Griffin's headlights beam down the drive, I pick up the backpack with the water bottles, flashlights, and a blanket from Dad, though I'm not sure how any of these will help find Ben.

The wind whips open the door, and I hear a cry behind me. "Don't go bye-bye, Auntie Claire!" Alisia stands in the hallway, her little nightgown nearly touching the ground, hair messy from sleep. She runs and clasps her hands around my legs.

"I'll be back soon, really," I say, trying to hurry away yet very aware of how this must appear to her. Another person disappearing into the night. "Griffin will take care of me. He'll bring me back, okay?"

I bend to her level, touching her face as the wind moves her hair. "I love you, Alisia. I'll be back soon, okay?"

"O-kay," she says with a tremble in her lip. "Love you too."

The wind lashes me about as I race for his truck. Slaps of water and cold strike my face.

"What happened?" This was the agonizing question I regretted not asking on the phone.

Griffin backs up and pushes the gas pedal farther down than he should for this weather, hands clenched tight on the wheel and eyes studying the road ahead. The dashlights illuminate the worry creasing his forehead.

"Ms. Fleming used Ben's radio, hoping he'd stayed in town for the night. The harbor checked and Ben's dinghy was gone so they called search and rescue. Friend of mine is on the team and called me, said I could go out in one of the rescue boats. Maybe we can get you to Ms. Fleming. She's probably frantic out there alone."

"I'm sure she is." I think of Sophia, worried and afraid out on the Point.

And Ben, dear Ben out there in this storm.

We arrive at the harbor master's office and squeeze our way through the groups of policemen, search and rescue, and other fishermen. They're looking over maps, checking ship logs and weather reports, drinking coffee. The radio is crackling, and someone is talking too loudly on a cell phone. I recognize a few people from church, carrying food and serving steaming cups of tea and coffee. Grasping the back of Griffin's coat, I meander through until he finds his friend Bobby.

"What's going on?" Griffin asks with irritation ripe in his tone.

"Storm's too much for a team yet," Bobby says, glancing at me as I come to stand next to Griffin. "Sorry, man, they just can't risk it. My captain can't put his guys in this kind of danger. A few hours and we might be able to try it. We've got hurricane-force winds on that water."

"Are they sure he's out there?"

"Few guys watched him go, said he left about five-thirty."

I glance at my watch—it's 1:00 A.M.

"I'm not sitting around here," says a voice beside us. Cap Charlie is buttoning his raincoat with determined fingers. "Us old codgers don't have any state mandates keeping us from saving an old friend. We know these waters like we know our way around a smorgasbord."

"I'm going too," Griffin says, gaining a nod from Charlie.

"Can you get me out to Sophia?" I ask.

Griffin and Cap Charlie exchange looks.

"Sorry, ma'am. It's too rough to get the boat close enough to Ben's dock."

"I think I can get you there," Bobby says. "We'll go by land. It'll be rough, but the four-wheeler will make it. That lady shouldn't be out there alone. Once the weather breaks even a bit, I can start checking the shorelines."

"Great," I say, thrilled to be able to reach Sophia, yet also knowing what Bobby will be checking the shoreline to find . . . possibly a body.

"Let's hit 'er," Cap Charlie says.

Griffin and I turn toward one another. "Be careful," we both say. I feel foolish for these mediocre words at such a time. He takes my hands, encased in gloves but fully feeling his grasp. "I'll see you soon."

I nod and wish to keep holding on. And then he's gone and I'm following Bobby.

We're all heading straight into the storm.

## Sophia

It seems I've been shivering for hours as I sit beside the CB and await any news. Darkness came in around me except for the rotating reflection of light from the bulbs above. Finally I rose to switch on the lamp and build a fire in the woodstove. The chill within the residence portion of the lighthouse begins to diminish, yet my shivering continues.

Ben is outside in this. I am cold within these walls, and Ben is outside.

Sitting here, I realize I've never been at Ben's this long. He comes to my house, and he has a chair that is his. I've visited his lighthouse, of course, but never for an extended amount of time. Now I gaze at the place he inhabits and study the man he is away from me.

He's fairly neat and organized. There's an extra pair of boots by the mudroom door, wool socks drying on a rack beside the woodstove. Across the room are a television and VCR that we've watched movies on from time to time. The kitchen is sparse in utensils and rations. He doesn't need much and doesn't stock up on many supplies except the essentials. A few pots and pans, several plates and glasses, a single set of silverware.

Magazines, his Bible, books—more books than I expected. Rising from the chair, I inspect his bookshelf and find both of my novels. I pull them from the shelf and notice torn pieces of paper marking pages. Inside, he's underlined passages and made notes on the sides. Once he told me that he'd read my books, said that he liked the second better than the first. I'd dismissed it as his way of encouragement, not that he actually meant it. Why didn't I let him discuss it with me? Why didn't I ask how he saw the stories, especially when the first was based on our childhood?

Back in his chair, I breathe in the smell of Ben's lighthouse. On the table are the pages of Josephine's memoir and the new paper, the letter from Eduard to his wife, the letter she never received. I brought them with me, telling myself that Ben would be here when I arrived and though annoyed as I'd be for the worry, we'd sit and discuss the incredible find. The words of Eduard are not lost in their significance—that he wrote them too late.

A dread fills me. A Christian woman I'm supposed to be. A woman of prayer. But as the storm beats upon these walls and windows and holds my Ben captive in its hands, I find desperation grab hold of me. This solitude maddening. My prayers caught in my throat and strangling.

Something in the wind and rain grows louder, a rumbling sound—an earthquake or tidal wave? Fear holds me frozen. The sound grows. Then I recognize it—a vehicle. Holiday and Matilda jump from their rugs and start barking. Someone is coming, and then someone is here. Before I can get up, there is a knock, and the door flings open with the wind.

"Sophia!" Claire calls.

"Did they find him?"

"No, not yet. Are you okay?"

And then her arms are around me, and I'm falling against her like a child in a mother's arms. The relief of her presence fills me even as the storms whips in from the yawning doorway.

Ben is still out there.

My short-lived relief is replaced by heightened alarm.

## Claire

The incessant *tick* and *tock* grow louder, the old German clock like a dripping faucet intensifying within the room.

For a diversion, we discuss the letter. If not for our worry, I would be fascinated by such a discovery. In one stack of papers are the words of Josephine. And then Eduard's letter, the epiphany of what they'd shared and lost and hopefully found again on the other side of this world.

The fire nearly goes out while we sit staring and worrying. Suddenly the cold creeps in as if it's been waiting in the shadows to catch us unaware. Looking over at Sophia, she gazes toward the waning flames but doesn't move as I rekindle the fire.

The storm beats upon the house. I feel a sense of guilt that I'm warm inside while Griffin, Cap Charlie, and Bobby are out there in search of Ben. And what of Ben? Every *tick* and *tock* reminds of the loss.

Coffee and soup are ready and waiting, so there's nothing more to keep our hands busy. As 3:00 A.M. approaches, I notice Sophia's inward turn toward deep silence. I try to think of something to say, but nothing feels appropriate, so I try to find something to do. But the energy is gone.

*Ticktock.* The bird awakens from his clock doorway and chirps the hour, a long time from winter sunrise. I want to be out there in the midst of the weather and searching. This sitting and *ticktock*ing are driving me crazy.

*God, help us, help them, help Sophia. Please, help Ben.* The most eloquent, structured prayers are abandoned in such times.

We both jump up at the sound of a vehicle.

"Well?" we say in unison when Bobby comes through the door.

"Nothing," he says with defeat in his tone. He warms by the fire, takes a cup of coffee, and talks on his radio for a while. We hang close to hear of any news. The *Melinda Rose* has radioed in through the night with nothing to report except bad weather.

He pauses for a moment. "Cap Charlie's calling the team," Bobby says, then listens. "They found Ben's boat."

# Sophia

There are times when you wish memory to leave you. Times when desired sleep or unconsciousness eludes. Times when truth is too painful to look upon.

The storm, still howling, has subsided enough for the search-and-rescue team to set up station at the lighthouse. The noise of voices, footsteps, and the rustle of heavy raincoats and maps chase the silence to the corners. Exhaustion comes in waves, yet the truth of what I see in their faces cuts deeper than my weariness. Many set out into the storm believing this is no longer a rescue but a retrieval.

I won't survive this. Losing Ben. I won't survive it.

Griffin arrived an hour ago, his features drained by worry and the sight of Ben's abandoned boat dashed upon the rocks. He loves Ben as I do; I can see that in his face. Claire offered coffee and soup, but he barely sipped them as he gathered the latest updates and prepared to join the team combing the shoreline.

"Go on now," I say to Claire, mindful of her battle between doing something and being here for me. With a little coaxing, she believes I'll be fine without her. Yet as soon as she disappears into that furious darkness, I want to call her back. What have I just done, sending her into the storm, a storm with quick arms to steal lives at every opportunity? I hurry to the window and see them hop on the back of the four-wheelers, Claire riding behind Griffin. For a moment her profile is illuminated by the headlights of another vehicle. She looks afraid but determined. And as before, she reminds me of another young woman who faced a storm on Orion Point.

Prayer has never felt as insignificant yet so very necessary as now.

# Claire

I could not have anticipated the anger of a storm. Wind and rain like tiny stones flung against me, howling and pelting my skin. Morning must be coming, but there is little to see except a few distinguishing shapes outside the rings of the headlights. Breathless and exhausted, I cling to the seat over the rugged terrain and search through goggles for anything unusual my flashlight might illuminate along the shore or in the water.

The four-wheeler jolts to a stop. Griffin shouts something that escapes in the wind. I look toward the foaming, moving mass of gray surf like furious in- and outtakes against the rocks and shore.

"What?" I yell toward his ear.

"A flare." Griffin points but I see nothing. My face wet from the spray and rain, I peer out earnestly. We're off the four-wheeler, leaving it idling. Griffin grabs the radio, then starts toward the rocks. Suddenly, a red flash is visible.

"Yes, there," I call, seeking a way toward it and searching for movement other than water.

Looking back, I see Bobby rumble to a stop behind us as I run to catch up with Griffin. He jumps and slips along the rocks, shouting back, "Be careful, Claire. Watch for—" His voice disappears again. I follow the boulders and crevices in his path, but slower, unsure and stumbling.

Griffin stands at the top of a large rock where another red flare blazes. I reach him, bending down with my sides burning, out of breath. The grayness has turned lighter, the sea and rocks visible though the darkness continues to reign.

"I don't see him, but he must have lit them!"

"There's another, down below," I shout, and then I see one extinguished and bouncing away from us on the waves. The tide is coming in.

"They last twelve hours. We need to check all the crevices, and Bobby can get someone into the woods—maybe he's making his way back to Sophia's cottage. That path we drove leads to her house. When Bobby gets here, let him know what to do. I'm going to start checking around here."

I watch Griffin leave, feeling as if one of the stronger gusts could lift me from the top of this rock. Bobby reaches me and I explain Griffin's thoughts. Then I carefully weave between the boulders, cutting my fingertips on the porous surface, to reach the tidal pools. The larger rocks form sea caves and hollows that could suck someone inside. I catch up to Griffin where he's stopped to search some rocks. We work our flashlights in and out, staying close together. There's a deep gash along Griffin's face.

"Are you okay?" I ask, touching his cheek.

He frowns, confused. I think he flinches from my touch, but he's inspecting a narrow cavern.

"I think I see him." He glances back at me, and the expression on his face freezes me with fear. "Stay here." Griffin hesitates, then plunges below the black rock and into the darkened cave.

He disappears for a few moments, lost in shadow and the back side of dark boulders, while the waves keep pulsing in, spray flinging itself over the shape of Griffin. He sloshes quickly through the tidal pools.

"Get Bobby!" he calls, then returns into the shadows of the narrow cave.

"Is he alive?" I shout into the wind that takes my words away. My feet are paralyzed, hearing Griffin's instruction and yet afraid of what the next moments will reveal. The cold and fear take my breath away, disorientating me a moment. And I haven't been out here all night like Ben. I want to crouch on this rock and have someone rescue me, sudden exhaustion taking over. *What if Ben has been in that cave all night?*

I recall that Josephine Vanderook reached for land along this very stretch of shoreline. Perhaps this very place. Lives have been lost here before. Pale twisted corpses tossed like driftwood upon the shore. The fury grasping for breath and ripping it from lungs.

*Lord, help us.*

How many voices pleaded those same words for the last time? For a moment, the bodies seem to return, the arms reach and sink into the waves, the tide rolling in chunks of the possessions of a ship's life.

I see Bobby's blue knit cap rising from the direction of the all-terrain vehicles. I start waving and rushing toward him.

"Griffin found him! He needs help," I say.

"Where?"

I point toward the rocky outcropping.

"Is he alive?"

"I don't know."

"I'll be right back." Bobby disappears into the cavern. I try to follow, but a spray of frigid water hits my face and hair.

Bobby appears before me so suddenly I scream. "Claire, go radio for help. He's still alive!"

# Sophia

———— ❖ ————

Tubes and machines, beeping noises and flashing numbers. That unmistakable hospital scent. I enter the room with tentative steps, so very afraid that relief cannot find a place in me.

He isn't the Ben I know—hollow cheeks, deathly pale, darker age spots, gray hair matted to his head. It's when I sit in the chair beside him that the dam of emotions bursts wide. Sobs choke inside my chest until I can hardly breathe, though I fight and fight to calm myself.

The doctors make no assurances. Hospital rules kept me from entering ICU until a host of supporters convinced the nurses to allow me some time with him. As I take Ben's hand, I can't help but feel like he's already gone, as cold and limp as his fingers feel. But I hold them and let myself cry for this man I love and yet have not loved enough. I cry for the years of unnecessary loneliness we've wasted. I cry for my stubbornness and my fear that someday I'd lose him, and yet because of that I never had him as I could have. I cry for Phillip and Helen and years cherished and years cried over. It seems I could spill enough tears to fill an ocean that would either drown us or rise around and help us to swim.

———— ❖ ————

Ben doesn't seem to be improving, but the doctors say that he is. We come and go in shifts. I sleep at Claire's and have her constant mothering, along with the calming grace of little Alisia. Whenever I awaken from my restless sleep, I'm disorientated by my surroundings—the scents and sounds are not what I've known, but it doesn't frighten me. Then I remember: We go to the hospital. I hold Ben's hand, read to him, and through it all, I pray. Time blurs together.

Then come the words we've waited for, the words that give me hope for another chance: "He's awake."

"Do I look that bad?" Ben says as I walk in and begin to cry.

"Worse."

"I've been thinking." He speaks slowly with eyes closed.

"Is that what you've been doing? And us all worried."

Ben's smile and nod make me laugh. "I had some time in a cave too. But what I was thinking is, how can the years pass so quickly?"

"I think of that every day that goes by. You'll be proud to know that I turned over the artifacts. There's a lot for you to catch up on." I try to hold back more tears, thinking how close I came to losing him. "So hurry and get well."

"I would like you to marry me, Sophia Teresa Fleming."

"Those medicines are getting to you," I say; then I reach for his hand. "You'll probably have a heart attack, or I'll get cancer just as we're finally together. But even if this is medically induced, I would like to marry you, Benjamin Harvard Wilson."

He smiles a long time without speaking, and tears stream down his cheeks. I'm crying again too.

"If we only have this moment, aren't we glad for it?" Ben says. "We can't live fearful of what will eventually happen. Old age carries many sorrows. But we have now. And we have forever when life really begins."

"You survived quite a storm."

"It's something I'll never forget."

## THE TIDAL POST

**ADVERSARY OF CHANGE ARRESTED**
Mrs. Hilda Crow was arrested last week and agreed to an interview with *Tidal Post* editor, Robert McGee. "I'll fight these charges. I was only doing what every good citizen in Harper's Bay should be doing," she said.

District Attorney Roberts said Mrs. Crow could get five to seven years in prison.

**RECOVERING AFTER DAMAGING STORM**
Local residents inspected the damage after Monday's hurricane-force storm. Trees blocked several roadways and downed power lines, leaving hundreds of people without electricity for several days.

# *Claire*

My car is running great, no glitches or hesitant reminders of the night it stranded me. I'm working on this story about Sophia, with her help even. The New York magazine wants a draft to see my progress. My brother is expected to be released next week.

And yet, why doesn't God make things perfectly clear? There I go again, back to the old questions and ponderings. You'd think at some point I'd reach a faith level where I didn't revert back here. I'm trying.

So I've packed up my car for a few days of driving down the coastline. A few days may give perspective, direction . . . something.

On impulse, I find myself driving down Rooftop Road, where

I park in front of Griffin's house. I look up into the animated face of the quirky superman holding the red-and-black earth as I approach the porch. Griffin opens the door just as my hand raises to knock. He's in his work clothing—his faded dungarees and a welding helmet with mask pushed up over his forehead.

"Hey," he says. "I came in for an $H_2O$ break and saw you drive up." He then seems to remember the helmet and quickly pulls it off, revealing hair sticking up all over his head. When I smile, he looks a bit embarrassed.

"I'm heading out of town for a few days and thought I'd stop by and say . . . well . . . good-bye, I guess."

"Oh," he says, glancing at my car packed with much more than I'll ever need for a few days: suitcase, laptop, books, magazines, food and water in case of a breakdown. "So what are you doing?"

"It's a little pilgrimage," I say with a grin, noticing that the scrape on his cheek might leave a slight scar. That night in the storm changed both of us, brought us close, but I'm not exactly sure what it means now. "I'm going down to the city, checking out a few possibilities. Not sure really."

"Well, watch out for those Pilgrims."

We laugh and he asks about Conner.

"He's expected to be released next week. I think he's moving into the little bungalow in back of Mom and Dad's house."

"Your dad's old inventor's studio?"

"That's the one."

"Well, I'll be here working on a sculpture when and if you need me."

We hear a creak and a groan, then a longer creak. Our eyes go to the giant superman guy on the front yard. And in slow motion, it seems, we watch the to-and-fro rocking of the great globe in Superman's hand. We stand there, unable to move. It's as if he's come alive and gently, so gently, he takes the world in his hands and releases it.

Right onto my car.

Griffin's face appears stunned, shocked, mystified, and surely mine reflects the same. We rush down the steps past the smiling superman to my car. The world sits snuggly crunched onto the hood.

"I was worried the storm might have loosened those welds, planned to check on that tonight," Griffin says in dismay. "Superman was one of my first projects when I wasn't the best welder."

We stare at the car and the earth, then at one another, then back at the car. Suddenly we laugh.

"You did it on purpose," I say.

"Wish I did, but it couldn't have been planned that perfectly."

"I got my sign from heaven."

That makes us laugh harder. Neighbors have begun to converge, and I'm bent over in pain from laughing so hard.

Sometimes God's ways are mysterious.

Sometimes he reveals them bit by bit over long periods of time.

Then sometimes they're just plain bizarre, but immediately clear—picture-perfect.

Guess I'm stranded again.

## THE TIDAL POST

**SHIPWRECK MYSTERY SOLVED AFTER 100 YEARS!**

After nearly 100 years, the mystery surrounding the fate of the *Josephine* has been solved.

*The Tidal Post*, working with scientists from the History Network, have discovered what caused the shipwreck that fateful night. Findings from the seafloor, the testimonies of survivors, disclosures from Josephine Vanderook's journal and Eduard Vanderook's ship log and letters used with the cooperation of former museum curator, Hilda Crow, have revealed substantial evidence in the demise of the ship and the 62 lost lives.

On the night of November 17, 1905, the ship journeyed north from San Francisco toward Seattle with an overburdened hold containing illegal gold when the storm hit. An alleged argument between the shipbuilder, Eduard Vanderook, and the captain of the ship may have caused the misguided attempt to reach Harper's Bay, where the ship impacted the rocks off Orion Point. Town rescuers included a young Doc Harper, who later recovered the gold for himself.

Amanda Rivans, spokesperson for the History Network, said, "Though we generally keep our findings confidential, this has been a unique situation in which we've enjoyed working with locals in finding the answers. Our full conclusions will be broadcast on a special next fall."

# Sophia

They've come to visit again.

With the new bridge complete, Claire drives out several times a week, sometimes bringing along Griffin, her parents, or her brother and Alisia—depends upon the day. I'm getting used to more company, welcoming them and finding I enjoy being hospitable.

"Who would've thought?" Ben says in amazement. I've surprised him further by going out to movies at the cinema, though we've only done that twice so far.

Today we're on our sea walk. Claire points out starfish in the tidal pools to Alisia; then I hear mention of a shipwreck and the women found upon these very rocks long ago.

Ben takes my hand, ever worried about the roughness of the ground. He smiles as he twists the gold band on my ring finger. Lately he again searches for flowers and plucks their petals until "she loves me" is the final result.

I often wonder about the lives before me and the lives that will follow. I wonder what I'll leave behind, if my prayers or my words have been enough, if even one will care to know who I am. We aren't really meant for this earth. Our record is written elsewhere and retold a thousand times. Maybe we're all contained within each story, little pieces found within. All lives eventually found upon the telling.

What comes from sorrow, watered by tears, grows something

of beauty. A salt garden. And so this I leave behind. A harvest for those who find their way into my life and I into theirs.

"This is for them," I whisper as Alisia holds up a near perfect seashell. "This is for you."

# Acknowledgments

As ever, thanks to my family and friends for their unending support: David (always), Dad and Mom, Cody, Madelyn, Weston, Jennifer Harman (McCormick power), Wendy Lee Nentwig, Jenna Benton, Tricia Goyer, Maxine Cambra, Cathy Elliott, Katy Pent, Shelley Chittim, Laura Jensen Walker, Marlo Schalesky, Anne de Graaf, Michelle Ower, Robin Gunn, Eleanor Martinusen, Serina Martinusen, the extended Martinusen clan, and the Tahoe family reunion group (McCormicks, Bentleys, Westons . . . and to Tim, Justin, and Jen, it must be mentioned that night in Tahoe was "something I'll never forget").

This book would not be completed without the following . . .

Amanda Darrah—unimaginable the events that bring people together, but gaining your friendship made those certain days well worth it . . . the beach lives on.

Katie Martinusen—you didn't know what you signed up for in third grade. Thank you for these decades of friendship, with more to come.

Janet Kobobel Grant—my agent and friend, thanks for believing when there was little there and for being my continued confidante and guide.

Anne Goldsmith—great editor and friend . . . that time at Mt. Hermon chapel continues to inspire.

Lorie Popp—you added such editing insight and polish to this book, and I hope you know how much you mean to me. Beware of golden people as I should have.

Ramona Cramer Tucker—the encourager & wonder editor, thank you, thank you.

Travis Thrasher—continued laughter and writing encouragement.

Ron Beers, the Beers Publishing Group, and the fine people of Tyndale House—for continued belief, my thanks.

Paul McCusker—you've encouraged my life and expanded my vision.

Al Janssen—for words you spoke long ago, never knowing the impact.

Several fellowships of writers (always near when the lonely writer needs another lonely writer): Quills of Faith, One Heart, Chi Libris, Mt. Hermon Advanced Track Group, and Joy Luck Club of Redding.

Mike Chittim granted solitude at the house in Mt. Shasta, which once again saved the day, or more accurately, saved the manuscript.

The Elegant Bean Coffee House—providing liquid comfort to the weary.

*The Valley Post* in Anderson, California—thanks to publisher Doug Hirsch and then-editor Steven Turney for the office tour and answered questions that helped in researching a community newspaper.

My gratitude remains to each one of you and to many others. . . . My hope is that each of you already knows. It's all remembered.

# About the Author

Cindy McCormick Martinusen lives in northern California with her husband, David, and their three children. Cindy and her husband were both raised in the small town of Cottonwood and continue to live there near their extended family and longtime friends.

Cindy's other Tyndale House novels include *Winter Passing* (Christy Award finalist), *Blue Night,* and *North of Tomorrow.*

Over the past few years, Cindy has traveled several times to Europe to research her novels, particularly focusing on Austria and the Czech Republic. She also includes many of the settings in California that are not only close to her heart but close to home.

In addition to writing fiction, Cindy enjoys coleading a writer's group, studying history, and hearing the stories of others.

Cindy invites you to visit her Web site at www.cindymartinusen.com. She also appreciates letters written to her in care of Tyndale House Author Relations, P.O. Box 80, Wheaton, IL 60189-0080.

# Visit us at tyndalefiction.com

Check out the latest information on your

favorite fiction authors and upcoming new

books! While you're there, don't forget to

register to receive *Fiction First,* our e-newsletter

that will keep you up to date on all of

Tyndale's Fiction.